RACING
MANHATTAN

RACING
MANHATTAN

TERENCE BLACKER

CANDLEWICK PRESS

Copyright © 2016 by Terence Blacker

First U.S. edition 2018

Library of Congress Catalog Card Number pending
ISBN 978-0-7636-9273-5

18 19 20 21 22 23 BVG 10 9 8 7 6 5 4 3 2 1

Printed in Berryville, VA, U.S.A.

This book was typeset in ITC Galliard.

Candlewick Press
99 Dover Street
Somerville, Massachusetts 02144

visit us at www.candlewick.com

In memory of my good pal Paul Sidey

Dress-Down Friday

A tall, gray-haired man in a heavy sheepskin coat is standing on the edge of his lawn. Beyond him are fields leading down to a wood. Now and then he puffs at a cigar.

My uncle. Bill Barton. Uncle Bill.

I watch him for a moment, a hay net over my shoulders, as I stand by his gold-and-black horsebox. The two ponies in the truck are racing today. There are three more ponies, and a horse belonging to Uncle Bill's wife, Elaine, in a row of stables beyond.

I can hear, above the early morning birdsong, the sound of Uncle Bill's groom, Ted, as he mucks out one of the stables.

Across a gravel yard stands Uncle Bill's big, modern house, Coddington Hall. An old, historic building with that name used to stand here, but shortly after my uncle bought it, a fire just accidentally happened to break out in the kitchen and the place burned to the ground.

"Every cloud has a silver lining," Uncle Bill says now when he talks about it. "Collected the insurance. Built a new house. Modern. Great facilities. Game room. More my style. Bish, bosh, done."

That's Uncle Bill's way. He is a determined man. Things don't stand in his way for long. If someone disagrees with him, he gives them the *look*. There's something about Uncle Bill's look that persuades people to change their mind.

He turns, zipping himself up (that's what he was doing there, like a big silver fox marking his territory). I hurriedly put the hay net in the back of the horsebox.

A few moments later, Michaela—Uncle Bill's daughter, my cousin and my most-of-the-time best friend—ambles from the house toward the horsebox. She looks amazing. Breeches. Shining boots. Silks in Uncle Bill's black-and-gold colors. She could be a real jockey, except in miniature and with long blond hair.

She checks her reflection in one of the side mirrors.

"Looking good, M," I say.

"Cheers, Jay." She smiles, then notices what I'm wearing. Sneakers. Jeans. Faded black T-shirt. The helmet on my head has a moth-eaten velvet covering and an old-fashioned peak. It looks like something out of *Antiques Roadshow*.

"I could have lent you some stuff," she says, frowning.

"No, it's fine. I'm comfortable."

Michaela does an odd little pouty thing with her mouth, a gesture she has picked up recently at her new school.

"*Comfortable?*" she murmurs. "What's comfort got to do with it?"

Now Uncle Bill is by the horsebox. A proud-dad smile appears on his face when he looks at Michaela. It vanishes when he catches sight of me.

"Blimey, girl," he says in that rasping voice of his. "Dress-down Friday, is it?"

"I had to get the ponies ready, Uncle Bill."

He swears quietly and gets into the car.

I take one last look in the back of the horsebox.

"Hey, boys. Everything all right here?"

Marius is looking restless. Dusty munches sleepily at his hay net.

"That's the way, Dusty."

Uncle Bill impatiently toots the horn.

I close the horsebox door. A movement in one of the house's upstairs windows catches my eye. My aunt Elaine stands there in a silk bathrobe, her hands around a mug of tea. She is Uncle Bill's second wife, Michaela's stepmother, and is not exactly thrilled by the idea of our going racing. I wave good-bye to her. She looks away.

I step into the cab, which is already thick with cigar smoke.

Uncle Bill looks across at us, grinning. "Ready for the races, girls?"

"Races, yay!" Michaela punches the air. "I'm so excited!"

"You've double-checked everything's in the back, Jay?" he asks, putting the horsebox into gear.

"Yes, Uncle Bill."

Bish.

Bosh.

Done.

A PONY ON THE NOSE

We drive for an hour or so. Beside me, Michaela chatters about the ponies, about school, about her friends. I can tell she's nervous.

My mind is fixed on the race ahead. I've been around Uncle Bill long enough to know that whatever he is planning, there will probably be something dodgy about it. He calls it "working the system."

I turn toward him. "Tell us about the races, Uncle Bill," I say.

He draws on his fat cigar and exhales. Spluttering, Michaela waves the smoke away from her face.

"It's mainly a bit of fun," he says. "With a little betting on the side to make it interesting for the grown-ups."

Here's a tip about my uncle: to get at the truth, you sometimes need to listen very carefully to what he says and then turn it upside down. Or inside out. Or back to front. Anything but the way he's told it.

These pony races, I'm now guessing, are mainly about betting. With a little racing fun on the side to make it interesting for the kids.

We bump down a long path until we reach a closed gate. Two men in combat jackets and dark glasses are standing in front of it. There is something about their body language that is not exactly welcoming. As we approach, they see who is driving and quickly stand back to open the gate.

A big, open field stretches before us.

"Where are we?" Michaela sounds a bit scared.

"This was once an air station," says Uncle Bill. "Now it's just derelict land. All sorts of naughty stuff goes on here. Raves. Hunting with greyhounds. The odd bare-knuckle fight."

"Bare-knuckle fight?" I look to see whether he's joking. He isn't. "What about the police, Uncle Bill?"

He gives a little between-you-and-me laugh. "They don't seem to bother with this, for some reason." He winks at me. "It's a sort of no-man's-land, law-wise."

"Oh, right. I see." (I don't, but with Uncle Bill, it's best not to ask too many questions.)

A few hundred meters away, there is a strip of old road where horseboxes, trailers, and vans are parked. This is different from the gymkhanas Michaela and I have been to in the past. No tents. No ring surrounded by straw bales, no jolly picnics, no man with a posh voice making announcements, no proud parents leading small ponies with braided manes.

Around the outside of the field, I can see poles and a white tape. The racetrack.

"Looks a bit serious," Michaela murmurs to me.

"It does." I smile to myself.

I feel like I've come home.

I get into the horsebox to check the ponies. Marius, a light-chestnut Arabian gelding, is trembling with excitement, while Dusty—dark bay, hairy heeled, big bottomed (my favorite pony in the world)—shows no sign of waking up.

You can probably guess which one I'm riding.

From the outside, Uncle Bill calls out, "Let's walk the course, jockeys."

He strides toward the white tape. As the three of us follow the track around the field, he points out to Michaela where the good ground is. He tells her that our race is longer than most, that she must wait to make her move. Marius has a turn of foot—he can beat any pony for speed at the finish— but he gets bored when he's in front.

I listen. Sometimes it can be useful, not being noticed.

There are three races before ours. Michaela stays at the horsebox with Marius. I watch the bigger ponies carefully. Most of the kid jockeys are going too fast too soon. They have forgotten that it rained during the week. The track is narrow in places, and already the ground is muddier there. With every race, the final bend is looking more and more like a plowed field in a thunderstorm.

Where the cars are parked, money is changing hands, and there seems to be quite a lot of drinking going on too. This isn't playtime—that's for sure. It's serious.

I like that.

When we get Marius out of the horsebox and saddle him up, one or two of the gamblers come over to look at him.

"What race is he in, mate?" one calls out to Bill.

"The fourth."

"Worth a pony on the nose, is he?"

Uncle Bill is tightening the girth. He ignores them.

"What's a pony, Dad?" asks Michaela.

"Just a little bet, love—twenty-five pounds," says the man watching us. "What d'you say, pal?" He calls out more loudly to Uncle Bill. "Worth a gamble, is he?"

"Save your money, mate," says Uncle Bill. "He's got no chance."

The men lose interest and wander off.

"He might win, Dad," mutters Michaela. "You never know."

"Might?" Uncle Bill laughs. "Will, more like."

"So why did you say he had no chance?"

There is a tight little smile on Uncle Bill's face, and suddenly I understand his plan.

"The fewer people who bet on you, the better your odds will be at the bookmakers," I say. "So if you win, anyone who bet on you makes more money."

"Never mind all that." Uncle Bill gives Michaela a leg up, and as she puts her feet in the stirrups, Marius looks around with a slightly superior air. Horse and jockey look magnificent.

"Jog him around a bit, love," Uncle Bill says to Michaela. "Warm him up." He watches her go, then turns to me. "You know too much, girl," he mutters.

Smiling, I go to fetch Dusty. He looks around, taking an interest in his surroundings at last. Uncle Bill slips the bridle over his head, and I saddle him up, murmuring beneath my breath all the while: *This is your day, boy. You're the one nobody thinks will win. We've got a little surprise for them, haven't we?*

Dusty nuzzles me. A stranger might think he's after a sugar. I know it's because he's listening to me.

As Uncle Bill takes the reins and holds Dusty's head, I flick some straw out of his thick tail with a dandy brush, then run a hand down his flank behind the saddle. Half Connemara and half Thoroughbred, he is no beauty, but he is faster than he looks.

"Beauty is as beauty does," Ted likes to say.

I jump onto Dusty's back and put my feet in the stirrups.

"Looks aren't everything, are they, boy?"

Uncle Bill shakes his head. "You and that pony—you're as daft as each other," he says.

"Ignore him, Dusty. He doesn't know you like I know you."

"Listen up, kid." Uncle Bill speaks in a low, casual voice as he checks that my girth is tight enough. "You keep out of Michaela's way, right? If she's coming up on the inside, let her through. Do not take her ground. Just don't get in her way. Understood? Be a good girl. Today's Marius's day."

"You want me to lose?"

"I want Michaela to win." He gives one of his trademark winks.

I feel a familiar lurch of rage within me. It is like a match being put to gasoline.

"Understood?" Uncle Bill repeats the word with a don't-mess-with-me harshness in his voice.

I clench my jaw and manage to nod. My hands are tight around the reins.

Red mist, it was called when I was younger. "Watch out for Jay when the red mist falls," my mum used to say. "She becomes a different person." But my anger, when it comes, is not like a mist at all. It's a red fire, raging in a forest in a high wind. It's dangerous, unstoppable.

Sitting there on Dusty, I hear in my mind the voices I have heard all my life at home and at school. Be a good girl. Know your place. Keep out of the way. Don't worry about Jay. Ignore her. She's nothing.

The red fire still burning within me, I canter Dusty down to the start. As we circle around, I breathe deeply and then, coldly and calmly, I pull my goggles down. There are eight runners in our race—five boys, a plump, scared-looking girl I recognize from gymkhanas, Michaela, and me.

Today's not our day, is it? Well, it is now.

As we circle around at the starting line, I notice that most of the ponies are tough, shaggy customers, a bit like Dusty. Beside them, Marius looks like a film star who has just dropped into a local unemployment office.

But I like the way Dusty is feeling. He's a moody old sort, and not the fastest, but I know one thing from riding him in gymkhanas: he likes to have his nose in front when it matters. He may not look the part, but he has racing in his blood. He feels alive beneath me, as if the fire that is still roaring quietly within me has somehow reached him.

Use your anger. That's what Mum used to say, Dusty.

I trace a heart shape with my finger on his shoulder.

We're about to give them all a surprise.

We line up beside a man holding a red flag. Michaela has been told to keep out of trouble, and now she takes Marius to the outside. Dusty and I, ignored by the others, are next to the tape.

When the flag falls, the starter roars, "Come on!"

"Go, boy!" I shout the words out loud.

I give him a dig in the ribs. He takes off as well as he can, but after a few strides, all we can see are tails. The boys are bumping and pushing for position, but it's the girl who has the inside rail. I notice Marius and Michaela going easily, slightly away from the pack to the right, as if the chestnut is enjoying his own private canter. I'm having to push Dusty along, like someone scrubbing the floor, just to keep in touch with the others.

Take your time. They'll come back to us. Let them run their race.

Dusty can't win. Of course he can't. The others are younger and faster than he is. Except . . .

They are going too fast for themselves. The boys are riding a finish and we've only just passed the halfway mark. The girl's pony, on the inside, is already losing ground. Marius, though, is still cantering, well within himself.

As we approach the final bend, I am three lengths behind the field, which is tightly bunched. The ponies are tiring, and so are some of the jockeys. They drift away from the inside tape toward the heavier ground. It's our moment.

Not that way, boy. Here we go.

The forest fire is raging now. It makes me stronger, more focused, than anyone could believe. I pull Dusty so close to the tape that I feel the posts banging against my left foot. I don't feel the pain. We've found a narrow strip of good ground that everyone else has missed.

This is where we start racing. Come on, boy—

Dusty seems to sense that the other ponies are faltering in the mud across the center of the track. As he feels the firmer ground beneath him, he lengthens his stride and puts his old head down, like a hound finding the scent.

"Go!"

I yell as I change my grip on the reins, and suddenly we're flying.

As we enter the final stretch, the other jockeys get their ponies back to the inside tape—and find themselves looking at the broad hindquarters of an old pony called Dusty. Before the bend we were last; now we're first. It is as if some strange magic trick has taken place.

Keep going. Don't break your stride, boy.

Dusty is tiring, but he's always been a brave little pony. Two hundred meters to the post. One hundred fifty. I know what to expect and am ready for it. I hear the pounding of hooves behind me and, out of the corner of my eye, a bright chestnut shape appears, gaining on us at speed.

As Marius's head reaches my right knee, instinct kicks in. I wave my arm and yell, *"Yaaaaahhhh!"* like a jockey riding a finish.

Marius may look good, but he's no hero. My waving

arm and my crazy battle cry spook him for a moment. He checks his stride, ears pricked in alarm. Michaela tries to get him going again, but by the time she does, it is too late. I flash past the winning post, a winner by half a length.

We did it, Dusty.

I pull up, patting my pony's neck as Michaela canters past me. Her shaded goggles are around her neck.

"What were you doing?" she shouts. "You scared Marius. You stopped us winning."

I shake my head and shrug, as if I have no idea what she is talking about.

But I do. The fire within me is dying fast now, becoming no more than the warm glow of victory. In my heart, I know that what I have just done wasn't exactly fair—maybe I was even a bit out of control for a moment—but there is nothing in the rules about a jockey waving an arm and shouting a bit.

I hear mutterings as I trot past the spectators. It seems that no one had their money on Dusty and me. For the first time since I pulled up after the race, I'm aware that my left foot is throbbing with pain from where the wooden poles banged against my sneakers.

Uncle Bill appears from out of nowhere. His face and neck are flushed a dark, dangerous red. He grabs the reins so sharply that Dusty throws his head up in alarm.

"Get off," he says to me.

I slide out of the saddle. My left foot hurts so much as I touch the ground that I almost fall over.

"What did I tell you?"

I shake my head, looking him straight in the eye.

"I said don't get in her way, right?"

A large man in a sheepskin coat wanders up and lays a hand on Uncle Bill's shoulder. "Well done, mate," he says. "Your daughter rode a blinder."

"Daughter? You're joking." The words are sharp, angry, like the crack of a whip.

Taken aback, the man holds up two hands in mock surrender and walks off.

"So." Uncle Bill drops his voice. "Did you forget or what?"

"I was riding a finish, that's all."

"Waving your arm and shouting. That's just . . . cheating."

I dart him a look. Uncle Bill worrying about cheating? I've heard it all now.

"I got six to one on Michaela," he hisses. "I could have bought another pony with my winnings."

"Sorry about that."

"*Sorry?*" He says the word between gritted teeth, his face close to mine. I can smell the sweat on him. "After everything I've done for you, the money I've spent on ponies, you're *sorry*? You little—"

Without a word, I take the reins from his hand and hobble off with Dusty. My pony needs a drink. The fire has gone now. To tell the truth, I'm beginning to feel a twinge of guilt about what I've done—I never wanted to upset Michaela.

"You said you understood," he calls after me. And I did.

I understood that I was going to do whatever it took to win.

I understood that if you're second, you're just the best loser.

I understood that no one was going to stop me from doing my best.

We drive home in the black-and-gold horsebox. There's silence in the cab — Michaela upset, Uncle Bill steaming, me a little bit frightened about what I've just done. My left little toe seems to be swelling up in my sneaker, but somehow it doesn't seem the moment to talk about a pain in my foot.

As we reach the village of Coddington, about a mile from the house, Michaela, sitting on the middle seat between her dad and me, murmurs something to her father about giving me some of the prize money.

Uncle Bill gives an angry little laugh. "You're joking, I hope."

"I don't want any money, Uncle Bill," I say. "It's OK."

"Come on, Dad," says Michaela. "It was a hundred-pound first prize."

"I lost a hell of a lot more than that betting on you."

Michaela looks away. "Jay didn't know that."

Uncle Bill shakes his head. "I can't believe you," he says. "You're actually sticking up for the person who beat you."

"Please, Dad. For me."

Uncle Bill sets his face, jaw clenched, and stares ahead. I watch him for a few moments, suddenly feeling sad at the distance he keeps from me. I used to wonder what it was like being Michaela and having a dad to say yes and no in your life, helping you, making decisions. When I was younger, I even tried to pretend to myself that my uncle was a sort of father to me, that he filled the great dad-gap in my life, but it never really worked. Uncle Bill made sure of that.

I turn to Michaela and say out loud the words I have been thinking all the way home. "I'm sorry, M. I wasn't just riding a finish like I said. I knew what I was doing. I spooked Marius on purpose."

Michaela looks at her hands, frowning. I know that I have hurt her.

"Why would you want to do that?" she asks quietly.

"I just have to win. It's in me, like a disease. Even when I know it won't do me any good, I can't help myself."

Uncle Bill glances across at me. There is a curiosity in his eyes, as if he is seeing me for the first time. "And when someone tells you to lose, that just makes you more deter-mined, right?" he asks quietly. "You've got the rage. You're going to show them. You couldn't lose if you tried."

"Yes." I nod. "How did you know that?"

He shrugs. "Just a guess," he mutters as we turn into Coddington Hall's long driveway. "All I know is it's cost me a bundle. Your aunt's right. You're a money pit. Everything you do costs us money."

"I won, Uncle Bill. What more could I do?"

The horsebox draws up in front of the stables. "In this life, doll," he says, "you can win and still lose." He stares at me. I stare back. "No need to sort the ponies, Michaela," he says, his eyes still fixed on me. "Jay will do it."

He gets out of the horsebox and walks away, his boots crunching on the gravel.

"That's not fair, Dad," Michaela calls out. "She's got a bad foot."

"Leave her." He speaks the words without turning around.

With a little wince of apology to me, Michaela follows him.

I get out, gasping as my foot touches the ground. My toe feels so swollen that I don't dare to take off my sneaker before the ponies have been unloaded, rubbed down, fed, and watered for the night.

I let down the ramp at the back of the horsebox, then the small door at the front. Dusty, mud spattered but content, is half-asleep. Marius is still warm and sweating.

"There you go, boys," I say. "Let's get you out."

I back Marius out and lead him to his stall, then turn my attention to Dusty. It will be an hour or so before I can go to the house and wash my foot, but there is the trace of a smile on my face as Dusty backs down the ramp.

My.

First.

Winner.

CUCKOO IN THE NEST

Now, that is the most revolting thing I have seen in a long, long time."

We are in the kitchen the following morning. Aunt Elaine and Michaela are inspecting the red-and-blue mess that used to be my little toe.

"It throbs a bit," I say.

Aunt Elaine gives a weary sigh. I am used to that sound.

"It always happens to you, doesn't it, Jay?" She stares down at my foot with an I-think-I'm-going-to-be-sick look on her face. "I do worry about you sometimes."

That's my step-aunt for you. The fact that I won a race means nothing to her. It is my messy toe that she sees. She believes that girls should be soft skinned and as ladylike as she thinks she is, and that is something I can never quite manage.

I am small, strong, and wear my dark hair cut short. I can carry a bale of hay on my shoulders as easily as an adult. When I ride the ponies, I like to go fast and jump logs around the estate. I am most at home in the stables. Nothing about me is the slightest bit ladylike.

"Is it broken?" Michaela is looking more closely at the toe.

"Maybe," I say.

Aunt Elaine winces. "Don't get too close, darling."

Michaela smiles at me. "I don't think you can actually catch broken toes, Elaine," she says, but returns to her seat.

"You know exactly what I mean."

We all know what she means. I'm different from them. What she could catch is me.

It is as if I am a part of the Barton family's past, which Aunt Elaine would prefer to forget. Michaela's mother, Maria, ran off with a Brazilian pop star and now lives in South America. Uncle Bill was what she calls "a little rough around the edges." His sister, Debs, my mother, had a life that was full of problems.

Aunt Elaine had been at Coddington three years when I arrived. Looking back now, I think maybe she believed that the family was just beginning to change thanks to her lady-like ways.

Then, suddenly and without warning, my mum died and I was there—unrespectable, unable to change, fatherless, and now motherless, an everyday reminder of the way the Bartons used to be before she came along.

These days, she likes to describe Uncle Bill as "an entre-preneur," while Michaela is becoming "quite the young lady." They all live at "the hall," which has "a bit of land" and "just a few horses."

But there is nothing she can do about me. When my mother's name comes up in conversation, my step-aunt quickly changes the subject. My father is never mentioned.

Two years ago, when Michaela and I finished primary school, it was decided that Michaela would be sent off to a private weekly boarding school while I would go to the local high school. According to Aunt Elaine, Michaela had been picking up "unfortunate habits" from the "kids" (she used the word as if she were picking up something unpleasant with tongs). It was time for her to become "motivated," to learn how to be a lady.

And what about me? It was never spelled out, because it never had to be. I was one of the kids. My unfortunate habits were just part of me. There was nothing to be done about them.

These days I feel like an outsider at Coddington, a cuckoo in the nest. If it were not for the ponies and for Michaela, who is a real friend and always sticks up for me, I don't know what I would have done.

I finish my breakfast and hobble out of the kitchen. Behind me, I hear murmuring voices.

"One has to make allowances, I suppose," Aunt Elaine is saying. "Given the circumstances."

I do my chores. Feed the hens, collect the eggs, sweep the small yard in front of the stable, feed and water the five ponies and Elaine's horse, Humphrey. A constant refrain over the past year is how much looking after me has cost. Without being asked, I have begun to do more work in the stables and around the fields. I try to earn my keep.

There was a time when Michaela and I did these things together. We both loved riding and going to the local shows and gymkhanas with Ted. Looking after the animals wasn't work. It was fun.

For a while we had quite a name in these parts, competing in pairs events in hunter trials. We were the Bartons—same age, same height, same last name but very different in every other way. Michaela used to ride Lysander, a brilliant half-Arabian bay, while I was on Tinker, slower, less fancy, but reliable. We were a good team.

There are photographs in the house of us receiving prizes—Michaela, blond, neat, smiling at the camera, and me, dark haired, scruffy, and straight-faced.

Things have changed a bit since then. These days Michaela rides with her new school friends on the weekends. She says she prefers riding around the fields to competing in shows. She has already told me that she will never race again. "It's so *rough*" is the way she put it this morning. I laughed but felt sad. We used to do everything together.

I muck out Dusty, Marius, Humphrey, Cardsharp, Lucky, and Bantry Bay as they look out of their stalls. As I sweep the yard, I wonder if Michaela has begun to think of riding in the way Aunt Elaine does. Something to dress up for, to be seen doing by one's friends, to talk about at fancy parties.

"No stopping the jockey, eh?"

I turn to see Uncle Bill watching me as he leans on the gate that leads from the garden to the stables. The first cigar of the day is in his hand. After what happened yesterday, I am surprised to see him.

"I can't exercise them today," I say. "My toe—"

"Never mind that." Uncle Bill sounds impatient, but then, as if remembering his manners, he smiles at me.

Now I know he is up to no good.

"D'you mind doing this stuff?" He nods at the broom in my hand. "Looking after the animals?"

"Of course not. I love being with the ponies. It gets me out of the house."

Uncle Bill raises his eyebrows. "It's that bad, eh?"

"I mean, I like being in the house, but—"

"I know what you meant." Uncle Bill opens the gate and wanders toward me. "I wanted to apologize to you, girl," he says. "Spoke out of turn yesterday. Said stuff. Lost it for a moment. Sometimes I get a bit carried away."

"I know how that feels."

He laughs. "We noticed."

"I'm sorry I upset Michaela."

Uncle Bill shrugs. "You're a winner. Found the best ground. Took your chance. That little pony had no right to win."

"He's faster than you think."

"Nah." Uncle Bill takes a long pull at his cigar. "I was an idiot. I should have put my money on you. You would have won on any of the ponies in that race."

"D'you really think that?" I look away and start

sweeping the concrete so that he won't notice the smile on my face.

"You showed the older kids how it's done."

"Thanks, Uncle Bill."

I wait. There is something else coming, I know. My uncle has never been one to stand around, handing out compliments for no reason.

"There are other meets like that." He speaks casually. "Little pop-up events all year round, organized outside the system."

"Are there?"

"I think you could do well in them. I'll get you a few rides. Drive you there. You'd have to skip school now and then. Is that a problem?"

It's my turn to shrug.

"We could make a bit of money between us." He makes a chirpy little clicking noise with his teeth. "What d'you think, Jay? Are you in?"

Just.

Try.

To.

Stop.

Me.

A Ghost on the Racetrack

For the next eighteen months, my life changes. I enter the world of what Uncle Bill calls "unofficial" pony races.

By unofficial, he means illegal.

Some of the most interesting hobbies are unofficial, Uncle Bill tells me. Hares are hunted by greyhounds. Men wrestle and fight. Ponies race. People gamble.

I go along with it, but the truth is, I don't like the men and sometimes the children I meet at the unofficial pony races. They have a wild, dangerous look to them. When they get together, on some big field or abandoned airfield, it is as if they have stepped out of normal, everyday life for a few hours into a world where there is only one rule.

Winning. Making money.

They make jokes, slap each other on the back, but there is always that scary, hard look in their eyes.

Uncle Bill actually becomes more Uncle Bill–like when he is racing. Away from Aunt Elaine, he is louder, ruder, swearier. He seems more alive. His light-blue eyes flash with pleasure.

"You know what I like about pony racing?" We're in the car, driving home one day after I've ridden a walleyed piebald to victory on an abandoned greyhound track in deepest Essex. My uncle has the smile on his face that tells me his back pocket is bulging with twenty-pound notes.

"The money?"

He laughs. "More than that. It takes me back to when I was young, getting on in the world. Before life became all respectable and boring."

I decide that it's best to say nothing.

"I like it when you know where you stand." He speaks as if he has forgotten I am there. "No messing around. No nannies. No rules about this and that. It's—cleaner."

"What were you doing then?" I ask the question that many people have wondered but very few have the nerve to ask.

"Hm?" He looks at me, as if surprised to hear my voice.

"You said you were getting on in the world. What were you doing?"

He shrugs. "Usual stuff. Import, export. Development. Bit of buying and selling. Same as anyone else, really. Only better." He laughs again.

"And unofficial," I say.

He gives an Uncle-Bill wink. "Attagirl," he says, and switches on the sound system in the car. He likes disco tunes from the 1980s. Sometimes he sings along. He sounds like a performing seal.

Maybe, I think now and then, this is what a gangster looks like. He's not like in the movies—wearing dark glasses, with a big hat over his eyes and a pistol in his belt. In real life, a gangster might wear a sheepskin coat, listen to disco music, and have a big house in the country, with stables and ponies out back.

Uncle Bill seems to make a good living, but he worries about money all the time. On his way to and from races, he makes calls on his hands-free cell phone.

He has his own way of talking on the phone. It mainly involves long, threatening silences. Sometimes I hear the other person squawking away until he runs out of words or finally gets interrupted by Uncle Bill—just a few words, delivered in a low, angry tone like a punch to the stomach.

He never seems to lose these conversations. He talks about "merchandise" and "satisfactory financial arrangements." When the squawking dies down, he'll ask, "So do we have a deal?" And he always does.

After the call ends, the cold look on his face remains for a few seconds, then slowly he remembers that I am there and that today is a race day.

"Thank you and good night," he'll say.

Or: "Game over."

Or: "Another one bites the dust."

When Uncle Bill and I set off to the day's races, there are no ponies with us. They will be supplied by their trainers.

There is no telling what kind of pony will be standing in front of me in the paddock. A few (a very few) are bright in the eye and well groomed. Most have that sorry, woebegone look of ponies whose lives have taught them that nothing good is likely to come from humans. Many are wild and shaggy, their coats crusty with mud or manure. Some, I swear, have hardly been broken in. They behave as if they have never been ridden before.

It's all right, pony. You're with me. I'll look after you in the race. Leave this to me.

I feel them trembling beneath me, and I calm them as we wait at the starting line with a method that Ted has taught me. With the finger of my right hand, I trace the shape of a heart on their shoulders, just below the withers.

"I call it the heart trick," Ted says. "It's where a mare nibbles her foal when they're in a field. It's comforting. Takes their mind off the job."

And each of the ponies changes me. As soon as I am in the saddle, my feet in the stirrups, I am no longer a scrap, a wisp, the kid in the shadows that nobody notices. I draw strength from the shaggy, quivering body beneath me. Like the pony I'm riding, I may be nothing in the eyes of strangers, but I have my own strength. I look down on the world, clear-eyed and determined.

Uncle Bill has bought me a racing saddle and I begin to experiment, pulling up my leathers so that my knees are near the top of the saddle and I am lighter on the pony's back. The other riders are told by their trainers not to ride short, like professional jockeys do, but it works for me. I can balance the pony better.

Almost by instinct, I learn how to get the best out of a

pony. Be quiet. Use soft hands on the reins. Don't let it use up energy fighting against you. Make it feel as if it is not at work at all but galloping free across a sunlit field. When a pony forgets that a human is on its back, it relaxes, settles. Only at the finish do I remind it that racing is work too.

I become an expert at avoiding trouble. The best way to ride, I discover, is not to be noticed, except where it matters — as we pass the winning post.

I am a ghost on the racetrack, a ghost that wins.

Now and then, in the early days, one of the older jockeys makes the mistake of thinking that because I'm small and young, I can be scared or pushed around on the track. They try to put me off by saying something nasty in the middle of a race, or they bump my pony deliberately, or they cross in front of me, causing me to snatch up my reins.

The red fire flares. They learn quickly that I can look after myself and my pony on the racetrack. The word spreads: don't mess with that one. She's a nutter. They keep clear of me.

My average is good. Most kid jockeys are too excited, too tense, to let their ponies settle, to wait for the moment, to be cool. I specialize in the longer-distance races — the ones where tactics count.

In the early days, Uncle Bill insists that I wear the same clothes, with the same tattered riding hat, that I wore on Dusty's day of glory. He can get fancy odds on a hairy nag ridden by a small, dark-haired nothing of a girl who looks as if she should be out herding sheep on a farm.

The regulars are not taken in for long. I hear them

muttering as I go past—"There she is, the little scruff"—and some of the other jockeys start dressing down too, as if what they wear will help their luck. Just for a while, untidy is the hot new look on the pony-racing circuit.

I love it all—when I am in the paddock, slipping my feet into the stirrups, checking the girths, getting the feel of the pony I'm riding (the way it moves, how fit and how strong, whether it is brave or scared). Soon the human world, with all its worries and problems, falls away. I enjoy the best view in the world: a racetrack, seen through the pricked ears of a pony.

"You know why I like you, girl?" In the car, on the way home from the races, he turns down the music and looks across at me as he drives.

"I hadn't noticed you did like me, Uncle Bill."

"You're a funny little thing—not much to look at, a scruffy, snot-nosed kid with as much charm as an alley cat."

"Thanks."

"No offense, but you'll never have what Michaela has. She just has to smile and doors open for her. She's got the personality thing. Her mum had it too. It's what I fell for."

"I've got personality too." I say the words quietly.

"Different kind of personality, doll. Everything about you says you're just another no-hope kid. Your father did a runner. Your mother, God bless her, was a bit too easily led for her own good. You've got zilch going for you. And yet you're a winner. It's in your bones." He looks across and smiles. "D'you know who you remind me of?"

"Surprise me, Uncle Bill."

"Me. Yours truly. You're a chip off the old block."

"Oh, great. This just gets better and better."

He laughs, and I can't help it—I find myself laughing too.

I'm fourteen. I've skipped school. I'm doing what I was put on earth to do.

Riding.

Racing.

Winning.

The Best Mother in the World

Imagine you are looking at a movie on a screen and, right in the middle, there is a big black square of nothingness. You can see what is going on around the square. You can try to imagine what is happening behind it. But you can never tell what the movie is really about because at the center of it all is this big square blotting it out.

It is time to tell you about my mother.

Her name was Debs. For the first eight years of my life, she was the best mother in the world. We lived in a small, second-floor apartment in Peckham, in South London. She was like me in many ways—quiet, untidy, a bit distrustful, not at her best with strangers.

"Us against the world, babe," she used to say, putting me to bed, and that felt just fine. We may have been alone (she never talked about my dad except to say he was very nice but moved abroad before I was born), and we may not have been rich, but with each other, we were strong.

I had started school and Mum was working part-time in a local shop. I had discovered that I loved sports—I could beat any boy my age at running. Now and then, she talked about moving to a bigger apartment. "Maybe your uncle Bill will help," she said. "You'll meet him one day. He's . . . quite a character."

Mum preferred to avoid people who had authority. "Men in suits," she called them, even if they weren't men and they weren't in suits.

The people who collected the rent on our apartment were men in suits. So were the teachers at my school. So were social workers. So were doctors.

For that reason, I was a bit surprised when she told me, one day after school, that she had been to the local health center. Then she told me that she had been having "tummy troubles" and "aches and pains." She said she probably needed a few vitamins, but that the doctor wanted her to have some tests at the hospital.

"Bloomin' men in suits," she said. But she didn't laugh this time, and neither did I.

I knew something was wrong as soon as I came out of school that day. She had been at the hospital and somehow looked paler and iller than she had that morning.

She was loving and tender to me when I walked up to the door—too loving and tender. She fussed over me. Her eyes followed me whatever I was doing.

I asked her about the tests. She said everything was going to be all right. Yes, everything was going to be all right. Even at the age of eight, I could tell that saying something twice made it less true, not more.

We were going to be fine. She kept saying that. Us against the world.

This is where we get to the center of the dark square on the screen. The next day, when I got home from school, there was a man and a woman in the kitchen with Mum.

He was tall and gray haired. She was small, and pretty in a not-a-hair-out-of-place, pointy-nosed way. They looked as if they would prefer to be anywhere but in the kitchen of our apartment.

I remember thinking that the woman was judging us. Her eyes took in the dirty dishes that had been left in the sink, the sweat suit my mother was wearing, me. She seemed not to put her whole weight on the chair, as if she were afraid that there might be something unpleasant on the seat. The man, across the table from her, sat silently with a dead-eyed look on his face.

"This is your uncle Bill. You meet at last." There was a desperate, let's-all-make-the-best-of-this cheerfulness in Mum's voice. "And this is Auntie Elaine."

"Aunt Elaine," said the woman with an insincere smile. "Auntie's a bit common, isn't it?"

"I'm quite happy with Uncle Bill." The man stood up and—what was going on here?—hugged me. His clothes smelled of stale tobacco.

"We have something very important to talk about." Mum spoke in an oh-by-the-way voice that didn't fool me for a second. "You'd probably better sit down."

And into the darkness we went. More serious than she had ever been before, my mother told me that we all have something called a pancreas and that there was a rather serious problem with hers. "The doctor said it's a bit of a nasty one." She laughed. It breaks my heart to remember that laugh.

That was when I heard a new, frightening word. Cancer. I noticed that the grown-ups tried to avoid using the actual word when they were talking about the situation. It was as if not saying those two little syllables out loud would help keep it away from us.

In the coming weeks, when I had gone to stay with Uncle Bill and Aunt Elaine, there would be miserable conversations about "it."

It was advancing. It would be quite quick. It was getting worse. There was nothing anyone could do about it.

But the sicker my mother got, the less they wanted to talk about her. Aunt Elaine would frown and glance in my direction. It was as if cancer was a bit vulgar and lower-class.

I would visit Mum at the nursing home where she now lived and in the early days, we were able to talk almost normally.

For the first time in my life, she seemed to want to tell me about my father.

"He was funny, strong—like no one else I had met."

"What did he do?"

"Musician. He was in a very wild band. We met after one of his concerts. We just stayed together after that. We were soul mates."

"What was his name?"

"Jerzy. He was Polish. I called him J."

"And that's why —"

"Yes. That's why you're Jay. Sometimes I can see him in you."

There was a long silence.

"I'll never know why he left me. He just disappeared a few weeks before you were born."

"Maybe he was frightened."

Mum shifted in her bed. "I don't think so. He was looking forward to being a father. Something happened."

She looked so sad that I changed the subject.

After a few weeks, talking became difficult for her. The smile on her pale face was more strained, more like a wince of pain. One Saturday, I went to see her to find that—how could that happen overnight?—her face had changed. Suddenly she had the look of someone who was dying.

We sat in silence. She smiled at me. All the life in her was in those dark, sparkling eyes.

"You're. Special. Jay."

Each word was spoken as if it had in it enough sentences to fill a book if only she had the time and the breath in her body.

"Never. Forget. That."

"I won't, Mum. You're tired. Rest."

The next time I saw her, she could hardly talk. Each word was an effort.

Don't.

Be.

Afraid.

She frowned with concentration.

You.

Can.

Get.

Through.

This.

You're.

Different.

Special.

My.

Jay.

I told her to rest. She didn't need to talk. I understood. But the words kept coming, in gasping breaths.

You're.

A.

Winner.

So.

Determined.

Proud.

Of.

You.

My.

Girl.

I told her she was the best mother in the world.

Just.

Be.

Strong.

True.

To.

Your.

Dreams.

Do.

It.

For.

Me.

I knew even then that her words would stay with me for the rest of my life.

After a while, she grew tired and fell asleep. Uncle Bill took me back to Coddington Hall. As soon as we got there, I went out to the stable.

In those days, even before I knew how to ride, the presence of horses soothed me. Their soft eyes, their smell, the gentle curiosity, the smooth warmth of their coat. Something about their silent strength made me feel stronger too. I felt more at ease in the stable than in the house.

Michaela had a black New Forest pony called Tinker. We got on well, Tinker and me.

I opened the stall door and rested my face against his neck.

Hey, boy. You understand, don't you? I'm going to tell you about my mum.

I spent the afternoon in Tinker's stall, sitting in a corner, thinking about my mother, hearing her words in my head. Now and then, Michaela came by to see that I was all right.

Sometime later, Uncle Bill looked over the stall door. His face told me all I needed to know.

No.

More.

Words.

TROT ON

It was a strange time after my mum died. I was in the countryside, in a big house, with a family I hardly knew. My
uncle was busy doing his deals, making money. Aunt Elaine
never liked me. Even in those early days, when she was being
all sympathetic and kind, there was something a bit forced
about her friendship. It was like a pat on the head that is
slightly too hard.

"I'm not your aunt. I'm your step-aunt," she once said
to me. "It's important to get these things right."

Michaela was different. She talked to me, filling in the
silences of my life, chatting away about her school, where
I would be going that fall too. She told me about how she
missed her own mother every day, but her happiness reminded
me that life goes on, even through the dark days.

We both loved ponies. Every morning when I got up,
the first thing I would do was look out my window toward

the stable, where Tinker, Lysander, and Humphrey would be looking over their stall doors. Those summer vacations, Michaela and I spent most of the day fussing over them, grooming them, braiding their manes, picking their hooves.

Michaela had been taught by expensive riding instructors, but I learned everything that was needed from Ted, their Irish groom.

I had the better deal. A man in his fifties, Ted was taken for granted by Uncle Bill and Aunt Elaine. He was dark, quiet, and talked more to the ponies than he did to people. He walked with a limp caused by a leg injury he had suffered when he was a boy.

It was Ted who first put me on Tinker in the manège, a small paddock behind the stable. He told me how to hold the reins, how my feet should be in the stirrups, how to make a pony go forward, stop, respond to the commands in your legs and hands.

"Quick learner," he would murmur to himself as I circled around him first at a walk, then at a trot, and it was true that he never had to tell me something twice. I felt at ease, as comfortable in the saddle as I was on my own two feet. It was as if this was something I had done in a previous life and my lessons were little more than reminders.

The ponies went for me. We understood each other from the start. I sensed how each of them needed a different touch on the reins or with my heels. Tinker needed to be kept up to the bridle; Lysander had to be settled. There was trust there, even when I was learning.

Now and then, I would notice that Ted was smiling as

I circled the manège. He was mock angry when I asked him to give me extra lessons, but he always agreed. I would pester him to allow me to go the next step. When I was walking, I wanted to trot. When I was cantering, I longed to gallop.

Once, after taking Tinker over some trotting poles on the ground, I turned him toward a low jump called a cavaletti and popped him over it. There was a shout of annoyance from Ted, but soon he was showing how to give with my hands when a pony was jumping.

"One step at a time, jockey. It's like with young horses. Overface them—do too much too soon—and you can spoil them for life."

After a while, the three of us could go for rides together around the fields—Ted on Humphrey, Michaela on Lysander, me on Tinker. "Heels down," he would say as we went. "Squeeze your legs. Give with your hands. Get him on the bridle. Wake him up, jockey. Trot on."

I did what I was told. Sometimes, even when I ride today, I can hear that soft Irish brogue in my head. *That's it, jockey. Settle him down. You'll be all right.*

I pestered Ted to let me jump logs and low post-and-rail fences when we were out together. When out riding with Michaela, I would try to get Tinker to gallop.

"Go easy," Ted would tell me. "You're not a jockey yet, young lady."

Uncle Bill said I was pony crazy, but there was more to it than that. I dreamed of riding and jumping, even being a jockey. I found an old book on a shelf in Coddington Hall called *Great Ladies: The Wonder Fillies of History* and kept it in my room, reading every night about horses that had raced years ago.

When I went to my new school in the fall, my thoughts were never far from Tinker and Lysander. In class, I was in a world of my own and drew pictures of ponies when I was supposed to be working. For math, I looked at the racing paper Uncle Bill received every day and studied which horses ran best over what distance. I would have been the despair of the teachers if it had not been for the big, dark shadow of personal tragedy that hung over me.

Everyone thought that my obsession with riding and ponies was my way of escaping from the pain of what I was going through. It took most of that first year for them to discover that I wasn't cracking up at all. Riding made me stronger. I was not running away from anything because every moment of every day my mother's voice, one word at a time, was there with me, keeping me calm, reminding me that I was never truly alone.

Leading.

Me.

Forward.

Private Charity Case

By the time I reach the end of my first year of pony racing, a lot has changed.

At my new school, there is no Michaela to be my friend and keep me supplied with secondhand cool and glamour. I am a misfit, even in sports. Because I am faster and stronger than boys my age, they think I am weird, half boy and half girl. I have a nickname, "the Freak." I am Freaky Barton.

Michaela, on the other hand, is happy at her private school, Northfield Lodge. The two or three years when we were the Bartons, winning at the local gymkhanas, seem a long time ago. Something is different between us.

Nothing alters more than her attitude toward riding. At the very moment when I am becoming more interested in racing, she heads in the other direction. For her, ponies are for grooming and fussing over, for looking pretty and neat when we are out riding.

I want to go fast and to win, and now that I am winning, she finds that completely ridiculous.

"It is kind of weird how much coming first matters to you," she says in the strange, singsong voice she seems to have picked up from her school. "I mean, there's a whole world out there that has nothing to do with horses. Maybe you should try it sometime."

For the briefest moment, I am about to try to explain to her how I feel, but it passes. No point. Waste of breath.

We are drifting apart, my best friend and I. Pony racing has toughened me up. I was never good at chatting about parties or boys or celebrities, but there was a time when I used to try and tag along. Now I don't bother. For Michaela, those things seem to matter more than ever. Almost every day, she tries to talk to me about something I don't care about before giving up in despair. I have zero conversational skills, she says.

Maybe it's true. Two years ago, we talked all the time—Uncle Bill called us "the wall of sound." Now we sometimes struggle to find anything we have in common.

The days I spend racing with Uncle Bill make things worse. Michaela never mentions them, even when I have—*particularly* when I have—won, but I sense that it annoys her that I am doing something successful with her father in a world she doesn't understand.

In fact, my life at Coddington Hall is different all around. The more I talk and think about riding, the more I irritate my aunt. She jokes to her friends, "Jay might as well *be* a horse," and laughs in a slightly embarrassed way.

These days Uncle Bill spends more time in his office. Sometimes he seems almost out of place when he is with Aunt Elaine and Michaela. If he is feeling brave, he might joke about how he's not posh enough for them, with a little secret wink in my direction. He only truly relaxes when we are off racing, and that worries me too. It is as if we are becoming two families.

I don't fit in at school, and now I don't really fit in at home either.

It is early summer, and Uncle Bill and I have had a good week. Two meets, three winners.

That weekend, two girls from Michaela's school come to stay — Emma (tall with dark hair that she swishes around as if she's in a shampoo commercial) and Flossie (loud voice, large, likes to think of herself as something of a character).

I have learned over the past year that they are a school gang. They have their own private jokes, bits of stupid-sounding slang from "the Lodge" that I don't understand. They chatter away together like three happy songbirds. Next to them, I feel like a scruffy little sparrow.

I try to join in, but I get a full range of unfriendly looks — the Who-are-you-again? look, the And-what-do-you-know-about-this? look, the Are-you-still here? look.

I can handle that. The weekends when the "gang" are staying, I go about my business, spending more time on my own. There's always something I can do in the stable.

That Saturday after breakfast, I'm in the stable yard, saddling up Dusty for our morning ride, but there's no sign of Michaela, Emma, or Flossie. When I go into the house, I find them watching TV.

"I'm going riding. Anyone coming?"

No answer. All eyes on the screen.

"Er, hello. Anyone?"

At this point, Michaela stretches. Without looking at me, she says, "Could you tack up Marius for me?"

"*What?*"

"Oh, and Lucky as well while you're at it. Em's riding Dusty, by the way."

"Michaela, what is this?"

"Cheers, Jay."

I stand there for a moment while the three of them gaze at the screen. I'm aware that I seem to be trembling. Flossie clears her throat and murmurs to Michaela, "Don't look now, Mick, but she's still here." The other one, Emma, gives a little laugh.

Michaela glances at me. "We'll be out when this is over. Oh, and make sure you remember to put a drop noseband on Marius."

I leave, but I don't go to the stable. I go to my room, then down the back stairs to find out whether the gang are more talkative now than when I was there.

They are.

"It's embarrassing," Michaela is saying. "She behaves as if she's one of the family when she's so not."

"Isn't she your cousin?" The question is murmured. I think it's from Emma.

"Cousins don't count as family." Michaela gives a little

laugh. "She doesn't, anyway. She's basically a stable girl. She's here to look after the ponies."

"So why does she stay in the house and eat with the family?" asks Flossie.

"We used to go to school together. There was this big tragedy. Her father had walked out. Then her mum—my dad's sister—died of cancer and she had to stay with us." Michaela drops her voice. "My dad has always wanted me to treat her like one of us—like a friend. He didn't want me to grow up to be a snobby bitch, basically."

"That's going well," Flossie mutters, and they all giggle.

"No, seriously." Michaela drops her voice, but I can still hear every word. "She and her mum used to live in this block of apartments where the stairs smelled of, like, you know, toilets. And her mother was always in trouble. I feel sorry for Jay and all that, but the fact is she's really lucky to be here. She's like our private charity case."

"Aaaah," coos Emma. "That is so nice of you guys."

"Yeah, and my stepmother says it's important we don't make her feel like a servant," says Michaela. "Although she is, totally. She goes to these gypsy races and makes loads of money for my dad."

There is a roaring in my ears. Red fire. I back away toward a side door leading to the stable. I've heard enough.

Ride.

That's the answer to those moments when life becomes too much. I can't use my anger now, but there is always that.

Ride.

In the wind, the air, looking ahead, a pony beneath you.

It simplifies things. It clears away the garbage. It reminds you of what matters.

Ride, ride, ride.

I walk quickly to the stable and make my way to Dusty's stall. Whatever the weather, he will come out of his stall, looking around, ready for the excitement of the day.

"Others coming, are they?"

Unusually, Ted appears as I'm putting on Dusty's bridle. The sun is behind him as he stands at the door, a shadowy figure with bowlegs, like a comedy cowboy.

I glance toward him, too angry to speak.

"Are you all right, jockey? You look a little flushed."

"Yeah. I'm fine, thanks." I tighten the girth roughly, and Dusty grunts.

"Easy, girl. Don't take it out on the pony."

I nod, muttering "Sorry" to both Ted and to Dusty.

I walk Dusty to the door.

"I'll be back later, Ted," I manage to say.

"Go easy, then."

It is his favorite phrase. He uses it with humans and, more often, with the ponies. He gives me a leg up.

"Easy, girl. Go easy."

We trot briskly through the woods, through a gate and into a sunlit field beyond. There's a slight rise in the ground. I click my teeth and Dusty breaks into a canter, then a gallop. As the wind hits my face, I open my mouth and scream, letting it all out. There's a jump in the fence at the end of the field—an oxer made out of dead elm trunks. Dusty soars over it.

After a while we are no longer on Uncle Bill's land. Feeling calmer now, I cross a field where the hay has been cut, until we reach a small country road. I think about my life. School, Freaky Barton, Uncle Bill, Aunt Elaine, Michaela and her private charity case. I can see clearly now.

The farther we go, the more Dusty is enjoying our ride. Whoa, a bridge—that's interesting! Crossing a river now— scary at first, but that's cool too! Hey, look at all these cars and trucks! Watch out, a pheasant's getting up in front of us! Where are we going next?

Come on, Dusty. Let's forget about them all.

Ride.

Ride.

Ride.

TIME TO GO

It is not running away. It is running to. As soon as the idea is in my mind during the long ride on Dusty, there is no escaping it. I begin to work on my plan.

Over the past few months, I have been saving the money that Uncle Bill has given me for riding in races — ten pounds, sometimes twenty if I have ridden a winner. I have 230 pounds in a purse in my drawer, enough to get me away.

By the time summer is over, I will be sixteen. The moment has come for me to start a new life where I am not in the way, a nuisance, a freak, a bad influence; where I can be myself, where there are other people with the same dreams and hopes as me.

I am going to the home of racing.

It is still dark the next morning when my cell phone vibrates softly beneath my pillow. I get up silently, get dressed. One more time, I check my backpack. Spare clothes. Money. A diary with telephone numbers in the back. My battered copy of *Great Ladies: The Wonder Fillies of History.*

Make the bed, slip the cell phone into my pocket. Out to the stable to say good-bye to Dusty.

I'm going, boy, but I'll never forget you.

Dusty looks at me, surprised to have woken up to find a human with her arms around his neck, her face pressed against him.

You taught me. When things are going wrong, you have a choice. You can keep going and hope things will work out. Or you can jump.

The pony gives a long, patient sigh. This is not what he wants in the early hours of the morning.

From now on, I'll remember the Dusty way of doing things. Ears pricked, head high, eyes on the path ahead.

I hold him close and, at that moment, I hear a sound outside. I stay still for one minute, two.

Bye, Dusty.

Silently, I let myself out of the stall. The door to the tack room is open.

I sense that I am being watched. Ted has come to work early. I raise a finger to my lips, then walk softly out of the stable yard and down the driveway.

Thanks, Ted.

It is light by the time I reach the bus stop in the local village. A young couple on their way to work glance at me without any particular curiosity.

The bus is on time. We travel from village to village until we reach the town. I walk to the train station. It is already full of people going to work, too absorbed in their own private worlds to pay any attention to me.

I buy a ticket, get on the train, open my copy of *Great Ladies*. I keep my head down as the train pulls out of the station and gathers speed, taking me away from the past. With every mile, I feel as if a weight is being lifted off my shoulders.

I smile. The train hurtles onward.

After we have been traveling for an hour, I take out my cell phone. I tap up Uncle Bill's number and tap out a text.

> hi uncle bill.
> gone to get a vacation job. be in touch when i've
> sorted things out. plse don't worry about me.
> i know how to look out for myself!
> love to michaela & aunt elaine
> jx

I press "send" and gaze at the screen for a moment before switching off the power. Casually, I walk down the train car. I open one of the windows between the cars, and, after checking that no one is watching me, I hurl the phone into space, then walk quickly back to my seat.

Gazing out at the fields racing by, I think of my mother.

Do.

It.

For.

Me.

HEADQUARTERS

In my mind, I know what Newmarket will be like. It is the place where some of the biggest, most famous trainers have their stables, where Thoroughbred racing started and has its home.

"Headquarters," they call it.

Every shop will have something to do with racing. I've read that there are sixty stables around this town, and over five thousand horses—a horse for every six humans who live here. Cars have to give way to horses on the roads. There will be breeches and riding boots and helmets and different types of saddles in the windows. The pubs will be named after the great horses of the past—the Eclipse, the Hyperion, the Crepello. In the mornings, strings of racehorses will walk down the main street on their way to the grass gallops, where they are trained every morning. There will be jobs in racing advertised on the message boards of the local newsstands. I'll make a note of the trainers who need lads—there must be a need for enthusiastic boys and girls who can ride—and find a place in a yard. I'll soon be on my way.

But when I arrive in Newmarket late that afternoon, I am in for a shock. It is a town like any other. I wander the streets, expecting to hear chat about horses and racing from the people I pass, but there is nothing. There are more bookmakers' shops here than in most towns, but no sign of a horse or lads or jockeys.

I'm hungry now, and tired. I go into a café with steamed-up windows and buy a hamburger. As I sit at one of the tables, I notice a man and a girl sitting nearby. They are wearing dark-blue breeches and riding boots.

The girl glances in my direction, and I smile. She looks away and says something to the man. They laugh.

Nothing to lose. I ask them if they work in racing.

The man, thin and ferrety looking with cropped hair, stares at me for a moment, then nods. "Jimmy Stafford's yard."

Stafford is one of the biggest trainers in Newmarket. "Clever Jonah," I say, mentioning one of his stable's best-known horses.

The girl raises her eyebrows. "You follow racing?"

I nod. "Actually, I'm looking for a job as a lad."

Now they both smile. "Is it that time of the year already?" Ferret-Face laughs.

"How d'you mean?"

"Summer vacation," says the girl. "We get no end of kids rocking up here, looking for a vacation job or a bit of weekend work."

"Yeah, the big adventure of the horses." There is a sneer in Ferret-Face's voice.

"I just want to get into racing."

"Good luck," says the man.

I bite into my hamburger, aware that they're both watching me.

"Are you running away from home?" the girl asks suddenly.

"No," I say rather too quickly. "My parents are picking me up later. I wanted to do this by myself." The lie hangs in the air for a few moments.

"Get them to call around," the man says eventually. "Someone will probably need a kid to do some mucking out over the summer."

He stands up and the girl drains her tea. "Racing's not as glamorous as you think, love," she says to me, a little more friendly now. "I'd go home and wait until you're a bit older."

And they're gone, before I can even ask if Mr. Stafford is looking for lads.

I leave the café and walk up the main street. A big clock tower tells me that it is almost six o'clock—too late to look for a job today. I reach for the wallet in my back pocket. The train ticket and the hamburger have left me with just over 183 pounds. It is enough to keep me going for a few days in Newmarket, but not if I have to pay for a bed.

A sign pointing to Newmarket Heath gives me an idea. I start walking. On my way out of town, I pass closed iron gates with a sign in gold lettering, which reads ELVEDON

STUD AND STABLES. Beyond the gates are neat hedges and lawn, and a driveway leading to a big house and stables.

I walk on, past the gallops. There is a small wood at the top of a hill with enough cover to hide me from the world outside. It is early evening, but I have been up since dawn and I feel tired to the marrow of my bones. I make a little den in a clearing in the undergrowth, put on a second jersey, and make myself as comfortable as I can.

It is a clear, warm night, and as the sun sets, I can see the gallops of Newmarket Heath sloping down toward the lights of the town. Cock pheasants are calling in the wood, giving one last shout before they go to sleep. In the distance, I hear a fox barking.

Racing's not as glamorous as you think. The words of the girl in the café this afternoon come back to me.

Perhaps she is right. Maybe I am just another silly runaway in love with a crazy teenage fantasy. I had expected Newmarket to feel like home. It would be a place where anyone who loves racing would belong.

Instead, there are neat lawns, trimmed hedges, iron gates closed to the world.

One hundred and eighty-three pounds. I can survive here for a week, ten days at most. I think of Coddington Hall. The panic about my disappearance will have calmed by now.

I'm almost a grown-up. It is summer vacation. Will Uncle Bill get in touch with the police? Only if he is truly desperate. The past two years of illegal pony racing and skipping school would be bound to come out.

Over the summer, memories of me will fade. Michaela

will have her new friends. Aunt Elaine will no longer have to worry about what I am doing to the family reputation. Uncle Bill will go back to his deals. Life without me will be simpler for all of them.

"I can't go back." Sitting, my arms wrapped around my knees, I say the words out loud. An owl in a nearby tree hoots his reply.

I lie down, pull my spare clothes over me, close my eyes, and soon I am asleep.

Cheek.

Against.

The.

Turf.

MAGIC

I am awoken by the sound of cantering hooves, horses blowing, the occasional human voice.

From my den, I watch as a string of racehorses canter by. It is cold and my clothes are wet with dew. Steam billows from the horses' nostrils with every stride they take.

I wait for them to pass. Then, packing up my backpack, I make my way to the road.

The sight of horses on the gallops makes me feel stronger. The morning will be a busy time for stables.

I'll make a note of where the yards are. Then, this afternoon, I'll make my move.

"Paperwork, love. You need the paperwork." A tall man in a cloth cap, his hands sunk deep in his green jacket, looks down at me with a pitying fake smile on his face. We are standing at the gate to a big stable yard. Beyond him, I can see horses looking over the stable doors. I feel like a small smudge of nothingness.

"I can ride." My voice sounds whiny and desperate. "I thought that was what mattered."

"The reference comes first." The man is backing away from me, with an I'm-a-busy-man look on his face. "We can't just take on any passing kid to work here. We're not a charity, you know."

And he is off, leaving me to look foolish and pathetic at the stable-yard gates. I turn to leave.

I have been brave today, but it has done me no good. Lads have laughed at me. I have been sent from one person to another. The tall man who has just dismissed me was the assistant trainer at one of the bigger yards.

The story is always the same. They need references from an adult, from my school.

It is midafternoon and I am beginning to lose hope. Wandering down a side street, I see ahead of me a small lad pushing a wheelbarrow full of horse droppings down the street, whistling as he goes. The tune he makes echoes off the walls of the houses above the sound of the traffic.

It is such a strange and funny sight that, for the first time today, I find I am smiling. Still whistling, the lad turns down an alleyway, and I watch him as he goes. At the end of the narrow lane, there is a small door in a high wooden wall. The lad pushes it open with his wheelbarrow and disappears.

I wait for a moment, then make my decision. Anything is worth a try now. I make my way down the lane and open the gate. It is a stable yard, but less trimmed and tidy than those I have seen today. The lad is nowhere to be seen.

To the right of the stable yard there is a pathway leading to a big, ramshackle house. It is so covered in ivy that it looks as if it has grown out of the ground.

Something draws me to the house. I walk around the edge of the yard, then push a small gate, which opens with a creak. I make my way up the path, up the steps of the house between two crumbling gray pillars. There's an old sign with the paint peeling off it. EDGECOTE HOUSE.

I hesitate, then ring the bell. Beyond the door, I hear a stirring of life, then footsteps approaching.

"Yes?"

The woman who opens the door moments later is dark haired, slight, and wearing a black pantsuit. She has more makeup on her face than you would usually see in the countryside. She looks like she is on her way to a very important meeting in a big office.

"Can I help you?"

I open my mouth but suddenly find myself at a loss for words.

"What d'you want, girl?" She has the sort of accent that seems to have been sharpened to a fine point by years of telling people off. "Spit it out."

"My name is Jay Barton." There is something caught in my throat. I sound like a sick frog.

"And?"

"I was hoping to talk to the trainer?"

"Don't be ridiculous, girl. What's this all about?"

"I want to work in a racing stable."

The woman groans. "Now, there's a surprise."

"I've ridden in pony races. I've had winners. I'd be a good lad, I just know it."

The woman looks more closely at me. "I don't believe this," she mutters. "Write to the assistant trainer, Mr. Bucknall. You'll find his details online."

She is closing the door in my face when, out of nowhere, desperation kicks in. "Please!" My voice is so loud that it echoes around the stable yard behind me.

The woman hesitates. "You've got nerve, I'll give you that," she murmurs.

"I really need a job."

To my surprise, the woman steps back and opens the door. "Oh, come in," she says impatiently. I step into a gloomy hall. "Wait here. Do *not* touch anything."

She walks down a corridor, leaving me alone. I look around me. On the wooden walls, there are paintings of racing scenes from years ago. An odd musty smell hangs in the air. The place feels more like a museum than a house.

The woman returns. "You have a minute." With a nod of her head, she leads me down the dark corridor, then pushes open a door. I walk ahead of her into a sitting room. A figure, broad and hunched, is at a desk in front of the window, silhouetted by the sun shining into the room.

"This is Mr. Wilkinson, girl. He's the trainer. I'm Mrs. Wilkinson, the trainer's wife. You have disturbed our afternoon."

The man looks up from the newspaper in front of him

and gazes at me wearily. I recognize him from the racing papers Uncle Bill used to have.

"Magic," I say.

"Hm?" the trainer grunts irritably.

"Magic Wilkinson. The only trainer in history to have trained all five Classics winners in one season."

Behind me, Mrs. Wilkinson gives a brief, snorting laugh. "Knows her racing, the girl. I'll give her that." Watching me, she sits at a paper-strewn desk in the corner of the room. Beyond her, on the desk, there is a computer that looks out of place in this old-fashioned room.

"Ride?" A surprisingly squeaky voice comes from the trainer. "Jockey, are you?"

"I've ridden a lot of winners in pony racing, sir."

"What was your name again?" asks Mrs. Wilkinson. "Some of the trainers' children ride in pony races."

"I was christened Jasmine, but I've always been called Jay. I'm Jay Barton."

She turns to the computer and taps at the keyboard. "They won't have heard of me," I say. "The racing wasn't official."

Mrs. Wilkinson stops typing.

"Gypsy racing?" Mr. Wilkinson looks at me with more interest.

"They said it was 'unofficial.' That's all I was told."

"Blinkin' cheek," Mr. Wilkinson mutters to himself. "Walk up to my front door. Interrupt. Girl. Job. Bloomin' nerve."

I keep quiet. He is not at all what I expected a trainer

to be like, this confused-looking man with a squeaky voice. When he talks, it is in short bursts, like a cell phone with bad reception.

"Wants a vacation job. Pocket money. Be with the 'orses. Same old story."

"Would you need somewhere to stay?" asks Mrs. Wilkinson.

I nod.

"We are short-staffed, Clive," Mrs. Wilkinson murmurs.

"Two lads. Walked out. No notice." Mr. Wilkinson looks at me with fury, as if all this was my fault. "Muck out?"

Again, I nod.

"Pay you pocket money. Give you a bed and board."

"Yes, sir."

The trainer picks up a telephone on his desk and dials a number. The person at the other end answers almost immediately. "Got a new girl, Harry," says Mr. Wilkinson in his high voice. "Calls herself Jasmine."

There's an explosion of angry noises from the other end of the line. I'm sensing that the person receiving the call is not thrilled by this news.

Now there's so much swearing and shouting on the phone that Mr. Wilkinson takes it away from his ear and, after holding it in the air for a moment, places it back on the receiver.

"I prefer to be called Jay." I say these words quietly.

He frowns, as if I have suddenly spoken in a foreign language.

"I've never really felt like a Jasmine," I explain.

There's a brief bark of laughter from Mrs. Wilkinson.

"See how you get on. Few days," says Mr. Wilkinson.

"Thank you, Mr. Wilkinson."

"Got to last the week first. In the yard. Office. Find the assistant trainer. Mr. Bucknall." He suddenly seems full of rage at what has just happened. "You're on your own," he snaps. "Remember that. Any problems. Out. No room for silly little girls here."

He jerks his head toward the door. As I make my exit, I look toward Mrs. Wilkinson. She is staring at me, narrow eyed, with a look I can't quite read.

Friend?

Or.

Enemy?

A Back-Yard Sort of Person

I walk down the pathway into the stable yard. It is as old and ramshackle as the house, with an overgrown lawn at its center surrounded by paths of black bricks. From stalls on every side of the yard, horses watch me.

Hey, guys, I'm here.

I feel stronger than when I was in the house moments ago. There is something about the presence of horses that makes me more at ease. Right now I may be alone in the world, but those eyes following me, those pricked ears, give me strength.

I walk to the corner of the yard where there is a small door marked OFFICE. I knock.

No reply.

I knock again.

Silence.

After my third knock, there's an angry "Yes! Are you deaf?" from inside.

The small room is more like a ship's cabin than an office. Behind a table, there sits a man in his thirties. He is reading a newspaper and ignores me.

I smile politely. "Mr. Wilkinson sent me."

The man looks up slowly and runs a hand through his heavy, slicked-back hair. He has reddish cheeks and a big face with sleepy eyes. He yawns, mouth uncovered, as I stand there.

Mr. Harry Bucknall, the assistant trainer. "Are you Jasmine?" he drawls. Jyaaasmine.

"They call me Jay."

"Do they, now? Well, I prefer Jasmine. Friend of the missus, are you? Bit of *girl power* going on, is there?" A cold, sarcastic smile appears on his face.

"I don't know."

"Oh, come on, Jasmine. How else could you have been offered a job here without even an interview? It's your friend, the empress Josephine in there—interfering as usual." He makes a sneering face and puts on a trilling, womanish voice. "Oh, we've got to have more girls here, Harry. It's about equal opportunities these days. Girls are just as good as boys with horses, Harry."

I say nothing.

"What does she know?"

"I don't know," I mumble.

"We've had quite a few girls here, in fact. They just don't seem to want to stay. Can't think why." Suddenly he seems bored by the conversation. "Can you ride?" he asks.

I nod.

"Not little ponies, Jasmine. I mean really ride — horses."

"I've ridden winners in pony races."

"Oooh." He makes a mocking little noise, then stands up, reaching for a tweed jacket hanging on a nail in the wall. "Better find someone to show you around." He strides toward the door. "Not that you'll be here for long."

We step out into the sunlight.

"Main yard. For the better horses," he says. "You won't be here." He walks toward an archway, his heavy shoes echoing on the bricks. A passage leads to a second, smaller yard. There is no lawn here, no hedge or brick paths. The stables are smaller, with a sad farmyard look to them. In the far corner, steam is rising from a heap of manure.

"Back yard," Mr. Bucknall mutters. He looks down at me. "You look like a back-yard sort of person, Jasmine," he says, and laughs as if at some private joke that I wouldn't understand. I notice one stall set back from the others and slightly larger, which has a grille across it. For some reason, I'm curious about it.

The assistant trainer notices where I am looking. "Keep away from that stall," he says. Before I can ask why, he has pushed open a door in the wall beside him. "Tack room." He walks into a room with rows of saddles, bridles, blankets, halters, bandages, and boots along the walls.

Seated on a chair at the far end of the tack room is a slight, long-haired man in his twenties. A tin of saddle soap is on the table in front of him, and he has a small sponge in one hand, a bridle in the other.

"On tack duty, eh, Deej?"

The man called Deej ignores him and nods at me. I smile.

"Now, Deej. This little nobody here is called Jasmine. For reasons that remain mysterious, she has been taken on by Mrs. Wilkinson for a few days."

"I like to be called Jay," I say. "And it was Mr. Wilkinson who took me on."

"I don't mind a chick in the yard," Bucknall murmurs to Deej. "But this one looks like something the cat brought in."

Deej smiles at me and shakes his head.

"I'd like you to show Jasmine the ropes, tell her what's what. Apparently, she's staying at Auntie's place."

Deej continues to clean the bridle. "How's that working, then?" he asks casually. "With the rent."

"We pay the rent, Jasmine." The assistant trainer clears his throat. "It gets taken out of your pay. Understood?"

I glance at Deej, sensing that he is looking after my interests. He gives a little nod.

"That sounds good," I say.

"Right." Bucknall puts his hands together in a nervous clapping movement. "I'll leave you to it."

As the door closes, Deej shakes his head. "Eejit," he mutters, and we both laugh. He hands me a sponge and a bar of saddle soap. "You can make yourself useful, Jay," he says.

I spit on the saddle soap and get to work on a bridle.

Deej looks surprised.

"Sorry, not very ladylike," I say.

He reaches down for a bucket of water and places it

between us. "Save your spit," he says. "You're at Wilkinson's yard now."

"Yeah. Magic Wilkinson. I can't believe it."

Deej gives a little laugh. "Don't hold your breath for any magic," he says, frowning as he rubs down a browband. "Just do your best one day at a time, keep on the right side of Angus, and take it from there."

"Who's Angus?"

"Head lad."

"What's he like?"

Deej thinks for a moment. "He's OK. Scottish. Bit old and grumpy. He has issues." Deej laughs, as if something has just occurred to him. "Pretty much everyone has issues at Wilkinson's—humans and horses." There are voices from outside. Deej glances at his watch. "Evening stables. Stick with me and keep your mouth shut."

Outside, there is an atmosphere of quiet activity in the yard—lads carrying buckets, pushing wheelbarrows. I notice that there's no shouting, that when the lads speak to one another, it is in low voices.

"Horses come first," Deej explains as we make our way into the main yard. "It's the guv'nor's golden rule. Lads can come and go. There can be all kinds of human stuff going on. But nothing must ever be allowed to disturb the horses. No cell phones in the yard. No smoking. No shouting."

A couple of lads walk by us. They greet Deej and glance briefly in my direction.

Over the next half an hour, we look after the three

horses Deej "does"—that is, looks after. We give them fresh hay and water and muck them out, then tie them up, ready for Mr. Wilkinson's evening inspection. I do what Deej tells me and keep my mouth shut. It is like being at a new school where you know no one.

Fetching a bag of bedding from the barn, I pass by the corner of the yard where earlier I noticed the strange, cage-like grille on a stall door.

I hear Bucknall's words in my head. *Keep away from that stall.*

Glancing around to check that no one is looking, I approach it. The stall is out of the sun and has no windows. It is as dark as a cave inside. At first, peering through the bars, I can see no sign of life.

So why should I keep away from it?

Then, as I stand there, I see a movement, like a dappling of light in the darkness where none should be.

"Hello." I say the word out loud, but softly.

Another movement. There's a horse in there—a big gray. A glint of a dark eye catches the light. From the shadows, there comes low, loud breathing, almost like the growl of a beast.

"Who are you?"

The eye gazes back at me. Whatever is in there shifts slightly. The splashes of brightness in the gloom catch the light for a second and quiver like sunlight on water.

"What the blazes are you doing?"

It is a low, angry rasp, in a strong Scottish accent from ten meters behind me. I turn to see a small, wiry man standing there, hands on hips. He is wearing dark-blue exercise breeches and looks much older than the other lads. His gray hair is neatly parted, like a character out of an old-fashioned film. Angus.

"I was just looking."

He strides toward me like an angry bantam rooster. And stands uncomfortably close to me. "And who the blazing blazes might you be?"

"I'm Jay. I'm new."

"Who the blazes says so?"

(I should explain that Angus never actually uses the word *blazes*. He is the sweariest person I have ever met. He swears like other people breathe.)

"I saw Mr. Wilkinson this afternoon. He said—"

"He'd take you on for some vacation work, I know." Angus laughs wearily. From the far side of the yard, a lad—dark haired and with a powerful, stocky build—walks toward us, carrying a bucket of feed. He whistles loudly and out of tune, and as he passes us, he says, "Pony Club day, is it, Angus?"

The head lad laughs. "Evening, Pete."

The lad called Pete heads for the stall containing the big gray. He reaches for the pitchfork and, entering the stall, makes a rasping growl. There is a clatter of horse's hooves from within the stall, followed by curses.

Angus glances at me. "Get on with your work, girl," he says.

"Which horse is in that stall?"

"A psycho called Manhattan."

There is more commotion from the stall, and then Pete emerges with the bucket, now empty.

"A psycho? How is he a psycho?"

Angus raises his eyebrows. Then, to my surprise, he smiles.

Not.

He.

She.

AUNTIE

You don't want to worry too much about Angus. He's not as fierce as he tries to make out."

Enter Laura—small, broad shouldered, and tough. Her blond hair is cut short, but the look in her eye and the muscles in her arms will tell you that she's as tough as any of the lads. As we walk together to the boardinghouse they call Auntie's, she chats away, staring ahead of her as if she doesn't want to seem too friendly too quickly.

"Does he ride out?"

"He does. He rides an old handicapper called Andy's Pet. He's a bit of a legend in his own way, Angus. He was a top apprentice in Mr. Wilkinson's early days as a trainer. He sacrificed everything for racing—his wife walked out, his marriage broke up, he had nothing to do with his kids. He has always lived for the game."

"But he never made it as a jockey."

"He didn't. Had a fall. Lost his nerve. You hear a lot of that in this town."

Laura strides ahead of me in silence for a few moments. She walks so quickly that I have to jog now and then to keep up with her.

"He's all right, old Angus, but he won't do you any favors. He's a tad bitter and twisted about women since his wife left him."

"Is that why you're the only girl in the yard?"

"Could be. Just be polite and don't let the lads wind you up. I'm sure you'll be fine." I hear the doubt in her voice.

We walk down the main street, then take a turn toward a housing development. In the distance, I can see the heath where twelve hours ago I was sleeping.

"D'you like being a stable lass?" I ask.

"Stable lass?" She laughs. "We don't call them that. Everyone's a lad in Newmarket—even the girls."

"But you like the job."

"Yeah," she says. "It's a bit of a weird place, Wilkinson's. Old school. Once you know that and look out for yourself, you'll be fine."

"I've already had Angus on my case."

"It's not him you should watch out for."

I think of the lad who took a pitchfork into the stall of the horse he was mucking. "Pete?"

"Here's rule number one at Wilkinson's: keep clear of Pete. Even Angus is scared of him. He would have been out on his ear long ago in any other yard."

We turn into a row of houses. Laura leads me up a short path, then unlocks the front door of a small house.

"New girl," she calls out.

"Another new girl?" The voice has an Indian accent. "What's going on?"

Laura and I walk into a brightly lit kitchen. A woman in a sari stands in front of a stove, her broad back to us. "Honestly," she is muttering. "All this coming and going. I don't know. How long's this one going to last?"

She turns and looks at us. There is something about the fake-angry expression on her face that makes me smile.

"Oh, my goodness," she says. "They're getting younger all the time. You should be at school, young lady."

"This is Jay," Laura says to her. "The latest victim." Laura turns to me. "Jay, this is Auntie."

I learn quite a bit about Auntie that evening. She likes to combine English and Indian food in a way that only sometimes works. Over sausage biryani, she tells me how she came to Newmarket as a young girl, when she was married to Jasminder, who called himself Jas. Newmarket is full of Asians now, but when Mr. Wilkinson took him on, he was one of the first to be employed here.

"Those were the days when Mr. Wilkinson was big news," says Auntie. "One moment, he is just 'the guv'nor.' The next he is Magic. It is Magic this and Magic that. The press was crazy about him, I tell you."

Laura listens, a smile on her face. I get the sense that she has heard this story many times before.

Auntie's real name is Sowjanya, but no one could remember that, so when her three children—a boy and two girls—grew up and left home, she was happy for her family nickname, Auntie, to be used by her guests.

About ten years ago, Jas decided he wanted to return to India. "I told him straight out. I'm not going. I'm happy here. Vamoose." She waves a hand dismissively. "That's what I said to him. You've done your bit. Now it is my turn." It was Mrs. Wilkinson who suggested she should be a landlady. "The rest is history."

"She's the best landlady in Newmarket," says Laura. "She's been in the local paper."

"Stop it now—load of nonsense." Auntie waves a hand, as if brushing away her fame, but there is a smile on her face. She stands up. "Laura will show you the ropes. She's a good girl. And you can start by doing the dishes."

After supper, as Auntie stays inside watching television, Laura and I sit in the little back garden, mugs of tea in our hands.

She chats casually about the Wilkinson yard. It's one of the oldest stables in Newmarket, she tells me, then laughs. "And it feels it."

"But he's famous, Mr. Wilkinson."

"He had his glory days." Laura sips at her tea. "Trouble is, they were a bit of a long time ago. Racing's moved on, and he hasn't."

In the gloomy evening light, she tells me that these

days there is only one decent owner who has horses with Mr. Wilkinson, a Saudi prince, and that even he is rumored to be about to take his horses away.

"Too many has-beens and losers," she says rather cheerfully. "And that's just the humans."

"What about the horses?"

"Couple of half-decent two-year-olds, but there's a lot of rubbish in those stables. They're just kept for the—" She rubs the fingers of her left hand together.

"The gray, Manhattan," I say casually. "Is she rubbish?"

"Worse than rubbish. You don't want to waste your time on that big freak. She's the joke of the yard, Nellie."

"Nellie?"

"That's what we call her. Someone said she looks like a giraffe. Someone remembered that kids' song 'Nellie the Elephant.' So Nellie it was."

"What's wrong with her?"

"You'll find out." Laura stands up and drains her tea. She suddenly seems a bit uncomfortable by the way our conversation has gone. "New lads get a little bit of a test. It involves the mare." She speaks in a low voice, as if one of Auntie's neighbors could be listening in.

"What?"

"Don't worry about it. Just keep your nose clean and you'll be all right. I'll see you in the morning."

Alone in the little garden, I listen to the distant sounds of Newmarket—some music, a train racing by, the occasional raised voice.

I have a job. I am in racing. There are all sorts of mysterious tests ahead of me. And I'm not a stable lass.

One.

Of.

The.

Lads.

SPECIAL RULE

And so my life as a stable lad begins.

I feel odd and out of place at first. The breeches, boots, and helmet Deej found for me in the tack room are slightly too big and have the stale smell of someone else's sweat.

Deej and Laura look out for me, but always quietly. I sense that if I make a mistake, I will be on my own.

Although they mostly ignore me, I get to know the other lads.

There's Liam, an Irishman in his twenties who was once a promising apprentice but became too heavy to make it as a jockey, and Tommy—older, balding—who tells bad jokes. Amit is a good-looking Indian guy who looks neat on a horse but has soft, scared eyes. Davy, one of the younger lads, can never stop talking.

Then there is Pete, broad shouldered and with a harsh buzz cut that makes his head look like some kind of missile. He is older than I first thought—probably in his late thirties—and there is something about him that seems to scare the other lads. They laugh at his jokes, step out of his way when he enters the tack room.

I'm curious about him. He doesn't seem to like horses, and judging by the way he slumps in the saddle, he sees riding as a chore. Deej is reluctant to talk about him. "Comes from London," he says, adding as a casual afterthought, "it's best to keep on the right side of old Pete."

Sometimes as I go about my work, I notice that Angus, the head lad, is watching me. He has given me the heaviest, nastiest jobs. I lug bales of hay my first morning. When I finish, Angus hands me a bucket and scrubbing brush.

"Toilet duty," he says. "Give the lads' lavatory a good going over, will you, lassie?"

As he walks away, he passes Pete and says something that makes them both laugh.

There is no riding for those first two days. I watch as the early-morning string of horses—"first lot," it is called—go to the covered yard where Mr. Wilkinson waits for them, a matchstick in the side of his mouth. I see them walk out to the heath.

Second lot, for the horses not racing in the near future, goes out at 8:45. Later in the morning, there is third lot—the two-year-olds who are still too weak to be galloping, and horses that are recovering from injury.

I look out for the big gray, Manhattan, but the only time I see her is as she's being led by Pete to the walker, a circular moving floor that exercises horses for forty-five minutes without their having to be ridden.

After two days of being treated like the stable dog, I finally get the chance to show that I can ride.

I am on the stack in the hay barn when Mrs. Wilkinson appears. As usual, she doesn't exactly fit the image of a trainer's wife. In tight designer jeans, a well-ironed white shirt, and shiny boots, she looks more like a busy city type on a weekend break in the country.

"I think it's time to find out if you're any good, Miss Barton," she booms. "Tack up Athlone Boy, Mr. Bucknall's hunter. Use his hunting saddle. I'll see you at the indoor arena in fifteen minutes sharp."

She walks briskly out of the yard.

I'm already halfway down the ladder.

Athlone Boy is a heavy, sleepy cob with a slightly bored look to him. When going out to the gallops with the string, he and Bucknall, with their two big bottoms and a slow, waddling stride, look strange and out of place. It is as if a couple of hippopotamuses have wandered into a ballet class. Right now he is none too thrilled at being asked to work for the second time in the day.

"Wake him up, Jay!" Mrs. Wilkinson watches me, arms crossed, as I take Athlone Boy around the outside of the big barn where the string gathers every morning before going on the heath. "You're like a sack of potatoes."

I give the old horse a kick in the ribs.

Come on, boy. Stop fooling around.

With an impatient grunt, Athlone Boy trots on. I give him another harder kick, clicking my teeth, and he breaks into a canter, grunting with every stride. It is good to be back in the saddle.

You can tell that he is used to being ridden badly. At first, he is unresponsive and determined to go at his own pace, but I squeeze him up to the bridle, slap him on the shoulder with the end of the reins. He needs to know who's boss. Soon I have him running easily.

That's it. This is how it goes with me. It's more fun, isn't it?

After circling and doing some figure eights, I even pop him over a low triple bar that is in the center of the arena.

Out of the arena, Mrs. Wilkinson walks in silence beside me. Now and then she glances in my direction. As we enter the back yard, Angus appears.

"The girl's not bad." Mrs. Wilkinson nods in my direction. "Strong legs, good hands, got the old boy going nicely. I think she should ride out tomorrow. Put her on something quiet."

"Already, Mrs. Wilkinson? She's just a wee slip of—"

"Good to see what she's made of."

The head lad looks away sharply in irritation, then says quietly, "I'd probably best wait for Mr. Wilkinson's instructions on that, ma'am."

"No need." A quick, cold smile flashes across Mrs. Wilkinson's face. "I'll tell him myself."

She walks off, her boots echoing on the concrete.

* * *

I arrive at the yard early on my fourth day of work and go straight to the tack room to look at the List. Those are our orders for the day, put up last thing at night.

The List has all the names of the horses in the yard, and beside each of them the lads who will be riding them that day first, second, and third lot. If there are special instructions about blinders or if a horse should wear a certain bridle or martingale, that will be on the List too.

My name is nowhere to be seen. I have no choice but to stay in the tack room until Angus tells me what to do.

When he arrives, later than usual, he behaves as if I am invisible. He collects his saddle and bridle. As he is about to leave, he mutters, "Oh, yes, there's you, girlie. Muck out Liam's and Amit's horses, will you? They're going racing today."

"Excuse me, Angus," I call after him.

He turns. "Aye?"

"I thought I was riding out today."

He walks slowly back to me.

"Third lot. But your friend Mrs. Wilkinson won't be around to look after you. They'll be off racing by late morning."

"Great. Who am I riding?"

An odd little smile appears on his face. "Oh, maybe you can ride Nellie. Let Pete tack her up for you."

"Manhattan?"

"Nellie to her friends. If she had any."

"Thanks, Angus."

"You're welcome." He reaches for one of the whips hanging on a hook beside the saddles. "You'll need this."

I'm confused. I have been told by Deej that only lads who are experienced enough to ride on the training grounds are allowed to carry a whip.

"Special rule," Angus explains. "You won't be carrying a whip normally. But you'll need it on the mare."

There is an odd atmosphere at the yard later that morning. The Wilkinsons have left for the races after first lot. There is more noise and laughter in the yard than usual.

Another odd thing. I am no longer invisible.

"What's going on?" I ask Deej after he returns from second lot. "Why are people smiling at me?"

"Just do your best on the mare," he says.

"I heard that new lads get a test."

Deej gives me an odd look. I sense he would like to tell me more but hasn't quite got the nerve.

"We all need a laugh now and then," he says. "Don't worry about it."

At 10:45, I put on my helmet and, feeling a bit self-conscious, I make my way to Manhattan's stall, the whip in my hand.

To my surprise, Pete has her saddled and bridled already. She seems calmer than when I last saw her. In fact, she is more than calm—she looks half-asleep.

"What's she like as a ride?" I ask Pete as I look over the stall door.

He tightens the girth. "That's for you to find out, isn't it?"

I walk into the stall. For the first time, I see how big she is. She must be more than seventeen hands.

When Pete gives me a leg up, it is as if he is lifting me through the roof. I land in the saddle heavily. To my surprise, Manhattan shows no reaction.

Pete leads me slowly out of the stable. The mare puts one foot in front of the other as if every step is an effort for her. Looking down, I feel small and slightly ridiculous. Several of the lads are standing around the back yard, as if waiting for this moment.

"Off you go, then," says Pete, taking his hand off the reins.

I give Manhattan a kick. She plants her feet firmly on the ground. Her ears twitch backward.

Come on, girl. Let's go.

There are jeers around the yard.

"What's up, Barton?" Pete calls out. "Got a problem? We heard you could ride."

"Give her one, girl," somebody shouts. "Bloomin' freak, Nellie. She's making a fool of you."

I see Laura crossing the yard, carrying a saddle propped against her hip. She stares ahead of her as if nothing is happening. I slap Manhattan gently on the shoulder with the whip. Now her ears are flat back against her head.

We're not freaks, are we, girl?

Manhattan sighs wearily, and somehow I know how she is feeling, surrounded by laughing, scornful humans.

I take my feet out of the stirrups, slide the long way

down to the ground. I put down the whip beside the stall door and lead her toward the indoor arena.

When we enter, the six other horses going out on third lot are walking around the outside. Bucknall is standing where Mr. Wilkinson normally stands. I lead Manhattan toward him.

"Having problems already, Jasmine?" he says, a little smile on his face.

I stand beside Manhattan and raise my left leg. "Just a leg up please, Mr. Bucknall," I say.

The assistant trainer hikes me into the saddle. "Blimey," he says, looking up at me. "You've got a long way to fall, Jasmine. Where's your whip?"

"She doesn't like it. I could tell when I slapped her on the shoulder."

"Not a clue," Bucknall mutters. "Hopeless little schoolgirl."

Manhattan is doing her statue act again. I think of Ted and wonder what he would do. Then I remember the heart trick.

I place my hand on her shoulder.

Just you and me. Forget everyone else. It's us.

I draw the shape of a heart on her coat. Her ears flicker uncertainly.

That's it.

Again, I trace the heart, pressing into her skin.

You're safe with me, girl.

"Come on, new girl," I hear one of the lads calling out. "Let's see how you ride."

I ignore him.

Don't worry, Manhattan. I won't hit you.

I sense the slightest relaxation in the horse's giant frame. I apply the gentlest pressure on her mouth and click my teeth.

Slowly, reluctantly, like a grandma with arthritis, she walks forward. I join the rest of the string.

It is a tough hour and a half. Manhattan is tense, as if expecting to be hit at any moment. As we follow far behind the other horses, there is a temptation to get angry with her, kick her up into the bridle.

But I talk in a low voice, all the way up the horse path toward the heath.

As I join the other horses on the gallops, Laura—who is riding a two-year-old called Crazy Days—glances at me and winks, a little smile on her face. I sense that the other lads are losing interest in the Manhattan and Jay Barton Show.

I am watching the dark-gray ears in front of me. I have never known a horse with such expressive ears. They tremble, flicker backward or forward, as if listening out for a signal no one else can hear.

She lays them back if another horse comes too close to her or if she senses that I am becoming impatient. I go still in the saddle, lay a hand on her coat in front of the saddle, and reassure her.

You're all right, girl.

At first, as we walk along an exercise path on the heath, she is slow, almost sleepy. Then, as the string gets farther ahead of us, she begins to look around her.

At some point, the other horses break into a trot. I give her a light squeeze of the legs and immediately sense rebellion beneath me.

Come on, girl. Don't let me down. Not now.

I drop my hands and let her stop. I hear the laughter of the lads, who have noticed what is happening.

I click my teeth. Slowly, the ears flicker forward. Manhattan walks and then, with a grunt that is almost human in its grumpiness, she breaks into a long, loping trot.

Liam, the lad in front of me, glances over his shoulder. I can see surprise on his face. He says something to Tommy, who is in front of him, and the word goes up the string.

"The freaks are doing all right, girl."

By the time we return to the yard, Manhattan is walking a little more easily. She is still wary of me, but more relaxed. She goes better, I have discovered, when allowed her own space at the back of the string. She likes to be alone.

Angus watches as we come in, his face showing no expression. "Stop," he says to me. I stand in front of him, Manhattan posing, head high, as if she were the star of the stable. "How did she go, lassie?"

"She went quite well, thank you, Angus."

A look of surprise crosses Angus's face. "Well, you'd better get your parachute and come down to earth. Off you get."

I slip out of the saddle and carefully let myself down the great height from Manhattan's back. I'm leading her toward the stable when Pete arrives.

Without a word, he takes the reins from me. Manhattan's

ears go back and she lowers her head. Suddenly there's a mulish look in her eye. Pete tugs downward at the reins, and she jerks her head up in alarm.

As he leads her into the stable, he calls over his shoulder, "Stay out if you don't want to get hurt."

As Pete reaches for the girth, Manhattan arches her neck and bares her teeth. Swearing at her, Pete manages to get the saddle off just before Manhattan kicks forward, the hind leg only narrowly missing him.

"Cow kick, they call that," Pete says grimly. "And she's a cow, all right."

Angus walks over and stands beside me at the door. "Look and learn, lassie." He nods in Pete's direction. "This is how you handle a difficult racehorse."

I want to point out that I've just handled a difficult racehorse pretty well, but I don't. "Yes, Angus," I say.

Pete is trying to reach Manhattan's bridle. He has managed to unfasten the throatlatch, so that he now just has to take the top of the bridle and slip it off her head.

But Manhattan is having none of it. She holds her head high, and she is so tall that Pete is unable to reach her. The more he curses, the more she throws her head in the air.

"Sort her out, Pete." Angus is irritated that the lesson is not going as well as he planned. "It's the only way with mares."

"Could I have a go?" I ask the question quietly.

"This isn't the Pony Club, lassie," says Angus.

"I know." I draw back the latch on the stall door.

Pete glances toward me, then at Angus.

To my surprise, the head lad nods. "Let her make a fool of herself, Pete. If she gets hurt—well, we warned her."

Pete pushes his way past me. Watched by the two men, I walk slowly into the stall and stand beside Manhattan, my hand on her neck.

OK, Manhattan. This is the part where you don't embarrass me.

She stands still, her neck tensed. She trusts no one.

You know what? I've got a carrot in this jacket.

I reach into my pocket. There's the tiniest flicker of interest from Manhattan's ears.

"Waste of time," Pete says from the stall door.

Angus says nothing.

I hold the carrot in the palm of my hand, near Manhattan's head. She can smell it, but at first is too proud to take it from me.

We stand motionless for a moment. Then, slowly, Manhattan takes the carrot and crunches it, more relaxed now.

"Grab the bridle—her head's down," says Pete.

I remain motionless for a few seconds.

While Manhattan is looking for another carrot, I run my hand up her neck and tug at her ears, then rest my hand on the top of the bridle. Waiting until she has finished her carrot, I slip the bridle off slowly, then pat her neck.

That's my girl.

I look toward the door. Angus has gone. Pete is staring hard at me.

"Like her, do you?"

"I've never seen a horse like her."

"Enjoy her while you can. Any day now she'll be taken away to the vet. One-way ticket. The bullet. They're putting her down—it's been decided."

"What?" I look at Pete to see if this is one of his nasty jokes. It isn't.

"Ask the others," he says. "She'll be dog food soon."

There is a sick, empty feeling in my stomach. "But why?" I try to sound as casual as he is, but my voice cracks.

"She's useless. And dangerous. The owner won't breed from her with that kind of temperament. Nobody likes her in the yard."

"I like her."

Pete makes a pistol shape with his hand, puts it against the side of his head, and pulls the trigger. "*Boom!* Dead as mutton," he says. With a little laugh, he walks off.

Manhattan stirs and looks toward me, expecting another carrot.

No. It can't be true.

Too.

Beautiful.

To.

Die.

COME IN, NUMBER NINE

The next morning, I get a surprise. My name is on the List for first lot, beside that of a four-year-old called Norewest.

I have seen him out with the string. He is big and angular, with a slightly downtrodden look. He has never won a race and belongs to an owner who has better, faster horses.

There is a chill in the air, and a low mist hangs over the gallops when the fifteen horses make their way onto the heath. The lads, slumped and still sleepy, ride in silence. Occasionally, there's a bit of disturbance in the string when one of the horses acts up. Tommy, the oldest lad in the yard, swears and gives a tug on the reins and calm returns.

We circle at the start of the all-weather track with rails on each side. It leads away from the town into the mist.

Deej has told me that the only horses who will be doing serious work will be going out with the second string. We'll be doing a gentle half speed—fast canter, really—leaving a gap of about fifty meters between each horse.

To our left, beyond some rails along the road, I see the battered old station wagon I had noticed outside Mr. Wilkinson's house. The trainer and his wife are walking toward a point halfway up the gallops.

Ahead of me, Tommy mutters, "The missus is out."

As Mr. and Mrs. Wilkinson arrive and we circle around them, I notice that Pete is following me with his eyes. He says something in a low voice to Angus, who is in front of him.

"New girl. Barton," he calls out. "Get off that horse and let Pete sort out its tack."

Puzzled, I bring Norewest into the center of the circle and get out of the saddle. I hold Pete's horse as he looks at my girth.

"She's only gone and put it on twisted." Pete's voice is loud, an announcement to the string. He glances in my direction. "Don't they teach you anything at Pony Club?"

I say nothing but I'm confused. There was nothing wrong with the way Norewest was saddled. I'm sure of that.

Pete unfastens the girth and, with much sighing and generally fiddling about, adjusts it. "Pull the girth tight before you're on your way," he says, giving me a leg up. Then, weirdly, he winks at me as if we share a secret.

I nod, putting my feet in the stirrups.

Norewest seems to have been upset by the interruption. He prances around restlessly as the first horses set off.

"Settle that horse down, Jay," Mr. Wilkinson mutters irritably.

Four horses have peeled off and are cantering away from us down the track. Soon it will be my turn.

I lift my left leg in front of the saddle and pull the girth as tight as I can.

With a sharp, pig-like squeal, Norewest launches himself as if a rocket has been set off behind him. He bucks and twists as he goes, sending the other horses scattering. I cling on desperately.

I've managed to recover the reins, but I've lost my stirrups. Norewest is careering toward the road. Somehow I manage to haul him in the direction of the gallops, toward where Mr. and Mrs. Wilkinson are standing.

We head off, parallel to the track, galloping as if something terrifying is on our tail.

"Easy, boy, easy," I say loudly. "Easy, easy."

I see the white faces of the trainer and his wife, who have turned to watch my progress. Because I've lost my irons, I can put no weight on the reins. Even if I could, it would make no difference. I might as well not be there. The horse beneath me has gone crazy.

We pass another trainer's string, who have just pulled up from their work. I hear laughter as we pass them.

"Easy, boy."

I look ahead of me. The heath stretches into the distance, but there is a high hawthorn hedge to my left between the heath and a wood. I manage to steer him in that direction, then pull him around, back toward where the Wilkinson string is circling in the distance.

"Easy. Back we go to the string."

My arms are aching, my legs weakening from the effort of staying in the saddle, but Norewest shows no sign of slowing down.

Once again, like a crazy comedy act, we pass the Wilkinsons, then reach the string heading toward town. One of the lads calls out, "Come in, number nine, your time is up."

Norewest is wet with lather now. He is so crazed that I'm afraid he'll have a heart attack or break a leg before I can stop him. I manage to turn him away from the town, back toward the wood. It's time for drastic action.

I guide him, straight at the hawthorn hedge, not allowing him this time to head back toward the string.

For a moment, I fear that he is going to take on the hedge — try to jump it or burst through it like a cartoon figure running through a wall — but at the very last moment, he stabs his front feet into the turn. Emergency stop.

There is a moment, like something out of a dream, when I feel myself sailing through the air.

Then the world explodes.

Followed by silence.

I'm conscious. I'm breathing. I'm alive. I try to move my arms, then my legs. Nothing seems to be broken. I can move my head.

And I'm deep, deep in a hedge. This fact enters my brain a split second before pain tears through my body, the sharp agony of hundreds of thorns tearing and gouging my flesh.

Behind me I hear a low snort. The surprise of seeing his jockey in a hedge seems to have released Norewest from whatever madness was gripping him.

He gives a little harrumph. Then I hear him trotting away from me.

Closing my mind to the pain, I move one arm, then the other. I writhe and turn, eyes shut, one hand in front of my face. Slowly I back my way out of the hedge.

I am just emerging, unsteady and covered in blood, as the trainer's car rattles into view.

Mr. Wilkinson gets out, ignoring me and scanning the horizon for Norewest.

"Horse all right. Heading back to the stable," he says.

Mrs. Wilkinson stands by the car. Her face is not exactly a picture of sympathy. "Well, that was bloody unimpressive, I must say." She glances at my face. "You look a mess."

"I'm sorry." The words come from me breathlessly, like a sob. "I don't know what happened."

Mrs. Wilkinson smiles sarcastically. "What happened is that you rode a racehorse and were unable to control it."

My eyes sting from what I take to be sweat, but when I run the back of my hand across my forehead, it is red with blood.

Mr. Wilkinson has returned to the car. His wife looks at my face more closely. "You should probably get that stitched," she says.

"I'm OK."

She smiles coldly. "Suit yourself." She turns back to the car and opens the back door. "Sit on the rug," she says as I climb in. "Do *not* bleed on the car."

As we speed down a lane and on the road leading back to town, the trainer and his wife converse as if I am not there.

"She said she could ride," mutters the trainer. "Shouldn't listen to you. Another useless girl."

"She looked perfectly competent in the arena."

"Managed to spook Norewest. Takes some doing."

"At least she did the sensible thing and pointed the horse at the hedge." Mrs. Wilkinson glances at me. "Gave herself a soft landing, if a bit sharp."

The trainer is shaking his head. "Liability. Blinkin' hopeless."

"Thank you, Clive. That'll be enough." The voice is quiet but firm.

Mr. Wilkinson mutters briefly, then falls silent.

The car draws up outside Auntie's house. I get out, and as the car takes off behind me, I hobble my way up the path. Every inch of my body seems to be aching.

I ring the bell.

Auntie opens the door. "Oh, my goodness, what's happened to you?"

"Sorry, Auntie. I left my keys at the stable."

She steps back and I walk in.

Standing in the hall, I try to sound carefree. "Had a bit of a tumble."

"Stay there." She looks more closely at my face. "Nasty cut above your eye. Maybe I should take you to the hospital."

"I'll be fine. Honestly."

All.

Jockeys.

Have.

Scars.

Who Is Bug?

I must be more shaken than I thought, because as soon as Auntie closes the curtains that morning, I fall into a deep sleep.

Sometime that afternoon, I open my eyes. There's still daylight outside, and the big, reassuring shape of Auntie is sitting on the end of my bed.

"It's alive," she says, and I hear the smile in her voice. "I just wanted to check that you're all right."

I try to sit up, but small stabs of pain all over my body make me fall back on my pillow. "Ow," I say weakly.

Auntie lays a cool hand above the cut on my forehead in a way that reminds me of my mother when I was small. "You weren't knocked out, were you?"

I shake my head and wince at a sharp ache in my neck. "No. The hedge broke my fall."

"That cut looks nasty. You should have it looked at."

"It's all right. I wasn't planning to be a model."

Auntie hands me a cup. "Tulsi tea," she says. "Special herbal tea from back home. I used to give it to Jas when he had a fall."

I sip at the tea. It has an odd taste, sweet but with a tang of bitterness.

Laura appears at the door. "You all right?" she asks.

"Bit sore."

"Glad you're OK." She looks at me for a moment and is gone, leaving me with the niggling idea that I've let her down in some way.

Auntie goes to shut the door, then returns to the bed. "Maybe you should be doing all this racing stuff a little later." She speaks casually, picking at a loose thread on the bedcover. "You're so young and small. It's tough, that business. The horses. The falls. The bullyboys." She looks at me. "It's not much of a vacation job."

"No." I speak the word with quiet certainty. "It's not a vacation job. This is my life now. I can't go back."

"Think about it." Auntie stands and looks down at me. "Sleep on it."

After she has left, the tulsi tea takes effect. I doze off.

When I wake, it is the middle of the night. I lie wide-eyed and alert in my bed. The events of the day seem clearer now. Nothing about what happened on the gallops makes any sense. Why did Angus let Pete adjust my girth? How could I have put it on twisted? I think of the wink that Pete gave me after he had given me the leg up, almost as if we were sharing some secret joke. What made Norewest change so quickly? What did I do to upset him?

I get out of bed and stare out at the lights of Newmarket. When I first rode ponies, Ted used to tell me that when jockeys fall, they want to get back in the saddle as soon as possible.

The clock beside my bed shows two a.m. Four more hours and I will be back in the yard. Back in the saddle.

I leave early for work.

As I walk slowly and painfully toward the stable, I catch sight of myself in a shop window. I'm hobbling along as if I've just been hit by a truck. My face is a tangled cobweb of scratches. I'd laugh if it wasn't too painful. The gates are open, but none of the lads are here yet. I hear someone in the forage room, and as I pass, I see Michael, the feed man, stacking sacks of horse nuts.

I walk to the tack room to see the List. My name is nowhere to be seen.

I walk to the main entrance to the yard and wait. The first lads to arrive at work, Liam and Amit, laugh when they see me at the gate.

"Whoa, it's Bug," says Amit. "Straight out of *Night of the Living Dead*."

"Glutton for punishment, aren't you, Bug?" Liam laughs as he walks on, but admiration is in his voice.

Who, exactly, is Bug?

Deej explains it to me when he arrives. It seems I have a new nickname. "Someone said you'd been clinging on like a limpet," he says. "Limpet became Bug. It's a good sign, getting a nickname. Bug Barton. It could be worse."

Angus is less pleased that I am here. He stops when he sees me, his hands on his hips.

"What the blazes are you doing here, lassie?"

"I'm working. I was hoping to ride out."

"After yesterday? Are you kidding me?"

"I could ride Norewest."

"You're blazing joking. He's staying in today, thanks to you."

"Is he injured?"

The head lad looks away. "You can muck out the stalls in the back yard if you're so blazing keen," he says.

After the first lot have pulled out, I walk into the main yard. The only person there is Frank, the old ex-jockey who is now the stable's yard man. I tell him that I'm going to check on Norewest.

Frank leans on his broom, smiling. "Looks like you're the one who came off worst," he says.

He walks with me to Norewest's stall. The horse is calmly eating hay.

"Are you all right, boy?" Frank opens the stall door, walks in, and runs an expert hand down the horse's front legs. "No warmth there. He seems—" Grunting, he slips down on one knee and looks more closely at Norewest's stomach. He reaches out to touch a spot behind the horse's front legs. There is a dark stain there, where purple iodine has been sprayed.

"Has he cut himself?" I ask.

"Oh dear, oh dear." Frank is shaking his head. "I've not seen this for a while. Let me see the girth you wore yesterday."

We walk to the tack room. My saddle is on its rack as usual, but something has changed. Yesterday, there was a yellow elastic girth on it. Now it has a leather one.

Frank looks into the big wooden chest where spare tack is kept. There, on the top, is my girth. He picks it up and smiles grimly. Halfway along its length, there is a dark stain, which is still damp. He touches it, then looks at his fingertip. It is red. Blood.

"Nasty old racing trick, that is. Someone slipped a filed-down tack into the girth sheath. As soon as the girth was tightened—well, there's why your horse bolted. Seems like you might have an enemy in the yard," he says, wandering off. There's no way he is going to get involved in any of this.

When first lot returns, I wait until the lads are leaving for their breakfast before following Angus into the tack room. He is looking at the List as I enter.

"I've seen Norewest," I say.

"I'd concentrate on your own horses if I were you, girlie," he says quietly without turning around. "You've done enough harm as it is."

"His stomach has been injured, Angus. Where the girth was."

"Oh aye? You're a vet now, are you?" I sense a hint of concern in Angus's voice.

I walk to the tack chest, open it, and take out the yellow girth. I hold it out.

"Someone put something sharp in the girth sheath. When I tightened it, Norewest was stabbed in the stomach. That's why he bolted."

Angus turns, looks down at the girth, then at me. "Put the girth back, girl." He speaks in a low, level voice.

"I could have been badly hurt. The horse could have injured himself. It's cruel."

"Pete told me the girth was twisted." He says the words quietly, almost talking to himself.

"I just wanted you to know."

"Yes. Thank you. Let's keep this to ourselves, shall we?" Angus looks at me for a few seconds. Then, as if suddenly remembering something, he adds, "Will you be all right on Manhattan for third lot?"

"Of course."

"That's good, then."

He struts away and, in my mind, I hear Laura's words of advice to me.

Keep.

Your.

Nose.

Clean.

JINXED

After second lot has pulled out and the yard is quiet, I make my slow, painful way to Manhattan's stall.

She stands with her head in the corner, resting one leg. Her ears go back as I enter the stall, but when I ignore her, she returns to her sad, sleepy state. I lay a hand on her neck.

We're both alone, aren't we? And no one quite gets us.

She tenses slightly. She has seen too much of human beings to trust any of them, but there is something about me today that seems to calm her.

That's my girl. We're in the same boat.

I've taken my grooming kit with me. When Mr. Wilkinson does his evening inspection, I've noticed that he never spends long at this stall. All the other horses have been groomed so that they shine when their lad takes their blankets off. Because the trainer never casts more than a glance at Manhattan, Pete hardly bothers with her.

There you go. This will make you feel better.

Every move makes me wince, but I fetch a bucket and stand on it so that I can reach the top of her back. Gasping from the pain, I run a dandy brush over her. I start gently, and after a few minutes, the aching in my muscles eases. Manhattan allows herself to be groomed, almost as if she can sense that I am in no state to deal with her mad-dragon act.

Soon the stall is thick with dust and dirt. The gleaming color of her coat begins to come through as I pick up the body brush. Her coat is dark with small, delicate blotches of lightness, like the sun shining through thundery clouds, and her tail goes from black at the top to the palest gray at its tip. Her head and mane are a lighter color, and she has a wild blaze of whiteness between her eyes and spilling down to her nose, as if someone has thrown a can of paint at her. She has the longest eyelashes I have seen on any horse, and they are pure white. She is the most beautiful horse I have ever seen.

You like being pampered, don't you?

Her eyes, dark against the whiteness, half close as I run the brush over her.

You're tired of being fierce. You don't want to fight everyone.

When I reach for the currycomb and start working on her mane, she sighs wearily. Perhaps she is thinking of what her life should have been.

Since Pete told me that she was going to be put down, I have asked around. I now know the sad story of Manhattan.

One of the lads, Liam, has told me that she is the

best-bred horse in the yard. Her pedigree goes way back to a horse called The Tetrarch, another dark gray, who was a brilliant colt a century ago and became one of the greatest stallions in the history of racing. Fillies bred from The Tetrarch, or from his equally brilliant daughter Mumtaz Mahal, share the dark, dappled gray color and are big, strong, and fast.

She was bred by the yard's best owner, Prince Ahmed, who was a member of the royal family in Saudi Arabia. The week that she was born, the prince had a heart attack. He died a week later.

When she came to the yard as a yearling, she belonged to Prince Muqrin, Ahmed's son, a man in his twenties. The lads remember how she was bigger and stronger than any other yearling that year. Mr. Wilkinson gave her to one of his best lads, a man called Charlie, to break in. He was leading her up in the covered yard when he was found unconscious. When he came around, Charlie couldn't remember anything that had happened.

Her owner had died. Her lad was badly injured. People in racing are superstitious, and the big yearling began to get a name for bringing bad luck. She had a jinx on her, the lads said.

Trouble, I was told, followed her. She was too strong for most of the lads on the gallops. She went crazy when the vet or the blacksmith came near her. She was somehow different from any other horse, and usually in the worst possible way.

But she had talent. Before she raced as a two-year-old, the stable thought it had a future Classics winner. Even at that age, she was fast and strong and could gallop other horses into the ground. But when she first appeared on the racecourse, she sweated in the paddock, reared up on the way to the start, and raced with her ears flat back. She finished ten lengths behind the rest of the field, tailed off. She ran three times as a two-year-old, each time worse than the last.

There was a rumor that something was wrong with her. She has a strange way of walking and trotting, putting one foot in front of the other—plaiting, it's called. Whatever the problem, whether it was in her body or her head, the result was the same. She was a big, expensive flop.

Manhattan. It's a great name, but I'm going to call you Hat.

When I've finished, her coat gleams. I want to put oil on her hooves, but she lifts her feet nervously as soon as I go near them and I'm not in the mood to insist. I put on her blanket. She takes a carrot from me, and I tug at her light-gray velvet ears. I stand back to look at her.

Better, Hat?

What Pete said was right. Her career is over. She is now five, quite old for a flat racer. Most owners would quietly sell her off to go steeplechasing or abroad—maybe breed from her. But the Saudis are great believers in bloodlines. No bad blood or dodgy genes should be passed down to future generations of Thoroughbreds.

Manhattan has had her chance. It is just a matter of time before she is taken away to be destroyed.

I won't let it happen, Manhattan. We'll be in this together.

* * *

Later that morning, we join the six other horses in the yard for third lot. Laura's there, and Deej, Tommy, Amit, Liam, and one of the younger lads, Fergus.

They glance at me, surprised, as I enter.

"Giving us another show today, are you, Bug?" Tommy calls.

"Nah, I think I'll take it a bit easier," I say.

"She's almost as tough as you, Laura," says Amit.

Laura smiles at him but avoids looking at me. "Don't mess with the girls," she says.

The guv'nor walks in, hands in pockets, and stands in the center of the arena, watching us.

"All right, Jay?" he calls out.

"Yes, sir. Fine."

"Angus spoke to me. Said business with Norewest not your fault. Horse spooked by something. Got a bit of a saddle sore. Noticed last night."

"Yes, sir."

"Glad you're back. In one piece."

When the string files out of the yard into the sunlight, I pull Manhattan aside and let the others pass so that she can take her normal place at the back.

Today I find that I no longer have to coax and kick her along to make her walk out. I talk to her as we go. She relaxes, looking around and taking an interest in what is going on.

There is a surprise on the gallops. The trainer is standing by the rails about halfway up the all-weather track.

"We're doing a half speed," Deej calls back. "Keep

twenty lengths between you. Bring Manhattan up last. If she won't start, we'll meet you back here."

We circle at the start of the track. One after the other, the horses set off. Ahead of me, Liam looks over his shoulder.

"She won't go, Bug. Last time she dug her toes in."

Four horses left, three. I feel Manhattan tense beneath me.

I lay a hand on her shoulder. I trace the heart.

Liam calls out, "See you back here, Bug."

All right, girl. Our first canter. Let's make this good.

I lead her toward the track. Her ears flick back uncertainly.

Forget the memories, Hat. This is different.

She is walking stiff-legged now. Liam is ten lengths ahead of us. I gather up my reins and, for a moment, Manhattan stops in her tracks.

Come on, girl. For me.

I click my teeth, as I used to with Dusty. Her ears go forward. With an unladylike grunt, Manhattan sets off.

Her head is low and she takes a strong hold of the bit. There is a sharp twinge in my back from the fall yesterday. She has such a giant stride that it takes me about fifty meters before I realize that, even though she is only cantering, we are closing in on the horse in front.

"Easy, Hat."

I take a pull on the reins and she slows, as graceful as a ballet dancer. By the time we pass Mr. Wilkinson, standing on the rails, a smile is on my face, the aches in my body forgotten.

It is only a canter, but at the top of the hill, Manhattan behaves as if she has just won a race. She shakes her head like a two-year-old, jogs sideways.

You like stretching your legs, don't you, girl?

Ahead of me, Liam shakes his head. "Are you giving that horse drugs?" he says. "I've never seen her do that before."

She has calmed slightly by the time we file past the trainer on our way back down the hill.

"All right, Deej?"

"Yes, sir."

"Tommy?"

"Yes, sir."

I've noticed that when Mr. Wilkinson asks how a horse has gone, he is not looking for conversation. Unless the horse has coughed or gone lame, there is only one answer he is looking for.

"All right, Liam?"

"Yes, sir."

"All right, Jay?"

"Yes, sir."

The trainer follows Manhattan with his eyes. He murmurs something to himself, then turns to walk back to his car.

"All done." That's what I think he said. Or it might have been "Well done."

The sun is shining on the heath; skylarks are singing in the blue sky. On our way home, the lads include me in their chat. I'm Bug; I'm one of them. Quietly, so that no one except my horse can hear me, I sing one of the songs that my mum used to love:

"*Row, row, row your boat,*
Gently down the stream.
Merrily, merrily, merrily, merrily,
Life is but a dream."

I'm still humming as we walk down the horse path toward the main yard. I loosen Manhattan's girth and give her a pat on the neck but as we get closer to the stable, her ears flick back and the spring goes out of her step.

There is a movement in the shadowy passageway leading into the back yard. Briefly, I see the outline of a figure carrying a pitchfork.

Eyes.

Watching.

Us.

RED FIRE

The wound above my eyes grows crusty. The scab comes off. The scar grows paler until it becomes a slash of white on my sunburned face. Summer passes.

Now and then, when I'm feeling lonely, memories of the past appear in my mind like uninvited guests. Drawing back the curtains in my room to see Dusty looking up at me from the stable yard. Riding across the fields with Michaela. Being driven home from pony racing by Uncle Bill. The voice of Aunt Elaine from the next room. *Jay might as well be a horse*. It is strange how distant it all feels.

Because now I am a real stable lad in Newmarket. Somewhere along the line, the idea that I am a kid on trial has faded like the morning mist on the heath. This is my new life.

My body is getting stronger. These days I ride out with all three lots. I have taken to spending an hour every evening at the Racing Center in town. There is a gym, free for stable lads, where I keep fit. I work out on the running and rowing machines. I lift weights. I spend time on the racehorse simulator—a mechanical saddle that helps you strengthen the muscles used when riding a racehorse at full speed.

Not that my life is easy. "Teasing is part of racing," Laura once told me. "Having a laugh is how we get through the early mornings, the cold, the long days. And sometimes the laughs are at someone else's expense."

"Particularly if that someone is a girl?"

"You got it."

I'm not only a girl. I'm young, skinny. I'm often annoyingly cheerful when I'm with the horses.

Soon after the Norewest incident, Tommy tells me that some new protective gear has arrived for the lads. When I open the chest in the tack room, watched by several of the other lads, I find a padded bra. There are jeers and laughter and shouts.

"Bug in a bra!"

"Put it on!"

"You need it, girl!"

Then the niggle is about Manhattan. In the early days, I find myself getting a bit annoyed when someone uses her nickname, Nellie. Big mistake. From then on, the tune of "Nellie the Elephant" follows me around—hummed, whistled, sung. Some of the lads even take to calling me Nellie too.

Sometimes as we ride out, one of the lads tells me a crude joke about women. It is a test that I can't win. If I laugh, I'm going along with the sexism. If I don't, I can't take a joke and I get teased even more.

So it goes on, day after day. Now and then, I catch Laura's eye while this stuff is happening. She shows no reaction — not a smile, not a laugh, not a look. It is a useful lesson that over that long summer I begin to learn.

Don't let them get under your skin. Refuse to play their game. Ignore.

Angus has taken to putting me on different horses when I ride out. At first, I think it is because I am the youngest person working here and have to fit in with the others, but gradually I realize that I am being given the experience of different rides — the mad, the lazy, the tricky, the scared. It is the Wilkinson yard's rough-and-ready version of training.

But on third lot, I am always on Manhattan. It is the best part of the day. She has discovered that she likes being out, stretching her legs, looking around, feeling the warmth of the sun on her beautiful coat. I keep her at the back of the string, where she has her own space. She walks briskly, occasionally shaking her head like a two-year-old.

My hope, my dream, is that one day Mr. Wilkinson will see how she is changing, how her giant stride eats up the ground on the gallops, but it is me he watches. His old turtle eyes look away from Manhattan, as if she reminds him of something bad — failure, perhaps.

Pete is still her lad. When I ask Deej whether I should ask Angus if I could do Manhattan, he shakes his head.

"Give up on the mare," he says. "She's finished. Look after yourself."

Later, it occurs to me that it was a slightly weird thing to say.

Why should I have to look after myself?

It is late one morning at the end of August. After third lot, I am checking on Ocean Pacific in the main yard when there is a clattering of hooves on concrete and raised voices from the back yard. I hurry toward the sound, a feeling of dread within me. As I enter the yard, I hear the snorting of a horse, half-threatening, half-fearful.

A group of lads are gathered around Manhattan's stall.

To my relief, Angus strides past me, an angry look on his face. He reaches the stall before me.

"Is she acting up again, Pete?" Angus looks over the stall door.

"Yeah. She had a go at me. I'm sorting her out for good and all this time."

Over Angus's shoulder, I can see that Pete is standing like an old-fashioned soldier in battle. Only it is not a bayonet in his hands but a pitchfork.

Manhattan is on the other side of the stall. Now and then she swings her hindquarters toward Pete. As he scrambles for safety, there is more laughter from the lads watching.

"What's happened?" I ask Liam.

"She's had a go at him," he says. "Pete's teaching her a lesson."

"She's just frightened." I say the words loudly. "Where's Mr. Wilkinson? Bucknall?"

Liam glances toward the main yard. "They've all gone to lunch."

Manhattan has turned to face Pete. The whites of her eyes flash in the gloom. I can see—anyone could see—that she's terrified.

"What are you doing?" I ask the question loudly to the whole group. "I rode her this morning. She was fine."

"Leave it, Bug," Liam warns me. "This is Pete's business."

"She turned on him," another of the lads, Tommy, calls out. "She can be vicious, that one."

"She's just afraid." I raise my voice. "You should leave her alone."

Pete looks over his shoulder. "Who let the little girl in?" he jeers. He raises the pitchfork sharply and Manhattan throws her head up. "Bloomin' freak," he calls out. "Shall I give her one?"

I feel a lurch of anger within me. "Angus, please!" I'm shouting now, and one or two of the lads are looking nervous. "This is wrong!"

To my amazement, the emotion in my voice has an effect.

"Aye, game over." Angus raps the stall door. "You'll be late for lunch, Pete."

The lads behind me begin to wander off. "Lunchtime, Pete," one calls out.

Sensing that he has lost his audience, Pete backs toward the door and lets himself out.

He brushes past me, bumping my shoulder as he heads back to the feed room, the pitchfork hanging in his right hand. Angus and the other lads follow him.

I look into the stall. Manhattan has her back to me; her hind leg twitches nervously.

There you are, Hat. You're going to be all right. He's gone now.

Her ears, half-back, are motionless. I don't exist for her.

I spend the afternoon in her stall. I talk as I groom her, but for Manhattan I have become one of the enemy. Now and then, her ears go flat against her neck and she swings her hindquarters threateningly toward me, but I hold my ground.

I know. You want me to leave. But I'm staying with you.

The red fire is there, but it's different from the past, slower, more dangerous. It smolders quietly within me all afternoon. I only realize that I have entered the danger zone when I notice that my hand holding the body brush is trembling violently. In the past, I've been afraid of what the flames will make me do when I am in this state.

Now I welcome them. Rage makes me strong.

I am just preparing to leave for the evening when one of the younger lads, Davy, calls me from the door of the tack room.

"Hey, Bug. A few of us are going out tonight. D'you fancy joining us?"

As politely as I can, I tell him I'll be staying in. He beckons me over. There's something odd about this.

As I approach the tack room, Davy ducks inside. I hear

voices. Normally I would be more careful, but not tonight.

I push the door open.

There are five of them, lounging against the far wall. They are the younger lads, except for Pete, who is at the end of the row, examining his fingernails like some bad guy in an old-fashioned film.

"Hey, Bug," he says.

I look to the right, where there is a doorway leading to the feed room. There are more lads, mostly the older ones—the spectators. I look around for Deej and Laura, but they must have left.

The door closes behind me.

Trouble.

Oh, yes, thank you. Trouble is on the way.

Among the lads over by the feed room, someone starts softly whistling "Nellie the Elephant." I glance in that direction and the tune quietly fades.

I step into the center of the room. The red fire is crackling, burning, gaining strength. All the pain I have felt within me since seeing Manhattan being taunted this morning is concentrated in the core of my being.

I smile at the lads in front of me.

"We're not here for a joke, Bug." Pete speaks in a low, tough-guy voice.

"No?"

"We're here for a bit of schooling. You know what this is, don't you?"

"Schooling? You mean, like you were schooling Manhattan this morning?"

Pete frowns. "What are you talking about? Schooling is the name we give to initiating you into the yard. It's traditional in racing yards — just a little game. A ritual. I got all my hair shaved off and a bit of carpet glued to my skull. We've all had it."

I look around me. There is something wolf-like in the way those eyes are looking at me.

"Have I done something wrong?" I ask.

Pete ignores the question. "Normally we wait a bit longer before we school someone, but we've decided to make an exception in your case."

"Take it as a compliment," someone says behind me. I can hear the excitement in his voice.

Now I see the setup. The younger ones, like Davy, Liam, and Amit, are here to prove themselves. The older lads looking on from next door are enjoying the laugh. Angus has left for the night.

There is only one person behind this, and he's the bully of the Wilkinson yard.

Pete.

"So here's what we are going to do to get the little Bugster schooled." He rolls his shoulders and sticks out his chin, reminding me of something you might see behind bars in a zoo. He sniffs, then smiles at the other lads. "Bring out the bath."

Behind me, Liam and Davy lift a zinc tub full of a dark, oily liquid, into the center of the room.

"Tractor oil." Pete steps forward. "Used. A bit dirty.

You're going in there. Then you're going to be locked in the feed house with the rats overnight."

There's laughter from one of the older lads standing at the doorway, looking on.

"Nice one," somebody says.

"Then, in the morning, you'll be what we call 'schooled.' You'll be part of the yard. All right, Bug?"

"What about Mr. Wilkinson? Angus?"

"They know about schooling. It's part of racing. They leave us lads to sort it out. In our own way."

I stare deep into his eyes. In my mind, I see Manhattan, her ears flat back against her head, the whites of her eyes flashing. My skin is burning now. I taste revenge at the back of my throat.

"No."

"What?" Pete glowers at me, as if I have just insulted his mother. "What did you just say, Bug?"

"No."

His eyes glittering with threat, Pete speaks more quietly. "You don't understand? Have I made it too complicated for you?"

I stay silent, waiting for my moment.

"Here's the thing with schooling, Bugster," says Pete. "It can be done the easy way. Or . . . not."

He wanders across the tack room, a big, stupid smile on his face. Leaning against the saddle rack is his favorite weapon, a pitchfork. He takes it, weighs it in his right hand like a spear, then ambles back to me.

He is relaxed, enjoying the moment. That's a mistake. As he approaches, he glances in the direction of the lads watching him. In that instant, I step forward and grab the pitchfork. Trying to hold on to it, he loses balance, and at that moment I kick his legs from under him.

There is such a thing as justice. Falling, Pete hits his head on the side of the metal tub. As he lands on the floor, he lies dazed just long enough for me to push the points of the pitchfork against his neck, holding him down. I press downward. Pete's eyes stare up at me.

The red fire is raging.

"How about the easy way, Pete?" I say. "Shall we try that?"

He looks up at me, then his eyes dart helplessly at the other lads. None of them makes a move.

More weight on the pitchfork. The skin of his neck is white where the points press into the flesh. Pete raises his hands, like someone out of a cowboy film.

"Easy, Bug," someone calls out.

"This is for Manhattan." I hiss the words.

"Wha—?" It is a croak of fear.

"Leave her alone." The words are a hiss of rage. "Right?"

"Right." His face is going red.

"Am I schooled now?" I ask, my face close to his.

Pete opens his mouth but seems unable to speak.

He nods.

"So everyone can go home?"

Pete is recovering himself. Never drop your hands

before the winning post. I give the pitchfork a little push against his throat.

"Yes!"

I allow my eyes to take in the rest of the room.

"Party's over."

Slowly I take the pitchfork away from Pete's neck. Then, carrying it in my hand, I walk calmly across the room. The lads make way for me as I pass. I glance back at Pete, sitting on the floor, rubbing his neck. Then I push open the door and walk into the daylight.

Outside, I lean the pitchfork against a wall, feeling suddenly tired and sad. I walk in silence out of the yard.

End.

Of.

School.

Too Far

The next morning, on the way to work, I tell Laura what happened. She gives me a funny look when I mention holding Pete down with a pitchfork.

"Whoa, psycho-babe," she says. I get the feeling it is not a compliment.

"What else could I do? I had to teach Pete a lesson."

Laura looks away. "Trouble is, you taught everyone else a lesson too. They won't like that, believe me."

She is right. I go to the tack room to look at the List. My name is nowhere to be seen. As I stand there, checking it once again, Amit and Liam walk in. They ignore me. I go to Ocean Pacific's stall and I find Davy mucking it out. He tells me he has been asked to do my horse today. The other two are being done by Tommy and Deej.

Walking more slowly now, I make my way into the main yard.

Angus emerges from one of the stables and brushes past me as if I'm not there.

"My name doesn't seem to be on the List, Angus." He keeps walking, so I follow him. "Am I riding out?"

"No." The word is spoken quietly. "And you're not doing your horses, either."

"So what should I do?"

"Muck out all the horses in the back yard, except the gray. Then go home and pack your bags. You're out, girl. You've gone too far. Go to see the guv'nor at six tonight."

"I had to do something, Angus. First Norewest, then Manhattan."

Angus shakes his head. "Why couldn't you just leave it to me?"

Because you did nothing. Because Pete was still mistreating Manhattan. Because I couldn't wait any longer. These are some of the things I could have said to Angus but didn't.

"Time," he mutters. "These things take time."

"Ah. It's Bug Barton." Opening the door to Edgecote House that evening, Mrs. Wilkinson gazes at me with chilly disapproval. I step into the hall. With the usual mustiness, there is another smell, one that I recognize.

Cigars.

I hear men's voices from the sitting room along the corridor. Mrs. Wilkinson leads me into the room. There, sitting on a chair beside the fireplace, a cigar between his fingers, is the man who, in the whole wide world, I least want to see right now.

"Uncle Bill. I don't understand."

My uncle winks, as if we are both enjoying a secret joke. "All right, doll?" he says.

Mr. Wilkinson, sitting in his normal chair, waves in the direction of the sofa. "Seat. Barton. Won't keep you long," he says.

I notice that there is a half-full glass of what looks like whiskey on the table beside his chair.

"Clive and Rosemary have been telling me how you've been getting on," says Uncle Bill in his best fake-relaxed voice. It's as if he's popped in to meet the teachers on parents' night. "Bit of a mixed bag, it sounds like."

"How did you know I was here?"

"Detective work, girl. I knew you'd go to Newmarket. I got my contacts to ask around. New girl in town. Nice little rider. Small, dark haired, young. You know me, doll. What I want I get."

There is an awkward silence in the room. For the first time, I realize that my uncle is wearing a bright-green tweed jacket and smart trousers with a crease. I have a horrible feeling he thinks this is what you should wear when visiting a racing stable.

"Your uncle has been in touch with us for a while," says Mrs. Wilkinson. "After Angus told us about your behavior yesterday, we asked him to come and get you."

A low rumbling noise comes from Mr. Wilkinson. "Have to fit in. Racing game. Not just about riding well. Attitude. Like the 'orses. Ability? Not enough. Character. Can't go off like a firecracker."

"The kid's got loads of character," says Uncle Bill. "Too much bloody character sometimes." He winks at me. "Eh, doll?"

Now all three adults are looking at me, as if expecting me to say something.

"I'm sorry about what happened to Pete," I say quietly. "It was just that Manhattan—"

Mrs. Wilkinson groans. "Leave that animal out of it," she drawls. "She's cost her owner a fortune, she's useless on the racecourse, and she is vicious in the stable. If the lads are a little tough on her, I don't blame them, frankly."

"And before that, there was Norewest. I didn't want to tell you this." I look at Mrs. Wilkinson, then Mr. Wilkinson. Their faces are telling me the same thing. "You knew."

"We're not idiots," says Mrs. Wilkinson. "But it's more complicated than you think. Pete's father worked here for years. The family has been very loyal to the yard. We've been looking for a job for Pete away from horses. After the Norewest thing, we gave him a final warning."

"Racing family," mutters Mr. Wilkinson. "Can't throw 'em out on the street."

"What about Manhattan? Doesn't she count too? I was told that horses came first in this yard." My words are an angry wail.

There is a moment's silence.

"Girl's got a bit of a temper on her," says Uncle Bill, trying to cover for me. "Too emotional for her own good sometimes."

"We noticed," says Mrs. Wilkinson.

"Horses is horses." The cold, watery eyes of Mr. Wilkinson are fixed on mine. "Mare. Jinxed. Nothing but trouble."

I know there is nothing I can say. Any words that leave my mouth seem to make the end of my life in racing more certain.

"Had your chance," says Mr. Wilkinson. "Messed it up."

"Big time," says Uncle Bill.

"I'm sorry."

And I am. I'm sorry for Manhattan and Norewest. I'm sorry for all the horses in the world who have to suffer the cruelty of the human beings who control their lives. I'm sorry that caring about animals has brought me to this.

"Really?" Mr. Wilkinson can see the defiance in my eyes.

"Yes, guv'nor." I manage the lie quite impressively under the circumstances. "Really."

"Learns her lesson." A big, chummy smile is on Uncle Bill's face. "Typical teenager."

Mrs. Wilkinson sits forward in her chair. "You ran away from home. You turned up on our doorstep and demanded a job."

"I—"

"Shut up and listen, Jay. You had a crashing fall and rode out the next day. You've gotten the most hopeless animal in the yard going rather well for you. You've"—there's an irritated twitch to Mrs. Wilkinson's lips—"stood your corner with the other lads, who are stronger and older than you."

"The girl's tough," says Uncle Bill. "You've got to give her that."

Mrs. Wilkinson ignores him. "Here's what we're going to do. Your uncle will take you home." She holds up a hand to fend off any interruption. "At the beginning of next month, there's a course at the British Racing School just outside Newmarket. We've found you a place in something called a Level Two apprenticeship in racehorse care. It's not just learning about racing. You'll do some schoolwork there — this is still part of your education because you can't work full-time until you're eighteen. If you pass the course, you'll complete your apprenticeship here."

"What?" I swallow hard, unable to believe what I'm hearing.

"Told your school back home," says Uncle Bill. "They were not exactly heartbroken."

"You mean —?" I look from the trainer to the trainer's wife and back again. "I'm being given a second chance?"

"No," says Mrs. Wilkinson in her coldest voice. "You're being given a last chance."

I smile uncertainly at Mr. Wilkinson. "Thank you, guv'nor."

"Don't thank me. Not my decision." Mr. Wilkinson suddenly looks annoyed, as if he has been tricked into making a decision he will regret later. "Behave yourself. Do what you're told. Keep your mouth shut."

Uncle Bill stands up, eager to get me out of there before I say the wrong thing again. "Better be making tracks," he says.

"You shall not visit this yard again until after you have finished racing school," says Mrs. Wilkinson.

"Of course," I say. "And what will happen to —?"

"Questions?" It's an angry grunt from Mr. Wilkinson. "Bloomin' cheek. Yes, sir. No, sir. Thank you, sir. All I want to hear."

"I suspect she was going to ask us about Manhattan." Mrs. Wilkinson sits back in her chair. "Right, Jay?"

"Someone told me she might be put down."

"End of the season soon." Mr. Wilkinson drains his drink. "Owner's got bigger problems. Decision over the winter."

"And of course Pete will continue to be her lad," says Mrs. Wilkinson. "Understood?"

Clenching my jaw to keep the words back, I nod miserably.

"Got owners to call." Mr. Wilkinson struggles to his feet. "Wasted enough time." He shakes Uncle Bill's hand. Ignoring me, he mutters, "Women," and stomps out of the room.

Uncle Bill and I are shown to the front door by Mrs. Wilkinson. Gazing over my head toward the yard, she says almost casually, "I've given you another chance. Do not let me down."

"Thank you, Mrs. Wilkinson."

Looking away, she says good-bye to Uncle Bill, then closes the door behind us. Uncle Bill walks ahead, but I stand for a moment on the front doorstep of Edgecote House. I look down the path toward the stable and think of Manhattan.

No.

Time.

For.

Good-bye.

HOOKED

As Uncle Bill's car turns into the driveway of Coddington Hall, it is as if the strangest of dreams is beginning to vanish from my mind. Manhattan, the yard, Newmarket, the lads, the horses on the heath—suddenly they all feel distant. They are slipping away from me.

"Home at last," says Uncle Bill. He has been unusually silent during the drive home. I sense that he is angry with me for putting him through the meeting with the Wilkinsons. He has had to be polite and grateful, like a man looking for a favor, and that is not exactly his normal style.

I'm not feeling chatty, either. Fact is, he tracked me down—he stalked me, spied on me. For him, I'm just an annoying kid to be brought back into line.

As the car draws up in front of the house, Michaela appears at the front door. Her arms are spread wide, and a big welcome-home smile is on her face. She is taller than she was, and her hair has been cut short. She looks even cooler than I remember her.

"Hey, cuz!" As I get out of the car, she hugs me.

"Hello, M." I manage a chilly smile.

"Why, it's Jasmine." Aunt Elaine appears at the front door and walks toward me. She gives me the lightest of kisses on the cheek.

"Come and see Dusty." Michaela grabs my hand.

"Yes, go and see the pony," Aunt Elaine says, and gives a great, long sigh.

Michaela stays close to me those first two days at Coddington. She gossips about her school, asks me about whether there were parties in Newmarket, what the stable lads are like, whether there is anyone special in my life.

To a stranger, we would look like the best, most loyal of friends.

But we aren't. Michaela has always been able to behave as if things said and done in the past never really happened, but I have never managed that trick.

For me, something said is said forever. The nicer Michaela is to me now, the more precisely I remember what she once said about me to her friends.

Servant. Private charity case. Lucky to be here.

Eventually, I crack and say what is on my mind. We are sitting on a slope on the lawn, looking down to a field below where Humphrey and Bantry Bay are grazing.

"It's so great, your being back." Michaela sighs with fake happiness. "It hasn't been the same without you."

I turn to her and look deep into her eyes. "You don't have to do this, you know. I'll be all right."

"Do what? You're my bestie. You're the Jayster."

"You know what I'm talking about."

She looks away, and I'm expecting her to start crying. Whenever Michaela is in trouble or embarrassed or doesn't quite know what to do next, she brings out her not-so-secret weapon—tears.

But now she stays dry-eyed.

"You heard me, didn't you? When I was with Emma and Flossie."

"Yes."

"And that's why you left."

I shrug. Right now, I don't feel like sharing how I felt that day with anyone, least of all Michaela.

She is staring at the ground. "I'm so sorry," she murmurs. "I'd do anything to take back what I said. I was just showing off."

I'm not convinced by this excuse, and my face shows it.

"All the other girls at my school are so confident," she says. "They've got these amazing families, with au pairs and housekeepers and people who help with the cooking. I was just trying to keep up."

"I embarrassed you."

"I was such an idiot. I wish I could tell you how sorry I am."

We sit in silence for a while. I'm just thinking that being a bit embarrassed is not the best excuse for betraying your best friend when she says something that surprises me.

"The truth is I was jealous of you."

"Oh, come *on*. You? Jealous of me? How does that work exactly?"

"I still am. You're lucky. You've got something you're really good at. I had been riding all my life when you came along, and suddenly you were better than me. Everyone was looking at you, not me. You were 'a natural,' they said. Like I was an unnatural. And you just had to be riding a pony to be happy—I so envied you."

"That's ridiculous, M."

"Even my father treated you differently."

"But your dad worships you."

"I'm his princess, right? But you're the one who does stuff. Princesses don't do anything. They just get adored."

I look at Michaela and realize that it has taken a lot for her to make this confession. I shake my head, unable to keep the smile off my face. "I don't believe it. You're almost as much of a mess as I am."

We both laugh at the madness of life. I open my arms and we hug, just like the old days.

"I really have missed you," she says into my shoulder. "The way we can talk about anything."

"Me too."

"Stuff that's really secret."

"Right."

"And private."

"Yeah."

"Really private."

It has taken a while, but slowly I'm beginning to get the hint. Michaela has something to tell me. "Er, things? Stuff?"

"I shouldn't say." She moves away from me. The smile is back on her face. "I've promised."

"Promised who?"

"That's what I can't say."

"Fine. Keep it to yourself."

"No!" She gives a great dramatic sigh and gazes into the distance. Then, in a breathy voice, she says, "Jean-Paul."

"John who?"

"Jean-Paul. He's French." She looks back to the house. She's actually blushing. "You've got to *swear* not to tell."

It had to happen. Michaela is in love.

Jean-Paul was in the sixth form at her school. He talked to her once or twice during the summer term. Now he has left school and wants to meet up. There has been a big texting thing going on between them.

I ask what he's like. Tall, athletic, dark-brown eyes, comes from a rich family. Very charming. Plans to become a film director. Dreamy. Hunky. Sporty, but kind of arty too.

"I think he really loves me," she says. "He's got a motorcycle. He makes the boys our age seem like kids."

"But he lives in France."

Michaela smiles, then reaches for the cell phone lying on the grass nearby. She goes to the message page and shows me the screen:

Party next Friday in Kensington at my friend's
house.
No parents. Sleepover???
Je t'embrasse xxxx

"That means 'I kiss you' in French," says Michaela.

Now I'm worried for my friend. "Sleepover? You know
what that means. You can't, Michaela. What will you tell
Elaine?"

"I'm staying with Emma, aren't I? Nothing wrong with
that. She's not going to check up on me in the middle of the
night, is she?"

"You really don't know this guy. Maybe he's not"—
suddenly I feel a bit young and stupid—"respectful."

"'Course he is. He's really grown-up for eighteen."
Laughing, she grabs the phone from me. "You're good at
horses. Now I've found something I'm good at. Parties!"
With a crazy smile on her face, she jabs at the keyboard, tapping out a quick, brief message. Then presses "send."

The phone gives a ping.

She holds out the phone so that I can read her reply on
the screen:

Oui!!!

I miss Manhattan. It is like an ache that is always there. Lying
in bed in the early morning, I wonder what is happening to
her, whether she is all right. I think of her beautiful, shining
gray coat the afternoon when I first groomed her. One night,

thumbing through my copy of *Great Ladies: The Wonder Fillies of History*, I come across a picture that makes me gasp.

It is a photograph, taken at Ascot, of a filly called Petite Etoile. She is cantering past the stands, ridden by my favorite jockey from the past, Lester Piggott. She looks big and is dark, mottled gray. Her ears are pricked, and she has a proud, don't-mess-with-me look in her eyes.

She is the spitting image of Manhattan.

I read how, over fifty years ago, she was the queen of racing, winning the Coronation Cup two years running in 1960 and 1961, beating the colts. She was "famously moody," according to the writer. She was not an easy horse to train and was said to be ferocious in the stable. Once, when she was racing in America, the assistant to her trainer, Noel Murless, poked her in the ribs, commenting to her lad that she was carrying too much weight. The wonder filly picked him up by the shoulder of his jacket and threw him across the stall! In an interview, Murless described the filly as "a peculiar animal . . . unique in every way."

At the back of the book, there are charts of the wonder fillies' pedigrees. I look for that of Petite Etoile. Her breeding went back to Mumtaz Mahal, the "Flying Filly" who was sired by The Tetrarch. Petite Etoile was related to Manhattan!

I'm so excited by this news that I lower my guard. That evening at dinner with Uncle Bill, Aunt Elaine, and Michaela, I tell them about Petite Etoile.

Uncle Bill is amused by my interest. "Glad you've read one book anyway, doll," he says. Michaela listens as I speak, but I can tell that she is in the small, locked room in her mind marked JEAN-PAUL.

"Even if that book is only about racing," says Aunt Elaine, a strained smile on her face. She turns away from me as if I no longer exist. "How has your day been, darling?" she asks Michaela.

"Fine, thanks."

At that moment, there is a soft, electronic *ping*. It comes from Michaela's cell phone, which was left on the sideboard. Elaine has recently banned cell phones from the dining-room table while we're eating. She reaches for it before Michaela has time to react.

"Elaine, give me my phone, please." There is quiet panic in Michaela's voice.

Uncle Bill frowns. "You do not speak to your step-mother like that."

Elaine looks at the message that has just come in. Her face, lit up by the screen in front of her, goes even paler than it normally is. She scrolls down the screen and reads some more.

Michaela sits, head down, eyes closed, waiting for the ax to fall.

"I thought there was a no-looking-at-cell-phones-at-the-table rule," Uncle Bill says, winking at me.

Elaine is now staring at Michaela.

"You have a text message, Michaela." Her voice is quiet, threatening. "Shall I read it to you?"

"No. Please, Elaine."

"Yes, I think I will. It says, let me see—ah yes, here we

are. *'See ya there, sexy. We're gonna parteeeee.'* There are several exclamation marks followed by something I don't quite understand. *'Je tembrasse.'*"

"*Je t'embrasse,*" says Michaela quickly. "It's French for 'yours sincerely.'"

Uncle Bill is giving Michaela a hard look. "French has never been my strong point," he says. "But I'm pretty sure that's not quite the right translation there."

"Sexy?" says Aunt Elaine. "And what 'parteeee' is this?"

There is a moment's silence around the table, just long enough for me to make my decision.

"Sorry." My voice sounds weirdly chirpy. "Didn't I mention it?"

All heads turn toward me.

"I wanted to go to a party. With my friend. I borrowed the phone to send a text. Thanks, M." I smile at her.

Michaela's eyes widen with surprise and relief. "You're welcome," she says quietly.

Uncle Bill is looking at us both suspiciously. "So what's all the French stuff?"

I shrug, trying (not very successfully) to look like a so-what-it's-just-another-guy party girl. "He's this French jockey who works in Newmarket. We hooked at a lads' party."

That doesn't sound quite right somehow.

"Hooked up," Michaela murmurs.

"Yeah, hooked up, that's what I meant. We hooked up big-time."

Aunt Elaine dabs at her mouth with a napkin. "I suppose that's all one can expect from someone working in a stable yard," she says quietly. She darts a look toward Uncle Bill. "I'm really not sure that this is the kind of thing Michaela should be exposed to."

"Elaine—" Michaela looks desperately at me.

"Don't stick up for her, darling. She's old enough to speak up for herself." Uncle Bill's eyes are on me. "What have you got to say for yourself, young lady?"

I shrug and reach as casually as I am able for the cell phone. "Sorry, Uncle Bill," I say, glancing at the texts between Jean-Paul and Michaela. There are a lot of kisses and pink hearts, I notice. And he certainly likes his *je t'embrasse*s. I press "delete."

"All gone," I say.

"Kindly leave the table." Elaine closes her eyes. "I think we've heard quite enough for one meal."

"Sorry about that, Aunt Elaine." I stand up.

My step-aunt shakes her head. "So like her mother," she murmurs to Uncle Bill. "No better than she should be."

"It could be my father," I say, trying to lighten things up.

"Quite possibly," says Aunt Elaine. "They were as bad as each other."

"You never even met my dad."

"No. He ran away before I had that pleasure. But he left quite a reputation behind him."

The match. The flame. I feel the familiar sudden lurch of rage, deep in the pit of my stomach. My muscles tense, and just for a split second, I have a vision of myself stepping forward and sweeping all the plates and knives and forks and glasses off her precious dinner table onto the floor.

No. No. No. I hold myself where I am.

Swaying, eyes wide, I breathe deeply, close my eyes. Slowly the raging fire within me begins to die down.

I open my eyes. Aunt Elaine is casually brushing a speck of dust from the table.

Somehow I manage to dart a not-your-fault smile in Michaela's direction. Then I'm gone.

A door closes that night. If I ever belonged here, I don't anymore. There are eight days before I leave for racing school, but in my mind I am already there.

Aunt Elaine has never liked me, and now she has her reason. Even if she were to know that the dodgy texts were not for me but her innocent little stepdaughter, nothing would change.

"Once I know something in my heart," she likes to say, "there's no changing me. That's just the way I am."

She and Uncle Bill make sure the last few days of Michaela's vacation are full of activities. She is taken by some neighbors to an exhibition in London. She stays with some family friends who live nearby. She goes with Uncle Bill to a county show.

Anything that keeps her away from my evil influence is just fine, in other words.

Uncle Bill talks to me now and then, but in a weird, new way—cheery, loud, with lots of winks and jokes that I don't understand. I notice that when Aunt Elaine is around, he becomes strangely distant and quiet.

I have taken to eating my meals in the kitchen. If they want me to be a stable girl, that's how I'll be. Sometimes as I eat, I hear Aunt Elaine talking about me to Uncle Bill. She makes no effort to keep her voice down.

"When she's had her fun at the racing stable, she'll just have to find a job."

Uncle Bill murmurs something.

"Jockey? That's not going to happen." Aunt Elaine laughs. "Of course, she'll have no qualifications. A hair-dresser, maybe. Or a shop assistant. I'll ask around."

More mumbles from Uncle Bill, but Aunt Elaine has hit her stride.

"Anyway, she'll probably be just like your sister. Some unsuitable man will get her pregnant and then run away. With her mother and that coward of a father, she was bound to be like this."

Alone in the kitchen, I smile. It is the first time my father has been blamed for me. Aunt Elaine must be getting desperate.

The night before I leave for racing school, Michaela sneaks to my bedroom while Uncle Bill and Aunt Elaine are busy with one of their favorite rituals—watching the ten o'clock news on the BBC.

"I just wanted to thank you," she whispers, sitting on the end of my bed. She has thanked me almost every time she has seen me without anyone around, and now I give her my usual reply.

"There's nothing to thank me for. I had nothing to lose. You did."

"You're a real friend."

We sit in silence for a moment. From downstairs, there is a sound of chanting and shouting from the TV. More bad news is happening somewhere.

"What did you tell Jean-Paul?" I ask.

"I texted him that my parents found out. He was really scared." Michaela laughs. "Suddenly he wasn't such a hero."

"He was taking it a bit fast, M."

She nods. "Suppose so. He was gorgeous, though."

"Yeah?" I yawn and, amazingly, Michaela gets the message.

Tomorrow I leave early.

Back.

To.

School.

OLD STONEFACE

O n the screen in the classroom, we are watching a stewards' inquiry—that's the investigation that takes place after something has gone wrong is a race. Three middle-aged men in suits are behind a desk. Two jockeys, in their silks, stand before them. They look a bit like naughty children called to the headmaster's office.

Behind the stewards are four monitors. They ask one jockey if he felt his ground was taken. We now know what that means—one horse has blocked another from coming through.

The jockey is young and tongue-tied. He seems nervous that anything he says will get him into trouble.

The other jockey, who won the race, is older. He has done this before. He has an innocent "who me?" expression on his face.

The stewards and the jockeys all watch the race on the screens. Now and then they freeze the footage, or rewind to catch the moment when the younger jockey snatches at his reins and stands up in his stirrups to avoid a collision.

Our teacher, Barry Swinson, a small, wiry man in his forties, switches off the video and turns to the sixteen of us in the classroom.

"Right," he says. "Who wants to tell me if the horse that passed the winning post is going to keep the race?"

And so the discussion begins, each of us pitching in. Some of us understand the rules of racing, but most are guessing.

When Mr. Swinson turns to me, the class listens. Although they are all older than me, they have seen me ride. I know more about racing than most of them.

"It's true the winner did hang toward the rails," I say. "But I don't think it affected the result, sir. The second horse was already beaten."

Mr. Swinson returns to the video and we hear the stewards' decision. I was right.

At first, I like the life at racing school. We are all here to learn. There's no pretending that we know more than we do. From the moment we get up at six in the morning to the end of evening activities (diet, fitness, cooking), all we think and talk about is looking after racehorses, about riding, about racing in the past and today.

Some of the students get homesick, while others discover that their nerve isn't as good as they thought it was. After the first two weeks, our course is down to eleven— seven girls and four boys.

The teachers are different from those I remember from schools. They may be strict and get angry sometimes, but they know what it is like to be in love with racing. They have worked with horses. They understand the fever, the madness.

There is more to racing school than riding and messing around in the stables. Every afternoon we have classes— about the rules of racing, about how important breeding is for horses.

The class that the others find boring, the history of racing, is the one I most enjoy.

On one occasion Mr. Swinson asks which jockey won the most Classics. My hand goes up. "Lester Piggott. He rode thirty Classic winners between 1954 and 1992. He was fifty-six when he won the 2000 Guineas on Rodrigo de Triano."

"Very good, Jay."

Because Piggott is my hero, I can't help adding, "They used to call him Old Stoneface because he didn't smile or talk very much."

"Bloomin' know-it-all," mutters Jimmy, who is sitting behind me.

It is the first time I have ever been called that, and I find myself smiling for the rest of the lesson.

I like the students here.

There is Nicky, who has been in trouble with the police. She loves horses, all right, but she likes boys even more. Hannah is small, nervous, with a world of trouble in her dark eyes. There is Joe, who comes from a family of travelers and has ridden ponies all his life, but never with a saddle. He thinks he has the answer to everything and has been at war with the instructors from the first day.

Racing, for most of them, is an escape. When we are talking in our dorms after a day's work, the truth emerges.

"Horses calm me down."

"This is my chance to get my life together."

"Racing is in my blood. It's all I want to do."

The dreams are still alive.

The staff at the school are tough, but they believe in us. They are more like teachers than racing people.

There are moments, though, when I become restless. I look at the students and know that few of them will pull on jockey's silks. Some will never even get out on the gallops. Winning is not in their souls.

The truth is, we're in a pretend racing yard with retired racehorses who will never race again. To my surprise, I find myself missing the hard world of a real stable, the hopes that come with every new day, even the disappointments.

Although I think of Manhattan most of the time, I remember Mrs. Wilkinson's warning about staying away from Edgecote House until I have finished my course.

I'll be there, Hat. I'll be back soon.

One day at school, I visit the library and go online to find out more about The Tetrarch, Manhattan's famous ancestor. I find a website about racing history with a page called "The Rocking Horse That Rocked the World."

The Tetrarch was always unusual. With his strange color-ing and extraordinary speed, he was called the "Rocking

Horse" and the "Spotted Wonder" when he was the talk of British racing in 1913 and 1914.

In April of his two-year-old career, his trainer, Atty Persse, tested him against more advanced two-year-olds and was astonished by the ease with which he beat them. When the horse was tried against an older handicapper and was given an extra fourteen pounds of weight to carry, the result was the same.

In his seven races as a two-year-old, The Tetrarch was unbeaten, his victories including the Gimcrack Stakes and the Norfolk Stakes. He ended the season as the champion two-year-old of 1913.

His giant stride sometimes caused his back hooves to strike into his forelegs, and an injury at the end of his first season ruled him out of the 2000 Guineas the following spring. While he was preparing for the Derby, the same injury recurred, and he was retired.

His jockey, Steve Donoghue, said of The Tetrarch, "To be on him was like riding a creature that combined the power of an elephant with the speed of a greyhound."

He would never have been beaten, Persse claimed. "He was a freak, and there will never be another like him."

Then down the page, included almost as an after-thought, are words that make me gasp.

Persse described him as having a beautiful head and an unusually powerful build. He had a huge stride and galloped straight at speed, but "plaited" in front when walking or trotting.

It is exactly as Manhattan does, but with her, plaiting has been seen as a problem.

Only two things were known to upset The Tetrarch: he hated being shod by someone he didn't know and being given medicine by a vet. To avoid the first problem, his trainer, Atty Persse, made sure that the horse had his own farrier traveling with him when he went racing.

Slowly, I begin to understand Manhattan's story. She was a strong character like The Tetrarch, and like him, she had a fiery rage within her.

She fought back, refusing to race, behaving fiercely in her stable. She's proud, like her great ancestor.

I sit alone in the library, gazing out of the window.

You never had a chance.

After two weeks at racing school, it is time for the better students to get out of the indoor arena and onto the gallops. Five of us, including Joe and me, are allowed onto the all-weather track, where we canter, receiving instructions through an earpiece from Mr. Swinson as he drives his Jeep on a road beside the track.

By now I am beginning to feel different from most of the others here. For some, racing school is an adventure, the first time they have been away from home. Others become a bit wild, get picked up by friends in town, smuggle booze back into the dorm. There are romances, arguments, rivalries, dramas.

In the early days, I sense that Joe is interested in me. I catch him looking in my direction. His teasing has an edge to it. He jokes about me living for horses as if to embarrass me into being more like the rest of them.

He soon discovers he is wasting his time. I'm not here for fun—at least, not the fun he has in mind.

When the others are relaxing at lunch break and on Sundays, I spend time in the gym, working out, building up my muscles, riding finishes on the racehorse simulator, getting stronger.

In my mind, there is one goal—to pass the course, get back to the Wilkinson yard, and ride better than any lad there.

During the last week, each of the eleven of us go to Mr. Swinson's office for a final chat. He has a report to complete for the trainers.

On his desk before him are the results of the exams and tests I took the previous week.

"You did all right," he says without enthusiasm. "Your spelling's not great, your math is pretty appalling, but we can help you with that. You know your racing history, all right."

I nod, knowing that more is to come.

"I worry about you." He takes off his glasses and sighs. "I can't make you out."

"Did I fail the exams?"

He shakes his head. "It's not just about exams in life, Jay. You have to have people skills. You seem a little"—he frowns—"solitary. You're allowed to have fun, you know. Go to parties."

I go Old Stoneface on him. "I know. It's just that I'm better on the horse side."

"Clive Wilkinson told me that there were one or two problems with you at the yard. It was why he sent you to this course at such short notice."

"Sometimes I used to get a bit angry," I say, choosing my words carefully.

He looks down at the notes in front of him. "I see we offered you an anger management module but you turned it down."

"It's all right. I've sorted that out now."

He nods. "Your behavior here has been fine. What was the problem at Wilkinson's?"

A thug. A bully. A horse being treated badly. The answers I could give him flare briefly in my mind like little fires, but they quickly die. "I've learned my lesson," I say quietly.

"You ride well. You seem focused, professional. A couple of the trainers who have seen you ride on the gallops have asked about you. Big yards. Successful."

"Great." My voice is less enthusiastic than he expects.

He glances toward the door and drops his voice. "I didn't say this, right?"

"Say what, sir?"

"You've got talent. It may be a sensible idea at some

point for you to further your career away from the Wilkinson yard." He holds up a hand when I try to speak. "It's a known fact in racing that a girl will never do well there."

"Maybe I can change that."

"I've had girls go there from here," says Mr. Swinson. "They never last more than a few weeks. If you want to succeed, I would seriously suggest that you keep an eye open for other jobs. There's a trainer who has seen you ride. He has suggested that, after a few months back with old man Wilkinson, you might like to have a word with him about joining his yard. I've agreed that your Level Two apprenticeship could be transferred. You'd be given a chance. He'd have an excellent apprentice. We'd be delighted for you too. It would be win-win for us all."

"Except for the Wilkinsons. They stuck by me."

"Of course." Mr. Swinson smiles coldly. "And loyalty's an excellent thing. Very commendable but—"

"I know. Racing's a tough game. People keep telling me that."

"Everyone looks after themselves. Clive knows the score."

"I have things I need to finish at Edgecote."

"Things?" He laughs. "I always thought you were ambitious, Jay."

I consider for the briefest of split seconds whether I should tell Mr. Swinson about Manhattan, but looking at his smiling face across the desk, I know that he would never understand.

"I'm going back and I'm staying there."

He pauses and is about to say something. Then he thinks better of it and he closes my file. "Suit yourself," he says coldly.

I thank him again and leave the office. Already I can imagine the words that will appear on my final report.

Stubborn.

Won't.

Be.

Told.

Vicious Brute

There is a chill in the early morning air on my first day
back at the yard. The flat-racing season is almost over. I
walk briskly through the gate, eyes straight ahead, trying to
look more confident than I am feeling. The last time I saw
most of these lads, I had a pitchfork in my hand.

I may have a diploma now, but reputations stick in the
world of racing, and I have a sworn enemy in Pete. There is an
empty feeling in my stomach as I walk through the main yard.

On the way to the tack room, I pass Liam.

"Hey, the Bugster is back," he says, half-friendly. "How
did it go at racing school?"

"Good," I say.

In the tack room, I look at the List. I'm riding out first
lot on Ocean Pacific, and then on a new horse called Poptastic
for second lot. On the next board, I read my name and see
the horses I will be doing: Ocean Pacific, Norewest, and a

two-year-old called Something Fancy. They are all main-yard horses.

No Manhattan.

I go to the back yard and walk around, stall by stall. Her stall is empty, scrubbed, smelling faintly of disinfectant.

I stand for a moment, alone in the back yard, gathering my thoughts. Be professional. For the first time, I realize that it is not the Wilkinson yard I've been missing, the riding out, the working on the gallops. It is one horse.

Laura is watching me from the passageway between the two yards. She was out last night and this is the first I have seen her since my return. She gives me a careful smile as I approach. "Welcome back," she says.

"Has she gone?" I try to sound calm, but the crack in my voice gives me away. "Did they take her away?"

She shakes her head. "She's here, but she's in trouble. I'll tell you all about it when we get home," she says in a low voice.

"What about Pete? Is he still doing her?"

Laura winces. "Pete's not going to be around for a while. You have some news to catch up on."

"But—"

She holds a finger to her lips and walks off.

I go about my work as best I can, mucking out and grooming Ocean Pacific, taking him onto the walker. I keep to myself, but there is none of the old hostility in the lads' eyes.

As we pull out for the first lot, I see Angus for the first time.

"She's back. Little Miss Trouble." By his standards, he sounds almost welcoming.

"Morning, Angus."

The string walks in sleepy silence around the covered yard. I get the nod from the other lads as they see me. There is no sign of Pete.

Mr. Wilkinson enters the arena, shoulders hunched, his usual matchstick between his teeth. "Morning, Jay," he calls out. "Welcome back."

As we file out to walk toward the gallops, Amit is behind me.

"So you did OK, Bug?"

"Not bad," I say over my shoulder.

"Better than that, we heard."

It is a small world, racing. By the time we reach the gallops, I realize that the other lads know that other trainers have been interested in taking me on. I am being treated differently now — almost respectfully. It explains the friendliness from Angus. I'm no longer the joke, the holiday girl.

I am rubbing down Ocean Pacific after first lot when Harry Bucknall looks over the stall door.

"When you've done that, pop into my office for a chat, will you, Bug?" he drawls.

"Yes, Mr. Bucknall."

Five minutes later, I'm knocking on the door of the tiny shed that the assistant trainer likes to call his "office."

"Come in."

He sits behind a small table, studying some paper-work, which I notice are the latest feed bills. With a busy-guy frown, he waves to a chair, on which are some new jodh-purs, boots, and gloves. I put them on the ground and take a seat.

"Those are yours, by the way," he says. "Replace that old gear you had."

I look down at the new gear. "Thank you. How much—?"

Bucknall waves a hand impatiently. "Just check that the sizes are right."

I do. "They're fine, Mr. Bucknall."

"Good." He lays down his pen and stares at me for a moment. "Seems you didn't entirely disgrace yourself at the school," he says, reaching for a sheet of paper on the side of the desk. He sniffs as he reads. "*Natural jockey . . . excellent hands . . . strong . . . professional attitude.*" He taps the paper. "Your end-of-term report. I've seen a lot worse."

"It was a useful course."

He stares at me for a moment. "Aren't you pleased?"

"Of course."

Bucknall looks down at the report. "*Conclusion. Has the potential to make a professional jockey.* They don't often say that in my experience."

"Great," I say.

"So—" He pushes the racing school report to the side of the desk. "You'll be riding work on a regular basis from now on. We want to get you a license as an apprentice. All being well, you might get a ride in a few lads' races—up against other apprentices. See how you do. One or two other trainers have been inquiring about your services, so there could be the odd outside ride. You'll have to do the apprentice license course at the racing school. It's just a week. We don't want to take you on too quickly."

"No, sir."

"You might find that some of the staff—the lads—are a little jealous. I don't want you getting into trouble, like before, with poor old Pete."

"I was just defending myself. I don't fight normally."

"So you say." Mr. Bucknall pulls the feed invoices to him, now bored by our conversation.

"Why 'poor old Pete'? Where is he?"

Bucknall does one of his odd gestures—a blink and a sudden jerk back of the chin, as if someone has squirted water in his face. "You haven't heard?"

I shake my head. "Heard what?"

"Pete's in the hospital. Smashed leg, three broken ribs, punctured lung, and a fractured skull."

"Did he have a fall?"

"Good Lord, no. He was attacked by a vicious brute of a horse. He would have been killed if Angus hadn't dragged him out of the stall."

And suddenly I know what is coming. "Manhattan?"

He nods, reaching for a copy of the *Racing Post* on his desk. "Nasty animal. One morning she just went for him—teeth, kicking, snorting, trying to crush him against the wall.

She's been put in a bull pen in the old cowsheds until she's
disposed of." He glances up at me and smiles coldly. "Shut
the door behind you."

On.

My.

Way.

Bull Pen

At first, I can see only little bruises of light in the darkness at the back of the bull pen.

"Hey, Hat."

It is a cast-iron cage at the back of the cowshed. From the sunlight through the main door, I can see the thick bars from floor to roof, the heavy reinforced door. And in the murk beyond, there is a still, dark-gray shape.

Oh, Hat. What have they done to you?

No reaction. No movement.

"I'm here, girl. It's me."

I slide back the heavy bolt on the door and walk stealthily into the pen.

The bedding beneath my feet is wet, and a sharp ammonia smell rises when I tread on it. No one has mucked out the pen for days, maybe weeks.

My eyes are becoming accustomed to the darkness. Manhattan has her back to me. Her head, held low, is in one corner of the pen. She looks like an old, exhausted workhorse that has reached the end of its days.

OK, girl. There's no need to be afraid. I understand.

Manhattan gives a low sigh and ignores me. Watching carefully for any movement in those hind legs, I move toward her.

He got back at me through you. The man who was supposed to be looking after you was angry with me. I made him look small. He knew how to get his revenge on me — by hurting you.

Two steps closer.

And you couldn't take it. You wouldn't take it.

I'm beside her hindquarters now. Her coat is dull and there are marks on it, which might be muck or scabs where she has been hit.

I long to touch her, but I don't want to startle her.

You're going to be all right, girl.

She turns her head toward me, as if noticing for the first time that I am there. The only sign that she has recognized me is that she is showing no fear.

I stroke her neck as softly as I can. Then, when there's no reaction, I put both arms around her neck and rest my cheek against her matted coat, breathing in the sharp, ungroomed smell of her, feeling the warmth of her. We stay like that, perfectly still, for a minute, maybe two.

I'm aware of a heaviness within me lifting. The noise in the world outside the yard. There seem to be tears in my eyes. My nose is running. I sniff and wipe it against Manhattan's neck. She stirs, then gives a long, heart-worn sigh.

Maybe I've got a carrot.

I'm reaching into my pocket when her head goes up, her ears flicker back. The sound of brisk footsteps echo on the concrete floor of the cowshed.

They won't touch you, Hat. I'm here now.

"What in the mother of mercy's name do you think you're blazing doing, Bug?"

As the unmistakable tones of Angus echo through the cowshed, I feel the muscles in Manhattan's neck tense. She moves, swishing her tail and lifting one of her hind legs.

Easy, Hat. Easy.

Angus is swearing quietly beyond the door. "Right, then," he says eventually. "Move very slowly away to the side." He's talking quietly like some bomb-disposal expert in a war. "I'll come around to that side and cover you through the bars with this pitchfork."

"No."

I hold Manhattan closer to me.

I'll be back soon, Hat.

Then I pat her, stand back, and face Angus.

"A pitchfork will only frighten her." I speak in a low voice.

To my surprise, the head lad leans the fork against the wall. I move calmly past Manhattan's restless hindquarters to the door, and out.

I bolt it behind me and face Angus.

"This isn't a blazing petting zoo, girl," he says. "It's a racing stable."

"I'd like to do her, Angus. In addition to my usual work."

"Got a death wish, have you, lassie?"

"She's not a bad horse, Angus."

"Aye, she's not." The head lad looks into the bull pen. "She's a lot worse than that. She's a bad mare."

"What?"

"Mares don't change, girlie." His voice takes on a steely tone. "You'll learn that when you've been in the game as long as I have. If you have a colt or gelding who's developing bad habits, you can sort them out. They learn. Once a mare goes to the bad, there's only one thing you can do. Try to break her. Show her who's boss. Doesn't always work."

"There's another way. You saw how Pete treated her. She was just fighting back. Let me talk to Mr. Wilkinson about it."

"You can, as it happens. That was why I was looking for you. The guv'nor wanted to see you at the big house." Angus's mouth does an odd little twitch, which may or may not be a smile. "You don't know when you're beat, do you, girl? You're a tough little thing — for a lassie."

"I'm not a lassie, Angus. I'm a lad."

"Och aye." He turns away, but not before I see the smile he is trying to hide.

When Mrs. Wilkinson opens the front door, she actually seems pleased to see me.

"Jay. And how was the course?"

My mind is still in the bull pen. "It was good. Can we talk about Manhattan?"

"No." The smile leaves her face as she turns to lead

me across the hall. "We have more important things to discuss."

I follow her into the dining room. Mr. Wilkinson is at one end of a long table, reading a copy of the *Racing Post*.

"Jay Barton is here, Clive."

The trainer, in a world of his own, glances up at her, then sees me. He makes an odd mumbling noise, which could be a groan or a grunt of welcome.

Mrs. Wilkinson takes her place at the other end of the table. She nods in the direction of a spare chair. "Jay wanted to talk about Manhattan, Clive. I told her we needed to discuss something else."

"I just wanted to ask if I could do her," I say. "In addition to my normal work."

"She's rather blotted her reputation, that mare." Mrs. Wilkinson sounds more bored than usual. "On the whole, it's not thought to be a terribly good idea for a racehorse to try to kill someone. People tend to disapprove."

"Just give me a few weeks. It'll be my risk if anything happens to me."

"Death wish," mutters Mr. Wilkinson, turning a page of his *Racing Post*. "Talk about. Something else. Reason you're here." He lowers his paper and looks at me like a sorrowful toad. "Put you down. Lads' race. February. Poptastic. Six furlongs. Kempton."

"Lingfield," says Mrs. Wilkinson.

"Lingfield, yes. Ride the horse second lot. Bit green. Never raced before."

I'm staring at him in amazement. "Thank you, Mr. Wilkinson. I won't let you down."

"Better blinkin' not." He reaches for his paper.

"So maybe now that you're going to be a jockey, a few second thoughts about Manhattan are in order." Mrs. Wilkinson gives me one of her polite society smiles. "The last thing you need is an injury before your first ride."

I don't even have to think. "I'll do both. I won't get injured."

Mrs. Wilkinson looks at me, surprised. "And if we say you have to choose?"

"I'll take Manhattan."

The trainer shakes his head, as if his worst suspicions have been confirmed.

"It would solve a problem, Clive," says Mrs. Wilkinson. "Pete's decided to get out of racing, and none of the lads want to do the mare. We can't have her looking like a hat rack if the prince comes down. Maybe we should take Jay at her word." She looks at me, a chilly smile on her face. "All your Manhattan work will be on your own time."

"Yes."

She nods. "I'll tell Angus."

"Thank you, Mrs. Wilkinson."

"Now, leave us alone," she says. "Second lot will be going out soon. You've got a racehorse to work."

I leave the big house, blinking in the sunshine as I stand on the steps, looking across the paddocks.

My heart is thumping in my chest. I'm no longer just

a lad. I'll be riding work with professional jockeys. Soon I'll take the first step to becoming one myself.

But none of that is the reason why a big smile settles on my face as I walk slowly back to the yard for second lot.

Something important has happened. I am riding into the future.

Me.

And.

Hat.

POPTASTIC

I change into my new clothes, dark-blue jodhpurs and boots, in one of the empty stalls in the main yard, then make my way to the stable of Poptastic, the horse I am riding for the second lot.

He is a big, gangling bay three-year-old who has yet to grow into his strength, but he is bred for speed.

His lad, Tommy, is running a body brush over him when I arrive. He glances at me in my new gear.

"Getting the leg up today, are we?"

"Yup." I undo Poptastic's halter, put the reins over the horse's head, and slip the bridle on him. "What's this one like?" I ask.

"Bit of a baby, but there's no harm in him. He wasn't strong enough to race as a two-year-old. Hasn't even done any serious work before today." Tommy pats him on the neck. "Got to look his best, he has. The owner's in today." He darts a look over his shoulder in my direction. "Now that you're a work rider, you'd better be at your best too."

I frown, not quite clear what he means.

"Look outside the door."

I do. There, on the ground, is a whip.

"Angus left it for you," Tommy calls out from the stall.

I pick the whip up. It brings back bad memories of when I first rode Manhattan, but I know it means a lot. Unless they are riding "problem horses," only jockeys and lads who are work riders can carry a whip. It is a sign of promotion, like the first stripe on the arm of a soldier.

On the way to the covered yard, Poptastic is on his toes, as if he can sense that today is the day when he has to grow up, become a racehorse. He jigs restlessly, looking around with wild-eyed, babyish enthusiasm.

Maybe because my thoughts are still on Manhattan, I'm completely relaxed. As we walk around the covered yard, I notice that the other lads are taking in the change in the way I look. I look smarter. I am carrying a whip. I am riding a main-yard horse whose owner will be watching this morning. I may be small, and I may be a girl, but I'm not the kid who helps out in the yard anymore.

Poptastic is seeing spooks in every shadow as we make our way out to the heath, and when the string does a slow canter on the all-weather track, he pulls hard, throwing his head around.

Easy, boy. You'll get your moment.

He's a strong horse, but he is clumsy and needs to

be held together to avoid him striking into himself. By the time we pull up, Mr. Wilkinson's battered station wagon has arrived. When the trainer gets out, there are two people with him—a small, powerfully built man wearing a green checked suit, the sort of clothes a city dweller wears when visiting the country, and, tottering behind him, a younger, taller woman with red hair and a short skirt. Her high heels make walking difficult on the springy turf.

One of the lads gives a low whistle. Angus mutters something sexist under his breath.

Behind me, Deej says, "Here come your owners, Bug."

I glance toward him, mouthing, "Who?"

"Pete Lukic. Most of the nightclubs in Essex belong to him. And I'm guessing that's probably not his daughter."

The eyes of the trainer and his guests are on Poptastic as the string circles around them.

"Jay." Mr. Wilkinson beckons me in.

"This my jockey?" The small man, Mr. Lukic, has an I'm-just-about-to-make-a-joke look on his face. "Shouldn't she be at school?"

I smile politely.

"That horse looks dead frisky, Pete." His girlfriend giggles. "A bit like his owner."

"Leave it, Paloma," mutters Mr. Lukic.

Mr. Wilkinson calls Liam and Deej to join us. Liam is on Poker Face, a useful three-year-old who has won a couple of races, and Deej is riding Norewest.

"Serious piece of work from the five-furlong pole," the trainer says. "Pass the two-furlong mark. Let them stride out.

Bug in the middle on the three-year-old. Bit green. Don't go crazy."

We canter away from the string, with Deej and Liam joking about the redheaded girl as they go. When we reach the five-furlong post, I pull my leathers up three or four notches. I want to feel and look like a jockey. Deej and Liam take their positions on each side of me. While they are not looking, I do the heart trick, tracing a shape on Poptastic's shoulder. It is more to calm me than him.

When we turn and set off, it takes a while to settle Poptastic. I play with the reins, changing the pressure on his mouth to keep him distracted, and soon he begins to relax into his stride.

There you go, boy. This is the way it's done.

I drop my hands on his neck and crouch lower in the saddle.

To my right, Liam is going easily. Deej, on the other side, gives a little whoop of joy as the wind whistles past our ears.

At the four-furlong pole, I change my grip on the reins and begin to push Poptastic out, hands and heels.

Let's see what you can do, boy. Here we go.

For the first time in his life, Poptastic gets a taste of what he has been bred to do. He lengthens his stride, and by the time we pass the group of onlookers beside the gallop, we are half a length ahead of the other two and going well within ourselves.

We pull up and canter back to the trainer.

"Said don't go crazy." Mr. Wilkinson is scowling at me,

but by now I know him well enough to see that he is quite pleased by what he has seen.

"I had a lot more in hand, sir."

"Oh, he's so sweet, Pete." Paloma is holding on to Mr. Lukic's arm and jumping up and down like a little girl at a birthday party. The owner turns and says something quietly to Mr. Wilkinson.

"Want you to keep him covered up at Lingfield, Jay," the trainer mutters.

Covered up? I have no idea what he is talking about.

Mr. Wilkinson senses my uncertainty. "He'll need the outing."

I'm no wiser, but I'd be a fool to give myself away. "Yes, sir."

"His moment will come." The trainer nods. "Take 'em home, then."

As I follow Deej back to the string, I call out to him, "What was all that about?"

"The guv'nor was telling you that you won't be riding a winner in your first race."

I laugh. "Just watch me."

"You don't get it," he says. "You're not riding a winner. That's what he was telling you."

"I don't understand."

"Covered up. Need the outing. Not his day. That's racing-speak, and it all means the same thing. You're not supposed to win."

I'm aware of a lurch of disappointment within me. I've been in racing long enough to know that races are sometimes

- 171 -

fixed. It's illegal, but not every trainer obeys the rules. Somehow I never thought that Mr. Wilkinson would play that game.

"I don't like it." I say the words quietly, more to myself than to anyone else.

"We're a gambling yard, Bug," Deej calls over his shoulder. "It's all part of racing."

The.

Real.

World.

No Funny Business

Yearling time has arrived. Day to day I have too much to think about to spend time worrying about my first ride in a month or so.

Throughout November, many of the older horses leave the yard. Horseboxes arrive and take them to their new futures—at stud or to steeplechasing or abroad. I try not to think too much about what is going to happen to the horses I've come to know so well.

Of mine, Norewest is to be trained in a jumping yard, and Ocean Pacific has been sold as a stallion to Japan.

As the yearlings begin to arrive, they are scruffy, wild-eyed, potbellied, more foals than horses. They look around, amazed and scared. Until now, they have been in a field. Some come directly from sales. For them, everything is new and different.

It is our job over the winter months to turn these babies, who have never had a weight on their backs or a bridle in their mouths, into racehorses.

The atmosphere in the yard changes at yearling time. Mr. and Mrs. Wilkinson are rarely to be seen.

Harry Bucknall, grumpy at being in charge during the darkest, coldest part of the year, shows how important he is by doing as little as possible.

The lads are in bad moods too. Most of them hate breaking in the yearlings, and some of the older ones, including Angus, avoid the work altogether. You have to be patient. The weather is miserable. Any day, you risk getting hurt by an overexcited yearling.

I love it all—getting them to stand and become used to human company, grooming them gently, picking up their legs, putting on a breaking bit, longeing them in the paddock, long-reining them around the yard and through the starting stall, getting them used to a saddle and girth, lying across them in the stable so that they become used to carrying weight, sitting quietly on them while they are led by another lad in the small paddock, then "riding away" when, snorting and confused, they are taken out for the first time to the part of the heath reserved for yearlings.

Each of them is different. One or two take a look around and accept their new life as if it was what they had been expecting all along. Others dash here and there whenever they can, act up when they should be learning how to work. A few want to fight you all the way.

It is like an unruly elementary-school class, but one where the students are big enough to kick you through a door or break your arm.

Whenever I have a spare moment, I am down in the bull pen with Manhattan. She has fresh bedding now, and whenever I can, I leave the door to the shed open. She can see sunlight, even if it is from the back of a cowshed.

Her winter coat has covered up the nicks and marks left by Pete. Some horses become restless when they are groomed for too long. Manhattan loves it as I whistle and sing while working. Once she wanted to be alone. These days, she has discovered she quite likes human company, as long as it's of the right sort.

"Routine, that's what the horses like," Ted used to tell me, and it was good advice. Manhattan has had so many shocks and surprises in her life that the reassuring rhythm of things being done in the same way and in the same order seems to calm her.

She has her own habits too. In the morning, she likes to wake slowly. I have learned that, when I arrive, I should walk quietly into the pen.

Morning, Hat.

I stand in front of her and gently rest my head against hers, forehead to forehead. We stay still for several seconds. It is a new day, and I am telling her that I am here, that she can trust me. It is our moment.

Later, as I muck out the pen, she can sometimes be

grumpy, like someone who wants to sleep late. When I ask her to move over, she swishes her tail in dozy irritation and at first doesn't move an inch.

"Hey, Hat, wake up! I've got three other horses to do."

She turns her head and gives me a look under those long white eyelashes. I am getting her princess stare. It says: "Excuse me, are you talking to me?"

"Enough, Hat!"

I slap her lightly on the hindquarters and, game over, she moves.

She is odd about her food, I have discovered. However hungry she may be, she will stand looking at her manger until I have left the pen. As soon as she hears the latch fall, she moves forward to eat.

Day by day, she is changing. The light is back in her eyes. She may be banished in disgrace to the back of a cow-shed, but in her own beautiful head, she is still special.

Two weeks after my return, Angus surprises me by visiting the bull pen late one morning. He watches me for a moment as I run the body brush over Manhattan.

"Don't spend too much time on the mare." He speaks more quietly than he used to. It is as if now that Pete has gone, he no longer has to pretend to be fiercer than he is. "Remember, she's not making money for the yard."

Manhattan turns to look at him. Her ears are half-back, but at least she is no longer rolling her eyes, baring her teeth, and swishing her tail.

"She's calming down," I say.

"Aye. So it would seem."

"Maybe I can start taking her out with second or third lot again."

"Your risk."

"Of course."

He looks from me to her, then gives a nod. "We'll try it tomorrow," he says, then walks briskly out of the cowshed, the heels of his boots echoing off the walls.

I wait five seconds after the door has closed, then give Manhattan a hug around the neck.

Yes. Yes. Yes.

I know she will be a handful. Since she attacked Pete, her exercise has consisted of being led around the inside arena and occasionally taken on the walker. Although her feed is more bran than high-energy nuts, she is still a racehorse in her prime.

When I saddle her up, she arches her back and gnashes her teeth, but by now I am beginning to understand her.

Leave it, Hat. No messing around today.

I clamber onto the metal manger in the bull pen and alight into the saddle. I let down my leathers a couple of holes so that I am riding long and low in the saddle, like an old lady going for a quiet ride in the park.

Out of the bull pen, into the daylight. Manhattan stops, stands stock-still, her head high, ears pricked. She gives a slow, superior snort.

I let her take in the sights and sounds of the day for a few seconds. Then I click my teeth. She walks toward the main yard, looking around as if expecting—assuming—that she is the center of attention.

And I catch it from her, this mad pride. I sit up straight in the saddle, a big smile on my face.

Let's go, princess.

The string is in the inside arena when we arrive.

"What's the big joke?" asks Liam, on a four-year-old bay in front of me.

"She's incredible."

"Nutcase," says Liam.

I don't bother to ask whether he's referring to me or the horse I am riding.

It's a cold day, and although it's late morning, a winter mist still hangs over the town.

As we make our way down the horse path toward the heath, I find I have to keep checking Manhattan, as her stride is so much longer than those of the horses in front of me.

We cross the road onto the heath. She's excited to be out. There is a rumbling, writhing feeling beneath the saddle, like an approaching earthquake.

Calm, Hat. No funny business.

We walk around the gallops, up Warren Hill, and I sense Manhattan's impatience. When we're about to embark on a second circuit, I call out to Deej, "Any chance of taking her for a canter up the all-weather?"

The other lads look at me in amazement.

"What d'you want to do that for?" Deej asks.

"She's jumping out of her skin. It'll calm her down."

Ahead of me, Laura looks over her shoulder. "Don't be crazy, Jay," she says. "The guv'nor will go mad."

"What difference will it make? If she's finished anyway, it'll just make looking after her easier."

We walk on. Then Deej calls back, "Your responsibility, Bug. Meet you at the top."

I peel off, and as I break into a trot, Manhattan shakes her head.

Easy, girl. It's just a canter.

No other strings are on the gallops. As she feels the all-weather surface beneath her hooves, Manhattan can contain her excitement no longer.

I gather up the reins, and we are off.

The mare drops her head, takes hold of the bit. We glide up the gallops. Now we are alone in the fog and the only sound is of my horse's hooves on the track, the rhythm of her breath with every stride. For one crazy moment, I feel like a superhero riding a magical winged horse through the clouds, a girl on Pegasus. We are covering the ground fast, but she seems to float effortlessly.

When we reach the end of the track, there are tears in my eyes, and they are not caused by the cold.

I'm back, Hat. It's you and me again. The old team.

We jog down the hill to the string. As I pass the other horses to take my place at the back, Laura shakes her head, but there is a little smile on her face. I notice the lads watching us. They still don't like Manhattan, but they know a real racehorse when they see one.

"She goes all right for you," Liam says, trying not to let on how impressed he is.

"She's amazing."

He laughs and repeats his favorite word. "Nutcase."

That night, when the guv'nor does his evening stable inspection and has reached my third horse, Something Fancy, I ask him whether he will be going down to the farmyard to see Manhattan.

"That screw?" He speaks dismissively and is about to leave. "Why? Something wrong with her?"

"She's the same as ever, Mr. Wilkinson," Angus says. "Nothing to report."

The trainer is looking at me. "Cantering her second lot. Trainer now, are you?" It is impossible to tell whether Mr. Wilkinson is angry or amused. "Spotted this afternoon. Little girl on big gray. On her own. All-weather track."

I open my mouth but no sound comes out. At last I manage to speak. "I just wanted to settle her, sir. It was my decision."

Mr. Wilkinson is staring at Something Fancy. "I wanted? My decision?" he mutters the words to himself. "Bloomin' cheek." He turns to Angus. "I'll see the mare," he says. "After I've finished the back yard."

I've been calming Manhattan for a good ten minutes by the time Mr. Wilkinson and Angus appear in the barn. She can be at her worst, I have noticed, when a group of people are looking into her stall. Now she swishes her tail when she hears Angus's voice.

Best behavior, Hat. Leave this to me.

The two men look nervously through the metal bars.

"Looks better. Tidier," says Mr. Wilkinson.

"She's still a bit light, sir." I slap her on the hind-quarters, and the trainer and head lad step back sharply. Manhattan, after a bit of fake-fierce head shaking with her ears back, moves over. I run a hand over her flank, where her ribs are visible through her coat.

"I've been keeping her light to calm her down," says Angus.

"She's eating well," I say. "And she was as good as gold when I rode her out this morning."

"Prince Muqrin. Soft spot for her," Mr. Wilkinson says to Angus. "Shouldn't look too ribby. Even if she is for the high jump. Feed her like the rest. Nuts. Oats. Vitamin supplements." He pauses, as if a sudden thought has occurred to him. "Bull pen. No place for a racehorse. Put her in the back yard tomorrow. Make her respectable. For the prince."

Before.

She.

Goes.

INSTRUCTIONS

The night before my first ride in public, I am summoned to Edgecote House after evening stables. Over the past month, I have managed to persuade myself that maybe I misunderstood what I was told the day that Poptastic's owner visited last year. Or that there has been a change of plan.

It would be a race like any other. We shall be there to win.

"Jay. Come. Race tomorrow. Talk." It is Mr. Wilkinson who opens the front door. He trudges down the corridor, and I follow. In the sitting room, he slumps into his usual chair beside a blazing fire. A glass of whiskey is on the table beside him.

He waves vaguely toward the sofa. I sit down.

Mr. Wilkinson reaches for a copy of today's *Racing Post* on the table beside him and tosses it onto the sofa. It is open on tomorrow's race card at Lingfield. The name of one race has been highlighted in red: *Albright Apprentice Handicap*.

And there's a blue line through one runner: *POPTASTIC (C. Wilkinson) 3 8–12 J. Barton (7)*

"Look good?" The trainer actually smiles at me.

"Yes, sir."

"Now. Need to talk about the race. Tomorrow." Mr. Wilkinson takes a sip of whiskey and looks at the glass in his hand. "Give the horse a couple of runs. Unplaced. Know what I mean? Time comes; horse trots up. Good odds at the bookies. You get a winner. Owner makes money. See you all right afterward. Way it goes in racing. Always has."

I know where this conversation is going but pretend to look confused.

Mr. Wilkinson gives a little twitch of irritation, as if I have said something that has annoyed him. "Owner likes a bet. Nothing wrong with that. Your orders. Do badly first two races. Win the third when no one's expecting it."

"You want me to lose?"

"No. Not lose. Just not win. Difference. Make it look good. Part of the skill of being a jockey. Thought you'd know that by now."

"I could get into trouble."

"Leave that to me. Takes as much skill not to win a race as it does to win it. Owner important to this yard. Mr. Lukic. Wants winners."

"I think he could have one tomorrow, sir."

"Wants them when he says! Not when some raggedy-pants yard girl goes glory hunting!"

"Yes, sir."

"Seen it before. Lads. Got promise. Go crazy. Ignore

instructions. Overexcited. Win races when it's not their day. Never heard of again. Unprofessional, d'you see?" He holds my eye, and I look away too slowly for his liking. "Want the ride or not, Barton?"

I nod. "I want the ride."

"Do what you're told, then. Not Poptastic's day. Have you got that?"

I look him in the eye, and I say the words that at that moment I really do believe.

Yes.

Sir.

Got.

That.

First Time Out

"It's no sweat to lose a race." Deej sits across the table from me at the lads' cafeteria at Lingfield Park racecourse. There is noise all around us, almost drowning his words. "You can be slow out of the stalls and never quite catch up with them. You can make sure that, accidentally on purpose, you're boxed in by the other runners so that you can't get your horse out to make its run until it's too late. You can pump your elbows out as if you're riding your horse out. If you're any good, you'll know how not to win."

"I guess." My words sound as gloomy as I feel. For most of my life, I have dreamed of riding my first race as a jockey. I somehow never imagined it would be like this.

There are nine runners in my race, the Albright Apprentice Handicap. Two of them, Minstrel Games and Divo, are previous winners. A couple of others, Whatadandy and Firefly, are nicely bred and come from large, successful yards. How difficult can it be to come in a respectable fifth or sixth?

"Can't think what you're worried about," Deej says, smiling. "All you've got to do is finish down the field and you've done your job. Where's the pressure there?"

I nod. "It's going to be fine," I say.

Mine is the fourth race of the afternoon. I watch the first two from the lads' stand and then go to get ready.

The locker room for women jockeys adjoins the larger one for the men. There are only a few women riding today — including Sally Jeffreys, who has had over seventy winners in her career — and none of us is the conversational type. Now and then, the noise and laughter from the male jockeys can be heard through the wall.

I am the only girl in the lads' race. When I am called to weigh in, I ignore the curious stares of the male apprentices as they wait by the scales. One nudges another and laughs. Even in a race for apprentices, it seems that I look ridiculously young.

Beyond them, I see Mr. Wilkinson in a baggy old brown suit. He studies his race card until I have weighed in and hand him my saddle and weight cloth.

"Right, Jay?" His small, glistening eyes gaze at me intently.

"Yes, thank you, sir."

"Ride your race. You know what to do," he says, and is gone.

Ride my race. Sitting in the weighing room, I think of those words. The race he wants me to ride for Mr. Lukic is not mine, but his.

We are called to the paddock. The other apprentices seem to know each other and chat easily, all fake grown-up and cool, as they make the walk from the weighing room, some of them casually slapping their whips against the side of their boots in the way they've seen proper jockeys do.

I walk behind them, alone. I'm distantly aware of the loudspeaker announcements, the feel of silks on my back, the whip in my right hand, the nervous emptiness in my stomach.

For one panicky moment, entering the paddock, I can't see anyone I know and I stand alone, looking lost, as the other jockeys walk confidently to their trainers and owners.

At last, I see the broad back of Mr. Wilkinson and, beyond him, my owner, Mr. Lukic, with an outsize pair of binoculars around his neck. Hanging on his arm is his girl-friend, Paloma, in a clingy orange outfit.

She notices me first and gives me a girlish wave.

I walk toward them, tip my helmet.

"Got your instructions, Jay," says Mr. Wilkinson. "Just remember them." When I glance toward Mr. Lukic, he gives an odd, twitchy wink that I'm hoping the cameras don't pick up.

There is sweat on Poptastic's neck, but he looks good. He has a touch of class to him.

"Been a bit of late money on our horse," Mr. Lukic says

as we watch him walking around, led by Deej. "I've got to admit he's the pick of the paddock."

The bell rings. I am given the leg up. The gateman lets us out onto the track. Leading me around, Deej looks up and gives me an encouraging smile.

"Good luck, Bug." Deej unfastens the lead rein and sends me off. As we canter gently to the start, Poptastic pulls hard against me. The sights and sounds of the racecourse slowly fade behind us.

We circle behind the starting stalls. Poptastic is one of the first to be put in. I sense his nervousness. Slowly, firmly, I trace the shape of a heart on his shoulder.

"Ready, jockeys," the starter calls out.

There is a mechanical click in the stalls that distracts Poptastic so that when they open with a clatter, he is back on his heels and makes a slow start.

The eight horses ahead of me spread across the track and for a few strides are advancing like a cavalry charge going into battle. Soon, they bunch up. Some, on the racetrack for the first time, are looking around, wandering first to the left, then to the right.

Easy, Tassy. This is just another gallop, right?

Poptastic has settled. Three-quarters of a length behind the last horses in the field, I would need only to steady him for a few paces for the gap between the two horses in front of us to close. We would be covered up, safely out of the reckoning.

Ride my race. I let out a notch on my reins so that we

have almost reached the horses in front of us. Somewhere in my jockey's brain, a decision has been reached. It is almost as if there is nothing I can do about it.

As we pass the three-furlong pole, the two horses beside me begin to lose ground. I look to my left. On the rails, a length ahead of me, three horses are being ridden out, stride for stride.

You want to win, don't you, Tassy? I can feel it.

We can hear the crowd now, but within me I am aware of a niggling, nagging voice.

Not his day. Not his day. Not his day.

"No." I say the word out loud. *Come on, boy. Let's go.*

Poptastic's strength is beginning to tell. A furlong out, there are four of us in a line. With every stride nearer the winning post, the voice of caution, protesting within me, grows fainter.

Poptastic drops his head and drives for the line. He is a battler, and so am I.

"Yaaarggggg!"

The roar that emerges from my throat sounds almost inhuman.

As if at a signal, the three other horses lose their rhythm. Two of the apprentices have pulled their whips through and are riding a finish, but their horses are unbalanced. I crouch lower in the saddle, driving my horse forward with hands and heels.

As we flash past the line, we've won by half a length.

That's my boy. That's my Tassy.

As we pull up, the apprentice riding on the second horse nods at me as he passes. For the first time since I've been on Poptastic's back today, a smile is on my lips. I've won.

Then, slowly, the excitement of the moment begins to seep away.

Oh, no. I realize the reality of what I have done. It is my first ride and I have broken racing's golden rule — I have ignored my orders.

Deej is waiting for me in the center of the track. He looks worried.

"You did it," he says. It's more an accusation than a compliment. Without a smile, he puts the lead rein on Poptastic and we head back toward the stands.

I pull down my goggles. "I got a bit carried away," I say quietly.

"We noticed. I hope you've got your story straight."

Led in by Deej, we pass a small crowd of racegoers, some of whom look at Poptastic and his female rider with curiosity.

In the winners' enclosure, Mr. Wilkinson waits with his owner. Neither of them is looking exactly thrilled by their victory. Behind them, I see Mrs. Wilkinson. She looks away as I catch her eye. There is a smattering of applause as I dismount. "Well ridden, love!" somebody shouts.

Behind me, I hear Mr. Lukic muttering what he thinks of me, mostly in four-letter words. I glance toward him and see that he has a sickly, fake smile on his face. He is not good at pretending to be pleased.

I undo the girth, take off the saddle, and am about to

go to the weighing room when Mr. Wilkinson puts a heavy
hand on my shoulder. His voice is in my ear like a threatening
rumble of thunder.

Warned.

You.

Didn't.

I?

ALSO-RANS

Not everyone is upset after I win my first race.

Auntie, for one, is thrilled. The night after the race, she cooks Laura and me a special meal (pizza with curried chicken on top) and opens the half-finished bottle of white wine that has been in the fridge for as long as I've been staying here.

"Her first ride a winner." Sitting between us at the round kitchen table, Auntie raises a glass in my direction. "Amazing."

Laura shakes her head, a little smile on her face. I shoot her a warning glance.

"Cheers, Auntie." I take a sip of the wine and almost choke. I had been hoping the wine would take away the taste of the curry pizza. Now I grab a mouthful of pizza to get rid of the wine from my taste buds. Maybe the two will cancel each other out.

"And you know what?" Auntie is holding the glass of wine like a trophy. "I think it was Laura who helped you get to that winning post. It's my team, I tell you."

I smile at Laura, who looks away, rolling her shoulders like a boxer about to get into the ring.

"She certainly did," I say.

"My Jas worked five years in Newmarket." Auntie tells the story as if we have never heard it before. "Not a sniff of a ride. And he was good—everyone said that."

"There's a lot of luck," I murmur.

"Luck be damned," Auntie says loudly. A glass of wine in her hand, but she has only had a single sip. She's not drunk but happy. "It's talent. This is the age of the girl."

Laura winces. "We may have a bit of a way to go, Auntie."

"Wait." Auntie leaves the table and goes into the sitting room. When she returns, she is carrying today's edition of the *Racing Post*. "Have you seen this?" She holds the report of yesterday's racing.

"No," I say, although I have.

"Here's what it says in the papers in black-and-white." She puts on the reading glasses that hang from her neck.

> "The highly fancied Minstrel Games disap-
> pointed in the six-furlong Albright Apprentice
> Handicap, finishing only fifth behind the
> eight-to-one Poptastic. In a blanket finish, the
> 'Magic' Wilkinson–trained colt prevailed over
> Divo and Firefly under the powerful driving of

newcomer Jay 'Bug' Barton. Both horse and jockey are ones to watch."

Auntie pinches my arm. "You're one to watch."

"Yeah, don't hold your breath about that," says Laura.

"Honestly, you're so negative sometimes, Laura." Auntie pours us both some more wine, although neither of us has managed to drink much. "Jay's ridden a winner. First time on a racecourse. Can you believe that?"

"No." Laura gives me her most innocent look. "None of us could believe it."

Later that night, just before I am going to bed, I get a call from Uncle Bill.

"You're a dark horse, girl." There's a throaty chuckle in his voice. "You don't even tell your own uncle when you're riding in your first race."

"I—"

"Luckily, I've got a finger on the pulse. Spotted your name. Had a little bet and, blimey, you bolt up at eight to one. Couldn't believe it, doll."

"It was Poptastic who did it," I mutter, but my uncle is not in a listening mood.

"I thought they liked to have a gamble at Wilkinson's. I'd have expected you to be one of the favorites."

"They didn't expect me to win."

"Never underestimate a Barton. I sent Michaela a text at her school. She'll be thrilled."

I smile.

"Just one more thing, doll."

"Yes, Uncle Bill."

"Now that you're on the inside, I'll be expecting a little bit of information. I'd like a few more eight-to-one winners, if you know what I mean."

"I'll try to remember that."

"No. You won't *try* to remember. You *will* remember." Suddenly the warmth has gone out of my uncle's voice. "Things haven't been so clever on the business front recently, doll." He clears his throat and for the first time I realize that he's sounded slightly odd throughout this call—a bit too loud and cheerful, like a man trying to keep up appearances. "Just remember you owe me," he mutters.

And with that, he hangs up.

That week at the yard, there is a strange atmosphere. I'm respected, yet pitied. No one can say that I rode Poptastic badly, and yet I have done the worst thing. I've won, but I'm a loser.

I still gallop the horses, carry a whip, ride work with the others, but everybody knows that I am no longer a jockey of the future. I am just another work rider—good with horses, useful to have in the yard, but unreliable on the track. I have become another of racing's might-have-beens. I could have made it, but on the racecourse—the only place where talent really matters—I blew it. I did the one thing my trainer told me not to do.

There is a coldness in the way Mr. Wilkinson watches me. The better I ride, the more disappointment there is in his eyes. Bucknall, on the other hand, has suddenly become chummy and jokey when I am around. My disaster has been the best thing to happen to him for weeks.

At the times when things go wrong in a yard, the lads close ranks. Now, if I'm around, no one mentions my race. People are friendly, but they keep their distance, as if failure is catching.

A week after the race, a horsebox arrives at the yard. Mr. Lukic has decided to move Poptastic and his other two horses to John Collings, a big trainer in Epsom.

We box them up. I say a last farewell to the horse who gave me my first (and probably my last) winner. As the truck trundles down the road, I stand beside Liam, the lad who did the other two of Mr. Lukic's horses.

"Good riddance." He smiles in my direction. "We don't need owners like that." He trudges back to the yard.

But we do. Every lad knows that. The Wilkinson yard needs any owner it can get. We have just lost three horses.

A week later, another couple of owners are gone. One is having money problems; the other wants his horses nearer where he lives. Coincidence? Of course not. There is talk of lads being "let go." Suddenly, the Wilkinson yard is on the slide.

And it is all my fault.

I spend more time with Manhattan. Like me, she has been written off by the trainer. We are both also-rans, outsiders.

As the days grow longer and winter slowly makes way

for spring, she begins to shed her winter coat. Her color becomes lighter, as if the sun is trying to break through those dark, dappled clouds on her neck and her flanks.

Her character changes too. In her new stable, she is less grumpy in the mornings. When I see her, she is looking out at everything that is going on in an interested, slightly superior way. She no longer lays her ears back when lads pass by her stall.

For the first time since I have known her, she is enjoying life. When first lot pulls out, I can hear her pawing at the ground impatiently. Once, when there are not enough lads for the horses who have arrived for the new flat season, I ask Angus if I can take Manhattan out alone during the afternoon. To my surprise, he agrees, and soon these afternoon rides while the other lads are resting become a daily ritual.

Quality time, eh, Hat?

We are both better alone. She is on her toes and excited as I tack her up. I get on her in the stable. We walk out into the yard. She takes two steps, then stops to look around her, ears pricked, head held high. Then we walk through the yard, her beautiful silver mane moving like a wave in the sea with every brisk step that she takes.

I love those afternoons, riding Manhattan. She has a way of walking, with a giant stride where her hooves seem to hover over the ground before she lowers them, as if there is something delicate in front of her that she is anxious not to crush. It feels like walking on air.

Although Manhattan likes routine, I discover during

our rides alone that she is also excited by change. If I take her on a different path to the heath or we go to a new part of the little wood on Warren Hill, she looks around, snorting the air.

You were bored, weren't you, Hat? That was one of the reasons you behaved badly. You're intelligent and need to be kept interested.

We walk the perimeter of the heath, trotting occasionally. One afternoon, when a hare gets in front of us, Manhattan shies and then, just for the hell of it, shakes her head, squeals, and does a mad little sideways dance.

I laugh. The heath stretches before us. The late-afternoon light is fading. The only person in sight is a woman walking her dog a few hundred meters away.

Come on, Hat. Let's have a bit of fun.

I click my teeth and give her the lightest of kicks. With a low grunt of relief and pleasure, Manhattan puts her head down, takes hold of the bit, and we are off.

There is no feeling in the world quite like this. Although we are only cantering, I can tell by the way the wind whistles in my ears and how the ground has become a blur beneath our feet that I should not be fooled by Manhattan's easy action. Her canter is faster than the gallop of many horses.

It becomes a daily event, and one that we both love. Every day when we reach a clump of trees, I look around to check that we are not being watched and then give the mare her daily treat.

We may both be alone in the world. We may have been written off by everyone who knows us. But we still have this.

Too.

Good.

To.

Lose.

PRINCE

The flat season is approaching. There is warmth in the March sun. One morning a stocky man with sleek blond hair is with Mr. and Mrs. Wilkinson to watch first lot.

The lads know him well. It is James Webber, once a jump jockey, now Prince Muqrin's racing manager. His presence usually means only one thing. A royal visit cannot be far away.

The atmosphere in the yard changes. The hedges are trimmed. Frank, the yard man, sweeps corners in the back yard that he usually ignores. The lads seem chirpier, smarter. Prince Muqrin is rumored to be a good tipper.

On Tuesday morning, after first lot, Angus tells us the news. The next day, the prince will be looking at his horses. Two of them will be working.

It is the moment of truth for Manhattan. Over the past few weeks, I have tried to forget the death sentence hanging over her, but now I know that today is when her future will be decided. During the afternoon before the prince's visit, I take her out for a shorter ride than usual, then spend two hours grooming her, washing her tail, pulling her mane, oiling her hooves. Her new summer coat is coming through and she seems lighter in color than she was last year.

Our winter rides have changed her. There is a brightness about her, a light in her eyes. The daily exercise has made her leaner, more muscular. She feels more confident in herself. She is a princess. She knows it, even if no one else does.

After evening stables, I'm surprised to find Laura in the tack room. Sitting on the blanket chest, she is cleaning her saddle. It's such an unusual sight that I have to laugh.

She glances up. "You'd be wise to do the same thing, Bug," she mutters. "The Saudis like things to look just right."

I look up at my saddle on the rack above my head and take it down. When Laura is prepared to put in overtime, I know things are serious.

Gouging out some saddle soap with a sponge, I give the saddle a quick once-over.

"I've been grooming Manhattan," I say. "She looks amazing. No way will she be sent to the vet's."

Laura sniffs. "I wouldn't count on it."

"What's he like, the prince?"

"He's all right." She stands up and, head to one side, looks at her saddle. "Quiet, polite, more English than most Englishmen. He was educated at a posh private school."

"So you reckon he'll give Hat another chance."

She laughs. "I didn't say he was crazy, did I?"

* * *

After first lot the next day, I am in Manhattan's stall when Laura looks over the door.

"Best behavior, Bug," she says. "The prince is in the main yard."

I put on Manhattan's blanket, then walk to the archway leading to the main yard. From the shadows, I watch as the visitors go from stall to stall.

Ahead of them is Angus, cap in hand, ready to open any stall if required. Trailing behind, ignored by the main group, is Bucknall, looking unusually smart.

Mr. Wilkinson walks between the racing manager, Mr. Webber, and a neat, small man in dazzling white robes. The prince. To tell the truth, I had expected something different—something a bit more impressive. I watch his face as he chats and laughs. Apart from the way he is dressed, he looks surprisingly normal. He could be a young actor playing the part of an Arabian prince on a stage.

Mr. Wilkinson leads him to the center of the yard where some matting has been placed on the grass.

One by one the two-year-olds are led up for him and stand as their futures are discussed. Then the older horses are brought for the prince to see. We have been told that his two best three-year-olds, Drive On and Ishtagah, are to have a trial this morning, ridden by the stable jockey, Pat O'Brian, and another experienced professional, Gary Fielding. Both horses have been entered in the season's Classics and need to be put through their paces before their summer campaign is discussed.

Eight of the prince's nine horses are led before their

owner. When the last one is returned to his stall, the prince turns to his manager to ask something. Mr. Webber points toward the back yard. Seeing me, Angus gives me a nod.

Manhattan time.

I take off her blanket and lead her out. She steps through the archway into the main yard, stops, then looks, head high, ears pricked toward the prince as if he is the one about to be inspected, not her. I take a gamble and let her stand there for a moment, even if she is keeping her owner waiting.

"Now, just behave yourself. This is the prince, Hat. You do not show him your teeth."

I lead her to the center of the yard. As we approach, Prince Muqrin smiles and bids me a good morning.

Morning, Your Highness.

Manhattan stands, gazing into the distance. Powerful, graceful, serene.

The prince is shaking his head. "What an awful pity it is," he says to no one in particular. "She looks like a champ, but she's an awful chump."

Mr. Wilkinson doesn't do jokes, but he manages to force a smile. "Had her chance," he says. "Good money after bad."

The prince is about to turn away, then seems to remember he should say something to me. "Bit tricky in the stall, is she?"

"No, Your Highness. She's lovely."

Mr. Wilkinson frowns and gives a slight shake of his head.

"Lovely? I heard that she's a bad lady," says the prince. "She's been nothing but trouble all her life. I just wanted to say good-bye to her."

"She's changed, Your Highness."

Mr. Wilkinson mutters quietly in my direction. "Speak. When spoken to."

The prince raises his left hand slightly and gives a graceful nod of his head to me. "You were saying?"

"She's a different horse this year, Your Highness. Not just in the stall but on the gallops. She goes really well. She's incredible."

The prince smiles. "What's your name?"

"Jay, Your Highness."

"Well, Jay." He pauses, frowning. "You'll discover when you're a bit older that it's no use looking handsome and going well at home. Good horses win races. This one has been an expensive disaster."

In spite of his strangely posh voice — *aaawful, baad, discovah, disaaastah* — I sense that he wants to believe me.

"Mare's a wrong 'un." It is a bark of anger from Mr. Wilkinson.

Manhattan turns toward him and gives him a cold stare.

"Hat's improving, Your Highness. I think she's worth giving another chance." There is emotion in my voice now. I have to speak up. "She has changed. Every day she goes better."

"Hat?" The prince looks shocked, but there is a twinkle of humor in his eye. "My horse is called 'Hat'?"

"Nickname," growls Mr. Wilkinson. "Silly girl. Treats the mare like a pet."

"And you say she's going better?"

"She's unbelievable, Your Highness."

Prince Muqrin turns toward the other two men, his eyebrows raised.

"Goes nicely for Jay," says Mr. Wilkinson. "When it doesn't matter. Had her chance, sir. Let you down. On the racecourse."

The prince is gazing sadly at his horse. "If only she behaved as well as she looks." He turns to his racing manager and the two men move away for a brief, muttered conversation. After a moment, the prince returns. "Jimmy's had a rather wizard idea," he says. "Let's see how she goes with the other two this morning."

Mr. Wilkinson looks even more irritated than usual. "Sir, we have only two jockeys booked. Not possible."

A determined look has entered the prince's dark eyes. "Well, perhaps young Jay here could ride her."

There is a moment of silence, and I am aware that all eyes are on me. I don't dare to breathe.

"Saddle her up, Jay," says Mr. Wilkinson. "What you waiting for?"

I bob my head in the direction of the prince and lead Manhattan away. As I go, I hear Mr. Wilkinson's words: "Last-chance saloon for this wicked lady."

There is no time to lose. Drive On and Ishtagah are already in the covered yard with their pacemaker for the trial, a four-year-old called Gatekeeper. I fetch a saddle and bridle from the tack room and hurry back to Manhattan's stall.

"No messing around, Hat. They're waiting for us."

To my amazement, she is calm as I tack her up. It is as if she senses that now is not the moment for games. I get on the manger, jump into the saddle, and we walk out of the stable.

Angus approaches. "Hang on," he says. He stands back, inspecting me, then fiddles with the noseband. "The prince's horses have got to look right," he mutters. "Even this crazy camel."

I look down and possibly for the first time since I have been in the yard, I smile at the head lad.

"Don't let her make a fool of us, Bug," he says quietly. "Good luck."

"I won't, Angus."

I am about to walk on when he calls out, "You're a work rider this morning." He holds up his whip. "You'll be needing this."

"I'm OK without it," I say. "But thanks all the same."

We walk briskly through the main yard and into the covered yard. The three lads there—Liam and Amit on the two three-year-olds and Deej on Gatekeeper—look at me in surprise.

"Manhattan joining you," Mr. Wilkinson calls out. "Making up the numbers."

We're going to show them, Hat. They are in for the surprise of their lives.

I like the way she feels this morning. She knows that something serious is about to happen. The moment for playing, looking around, and showing off is over.

I follow the three other horses out of the inside arena, down the path toward the heath. Liam and Amit chat to each other easily, knowing that when we get to the gallops, they will be making way for the jockeys. Deej, who has the serious job of setting the pace for the prince's horses, looks tense.

When we reach the heath, we trot to the trial gallops where three cars are parked — Mr. Wilkinson's old station wagon, the sleek Bentley with darkened windows that belongs to the prince, and Pat O'Brian's flashy red sports car.

The jockeys have arrived.

We circle around the group, which I notice now includes Mrs. Wilkinson. All eyes are on the two stars of this morning's show, Drive On and Ishtagah.

Liam and Amit pull in, and as Mr. Wilkinson and Bucknall hold the three-year-olds' heads, Pat O'Brian and Gary Fielding — a wiry, hard-eyed old-timer who has won a couple of Group One races in his time — are given the leg up.

We circle in silence for a moment. O'Brian glances in my direction. Good looking and a favorite with interviewers, he is not, according to the lads, as friendly in everyday life as he likes to pretend to the outside world.

Mr. Wilkinson steps away from the group.

"Pay attention, jockeys," he calls out. "Serious piece of work. One-mile gallop. Ride them out at the end. Proper trial. See what they're made of. Understood?"

We murmur our agreement.

"And Deej, take them at a good, brisk pace."

"Yes, sir."

We canter down to the end of the gallops, Gatekeeper at the front, followed by the two three-year-olds. The professional jockeys are chatting away as they go, but now and then they glance back at me. I can imagine what they are saying.

At the start of the gallops, we walk in a circle. I stop to check my girth. Then, slowly and firmly, I trace a heart on Manhattan's shoulder. We need the heart trick today.

O'Brian trots past me. "Just don't get in the way, right," he says in a quiet, threatening voice.

I nod, and at that very moment Gatekeeper takes off, followed by Drive On and Ishtagah. Unprepared, I haven't gathered up my reins and Manhattan is left flat-footed. As we pass the first furlong pole, we are already ten lengths adrift of the other three.

I settle on Manhattan, my hands moving down her neck, my body in the low crouch that I now find natural when I ride. The mare is running well within herself, covering the ground effortlessly with her giant stride.

Yeah, that's it. Easy, girl. This is where it's all going to change for you.

We pass the four-furlong pole. Halfway. We are now only five lengths behind the two three-year-olds, who are closing on Gatekeeper.

Three furlongs. Gatekeeper is losing ground. His job as pacemaker is done. Drive On and Ishtagah ease past him. I notice that O'Brian has begun to niggle at Drive On. Fielding has yet to move on Ishtagah. Manhattan is still as relaxed as a pony going for a canter on a beach.

Two furlongs. I pass Gatekeeper as if he is standing still, catching Deej's startled look as I go. I'm alongside Drive On. O'Brian glances across at me, almost doing a double take as he sees that I have yet to move on my horse. One furlong. Ishtagah is a length in front of me and Gary Fielding is riding him out, going for home. I change my grip on the reins, and suddenly it is as if Manhattan has decided to get serious.

She lengthens her stride, and I feel a surge of astonishing power beneath me. For the first time, I experience what she is like at a full gallop. In a matter of yards, we are at the front of the field.

Manhattan's ears go forward. She is like a caged animal who has tasted freedom after a lifetime of waiting. She stretches her sleek body and — I can't help it — I give a whoop of joy as she accelerates.

"Go, girl!"

As we flash past the group standing at the end of the gallop, I take a quick look over my shoulder. Ishtagah is a good five lengths behind me, and Drive On is well beaten, several lengths behind him. Manhattan is moving as if she wants to go another mile.

That's it, Hat. Easy, now. They've got the message.

I pull up and turn to canter back toward the trainer and Prince Muqrin. Fielding and O'Brian pass me on the way, staring straight ahead, as if I don't exist and that getting totally hammered by Manhattan was all part of their plan.

Suits.

Me.

Just.

Fine.

PAYBACK TIME

Manhattan is now in the main yard. I ride her out every day with first lot. Even when one of the lads, trying to provoke her, bumps against us in the string or waves his hand in her face, she is as dignified as a queen might be if one of her subjects had behaved badly in front of her.

That's my girl. That's my Hat.

She trusts me. As long as I am with her, she is above it all. Together we grow stronger and more confident every day.

Sometimes, just for old times' sake, she misbehaves for a few seconds while working, throwing her head around like a yearling being broken or pretending to take a bite out of a horse galloping too close to her.

"Cut it out, Hat!"

And she settles down. It is as if, hearing my voice, she remembers how life used to be before I looked after her.

Deej and I laugh about how quickly the lads have changed their attitude toward her. Group memory loss, he calls it. Once I was a funny little Bug who fell off horses and Manhattan was something out of a zoo—the crazy camel, the psycho giraffe, Nellie the elephant.

Now the joke changes. My name is still Bug, but no one quite remembers why. They call Manhattan "the big mare." One morning when we make our entrance into the indoor arena, Liam calls out, "Here they come, the darling divas."

Manhattan pricks her ears and shakes her silver mane in a way that, I have to admit, has a touch of the film star to it. I smile. For most of my sixteen years, I have done everything I could to stay out of sight. Yet here I am, riding high, a darling diva.

Then, one evening, I get a call at Auntie's.

"Hi, Jay." Michaela has never been one to hide her feelings. Now she manages to get more despair into those two words than in all the miserable books and songs and plays ever written. "How's it going?" she croaks.

"I'm fine. What is it, M? You sound terrible."

"I'm not going back to school."

"But it's vacation now."

"Ever," she says tragically. "No more Lodge. *Ever.*"

"What? Have you been expelled? Was it the Jean-Paul thing?"

She gives a bitter laugh. "No. Just for a change, Jay, it's not my fault. It's Dad. He says he can't afford the fees. I've got to go back to the high school." Her voice cracks. "I hate that school, Jay. And you won't be there, either." She starts crying.

Uncle Bill? Can't afford? Those two phrases don't even belong in the same sentence.

"Everything's different around here," Michaela mutters. "Ted's going. All the horses are being sold. We might have to get rid of the house."

"But what happened?"

And out it comes, between sniffles and sobs. Uncle Bill has had "business problems." Something about some tax that hasn't been paid. The police have become involved.

"He has to pay back this humongous amount or he'll end up in court. He wanders around the house saying things like 'I'm finished' and 'We're wiped out.'"

For some reason, a phrase Uncle Bill liked to use comes into my mind: Another one bites the dust.

"What about Elaine?"

"What about her? All she's worried about is that she might have to go back to work. As if that's the biggest tragedy on earth."

"Oh, Michaela."

"Come home, Jayster. We need you back here. You're good when life is crap."

I pause for a moment, trying to work out whether this is a compliment or an insult. Either way, I know my answer.

"I can't, M. I've got a job. It's—" I am about to tell her that my work is going well, but I sense that's not the news Michaela wants to hear right now. "It's important to me."

"Yes, of course," she says bitterly. "Horses always have to come first, right? I'd better go. I just thought you'd like to know."

And she hangs up.

Concentrate. Don't get distracted. The news from home is upsetting. It worries me that the world of Uncle Bill, the sunny security of Coddington Hall, is in danger of being shattered, but I tell myself there is nothing I can do.

At times like this, I think of my mother when she was in the hospital. I remember the advice she gasped out to me when I was alone with her there.

Uncle. Bill. Survivor. Gets. By. Do. Like. Him. Own. Life. Be. Strong.

One day in April, I am on Manhattan and, with the rest of first lot, we are circling around Mr. Wilkinson, having just done a half-speed gallop up to Warren Hill.

The trainer seems to be taking a special interest in Manhattan. Suddenly he calls out to me, "Going to run the mare."

At first I can't believe what I'm hearing. "This mare?"

He gives a brisk, impatient nod.

We continue to circle. I try to keep the smile off my face. Be professional.

"Changed?" The trainer could be talking to himself. "We'll see. She's a mare. Don't hold your breath."

I ride on, saying nothing.

"York races. Mile and a quarter. Middleton Stakes.

Group Two. For fillies and mares. Four-year-olds and up. No point in putting her with rubbish."

"No, sir."

We continue to circle in silence while Mr. Wilkinson seems to have drifted off into a world of his own. Then he looks at me sharply, almost as if I have insulted him in some way.

"Got nothing to say?"

"About what, sir?"

"The mare. The race."

"Sounds good, sir. I think she'll run well."

The trainer looks more displeased than ever. "You're up," he mutters.

At first I think my ears are playing tricks on me. Up? It is an old-fashioned term, but I know what it means.

"Me?"

"You deaf, girl? Putting you up. In the bloomin' saddle. For the race. Must be blinkin' crazy."

Yes, yes, yes.

I lay a hand on Manhattan's shoulder. It is all I can do to stop myself from leaning forward and hugging her around the neck. I'm aware that the other lads are staring at me.

"Mare goes for you," says Mr. Wilkinson. "We can use the claim. Apprentice on board. She gets seven pounds less to carry. Missus says you should be given a chance." He stalks off, hands deep in his pockets.

"Thank you, sir," I call out. "Thank you so much."

"Don't thank me," he mutters as he gets into his old car, slamming the door. As soon as he has driven off, the lads start on me.

"Ooh, yes, sir. Anything you say, sir," Davy says in a sweet-little-girl voice. The others coo and trill like a flock of pigeons.

"She's blushing," says Liam.

I laugh. Then I clench my fist like a boxer. I shout, "Get in there!"

"The Bugster's back," says Deej.

Manhattan is jogging restlessly at the back of the string. On an instinct, I pull out and trot past the other horses. "Where's she off to?" Davy says as I pass.

"It's diva time," says Liam.

When we reach the front of the string, I slow to a walk. Ahead of the other horses, Manhattan points her toes, pricks her ears, and takes us home.

"Where we belong," I call over my shoulder.

That night before I go to sleep, I read about Petite Etoile in my copy of *Great Ladies*. The book says that "like all females, the gray had her little foibles and moods." One of her habits, according to the author, was that she would sulk when out with the string unless there was a gray horse in front of and behind her.

It sounds crazy to me. The man who wrote it was always going on about the "ladies" and their "foibles" and their "moods." I wondered if he would write the same about the "great gentlemen." Then I think of how much happier Manhattan is when she is at the head of the string, and her other habits—how she likes to stand for a moment or two outside her stall before joining the string in the covered yard, how she frets if I am too silent in the stable, how she's sensitive to noise, how she doesn't like her feet being touched, how she hates it when other horses get too close to her, how she distrusts men.

The lads kid me about how I treat Manhattan but in their hearts they understand. Horses may not be the most intelligent of animals, but they are sensitive and have a memory for what has been good and bad in their lives.

Manhattan senses that things have changed. Now in the main yard, she is the lead horse of first lot; she is more settled, more focused on the job. On our way out or back from the heath, people look at her.

On the gallops, she pulls hard against me but settles down easily. It is as if she has decided at last to behave like a serious, grown-up racehorse.

I am changing too. All that is in my mind is the big race at York, the Middleton. Every night I am in the gym at the Racing Center, doing circuits, getting fit. It becomes a bit of a joke down at the center, the time I spend on the machines, the way I drive myself to exhaustion every evening, but now it no longer worries me if people laugh at me or find me strange.

There is just one thought in my mind. York. Manhattan. If she runs a good race, her life will be saved. Nothing else matters.

Perhaps that is why when something unexpected happens two weeks before the race, it worries me less than it should.

I am on my way home after finishing my workout at the center. A Mini Cooper with darkened windows is parked by the side of the road. As I approach it, the door of the car opens.

"Hey, Jay." It is a familiar voice.

I hesitate for a moment. The man leaning across and looking up at me is unshaven and wears dark glasses. But there is no mistaking who it is.

"Hello, Uncle Bill. What are you doing here?"

"Step in, doll. We need a word."

I get into the car. Close the door. It is odd seeing my uncle in a tiny car. He looks uncomfortable, like a man who is wearing a suit that is a couple of sizes too small for him.

"How's it going, girl?"

The voice is rougher than it was, and Uncle Bill looks older.

"New car?" I say.

He looks almost embarrassed. "Old car," he says. "I decided to downsize a little."

"Michaela mentioned something about that."

"She did?"

"Just that things were a little tough right now."

"Tough." He shakes his head, as if trying to get rid of a poisonous thought in his brain, then looks me hard in the eye. "Remember what I said to you last time? About you owing me?"

I nod, a cold chill of dread in my heart.

"You're doing well now. Going places. Wilkinson says he's giving you another ride."

"There's this horse, Manhattan—"

"You. Owe. Me." He points a finger at me, stabbing the air.

"I've left home now, Uncle Bill."

"When your dad got your mum into trouble, I sorted it out. You lost your mum—I was there. I took you in, looked after you. I know your aunt Elaine wasn't too happy with you sometimes, but you did your riding, right? Thanks to me, yeah? And then there was the pony racing."

"Yes."

"I sorted out the school when you came here. Not easy, but your old uncle was there for you."

"What d'you want from me?"

He smiles, and I notice that his teeth are yellower than I remember them. "It's payback time. I need some money fast, and you're going to help me."

"But—"

"Shut up and listen." He reaches into his jacket pocket, takes out a cell phone, and gives it to me. "Present for you, doll. You are going to call me on this every couple of days or so and give me information. Which horses are going well on the gallops. Who's worth a bet. Maybe some of the gossip from the other yards in Newmarket."

My first thought is that my uncle must be pretty desperate to be asking for my help. My second is that I'll get into trouble.

"It's not allowed, Uncle Bill. Lads can't give information to outsiders. I'll get sacked."

"You can do it, doll." Uncle Bill turns to me in his

seat. I see my face, still flushed from my workout at the gym, reflected in his dark glasses. "Information. Good, inside stuff. Call me next week."

"Uncle Bill, please."

"You remember what you said to Michaela after the first race you rode on Dusty?"

"Not really."

"'Course you do. You said you had to win. You tried to explain to her that it was just within you, something you couldn't do anything about. Like a disease." He lowers his dark glasses and fixes me with his piercing blue eyes. I want to look away but somehow I can't. "You and me, babe." He says the words softly. "Family. We're the same. I know how you felt. That rage. That need to show the world, even if it means not playing by the rules. Winning, whatever the cost. That's you. But that's me too."

"I'm not like you, Uncle Bill. I'm really not."

He laughs bitterly and pushes his dark glasses back into place. "It's not such a bad thing to be, like your old uncle." The laughter dies. He reaches forward and holds my chin. His face is so close to mine that I can smell his stale breath. "Unofficial. Just like the old days." He pushes me away, then starts the car. "Good night, Jay."

I step out and watch as he drives off.

Disco.

Music.

Blaring.

A Bit of a Character

It is four days before the race. The *Racing Post* publishes the runners declared for the Middleton Stakes. The race is one of the biggest of the York meeting. It's for fillies of four and up, and the small field includes several winners of good races last season. Beside their name is their past form, showing whether they have won or been placed in recent races. The favorite, Touch of Class, reads "11221," meaning she has won all of her last races except two, where she was second.

Beside Manhattan's name is her form: "00000."

Unplaced in all her races and ridden by an unknown apprentice, Manhattan is the outsider of the field, with odds of thirty-three to one.

"I'm not surprised with that form." Deej is going over the runners and riders as we have lunch at the café three days before the race. I sip at my soup, looking hungrily at his hamburger. I need to watch my weight before the race.

The row of zeros beside her name gives me a twinge of worry. What is it that makes me think I can succeed where other jockeys have failed?

"She loves galloping," I murmur. "So why does she hate racing?"

"She's difficult," says Deej. "She thinks too much. You could tell as we loaded her into the horsebox for races in the past. She wasn't in the mood for it."

"You think it's the traveling?"

"She's calm when we arrive. It's not that."

Deej's words get me thinking. I have always assumed that Manhattan's problems when racing in the past happened on the course. Now I am wondering whether the problem starts at home, as she is being prepared.

Then I remember something I read about Manhattan's ancestor The Tetrarch. I look for the notes I had printed out from "The Rocking Horse That Rocked the World" when I was at racing school. Near the end, I find these words:

Only two things were known to upset The Tetrarch: he hated being shod by someone he didn't know and being given medicine by a vet. To avoid the first problem, his trainer, Atty Persse, made sure that the horse had his own farrier traveling with him when he went racing.

I might be reading about Manhattan. I think of how she hates to have her feet touched, even by me. Picking out her feet and oiling her hooves have become a daily game between us, with much flashing of eyes and swishing of tail from her and quiet persistence from me.

The game becomes more serious when Ivor, the farrier who shoes all the horses in the Wilkinson yard, visits every month. Ivor is, like many blacksmiths, a big, muscular man. As soon as he enters the stable in his heavy boots and leather apron, she becomes upset.

Ivor refuses to go near her unless I hold her with a twitch, a device that involves putting a tight rope noose around her nose to quiet her. She looks at me, wide-eyed and enraged, as Ivor works on her feet. After he has gone, she sulks. When I ride her out, she is moody and difficult. Sometimes it takes days before she is herself again.

And here is the problem. When a horse races, it has to wear light shoes called "racing plates." Made of aluminum, they are too soft and fragile to be worn for any time but a race.

In other words, Manhattan will have lost her race before she even leaves the yard—at the moment the farrier arrives the day before to put on her racing plates.

I have no choice but to mention the problem to Mr. Wilkinson when he does his rounds with Angus that evening.

To my surprise, Angus backs me up. "Bug's right," he says. "The mare is good for nothing after Ivor's been here. She'd be too upset to race."

The guv'nor shakes his head. "Trouble," he says, eyeing Manhattan. "Nothing's ever simple. Bloomin' mare."

"The Tetrarch used to have his own farrier," I say. "Hating blacksmiths runs in the family."

Both men stare at me. Stable lads are not supposed to

know this kind of stuff. "I learned it at racing school," I say weakly.

"The Tetrarch? He was a champion two-year-old. A hundred years ago." Mr. Wilkinson gives a great sigh. "Big difference."

He moves toward Manhattan, and standing by her head, I sense her tensing up. When he runs a hand down her near foreleg, she arches her neck and, in a casual threat, lifts her hind leg.

The trainer jumps back, moving more quickly than I have seen him move before.

"Easy, Hat."

"Bloody animal." Mr. Wilkinson has turned quite pale.

"It's only when her feet are touched," I say.

"Horse not racing in plates? Heard it all now," Mr. Wilkinson murmurs to himself. "Bloomin' Queen of Sheba." He glances at Angus. "All right," he mutters. "Tell Ivor. Leave the mare this time."

With a nod in my direction, he walks off, followed by Angus.

"Does that mean she's in with a chance?"

Every night after dinner, my Uncle Bill calls. I make small talk with him, then wander casually out to the garden. There, away from the ears of Auntie and Laura, I give him the information he's looking for.

"I don't know, Uncle Bill."

"Thirty-three to one. Those are pretty good odds. I could make some serious money here."

I glance back at the house and notice Auntie looking out of the window. She knows me well enough by now to see that I am not enjoying this call.

I drop my voice. "I can't talk to you here."

"Your problem, kid. Maybe you should call me from a safe place. Is there a park nearby?"

"Yes."

"Well, then. Pretend you've got to see someone—a boyfriend maybe. Call me from there."

"No one would believe I've got a boyfriend."

"I need some winners, Jay." Uncle Bill puts on his scary, take-no-prisoners voice. "You've given me a couple of half-decent tips. Now I need to know about this Manhattan nag."

"She's not a nag." I hesitate, then dive in. "She might be worth a little bet, but she's a bit of a character. She needs to be in the right mood."

For the first time in our conversation, Uncle Bill laughs.

She'd.

Better.

Be.

JOCKEYS HAVE WHIPS

A pale spring sun looks down on us as we arrive at the York racecourse stables. Mr. Wilkinson's other runner, a three-year-old called Whirling Dervish, is first out of the horsebox, led by his lad, Tommy.

Then I bring out Manhattan. She walks down the ramp carefully, then looks around. Ears pricked, her dark eyes alert, she snorts in the air.

That's it, Hat. You're a dragon today.

She lowers her head in my direction, too proud to ask for a carrot but prepared to accept one if I just happen to have one in my pocket.

And you don't even think of behaving badly. Right?

I give her the carrot.

It is late morning and I am in the racecourse stables. I have walked the course with Deej. I am giving Manhattan a last relaxing groom with a body brush when I am interrupted by the sharp, irritated voice of the trainer.

"Not a lad now. Jockey."

"I'm just helping Deej, sir. I had nothing else to do."

Mr. Wilkinson nods in the direction of Manhattan. "Blanket her up. Talk. Outside."

I throw Manhattan's blanket over her back, fasten it, and give her a pat.

Outside the stable, Mr. Wilkinson is standing, hunched, hands in the pockets of his scruffy jacket. He is gazing, as if in a dream, toward the racecourse.

"Sir." I stand beside him.

"Big difference. Lad. Jockey. State of mind. Winner." He looks at me sharply. "You a winner? Are you?"

"Yes, sir."

"Grooming? Not Pony Club camp." He frowns. "Got to carry a whip today. Jockey. Professional."

I was hoping that he would forget about that. My plan—ridiculous now that I think about it—was to arrive in the paddock not carrying a whip and hope no one would notice. After all, it is how I ride Manhattan at home.

"Sir, she really hates—"

"Carrying a whip today!" It is an angry bark. The trainer stares at me, his eyes dark and small in his face. "Letting me down already. Shouldn't have listened. Need a pro on board. Still could, you know. Change jockeys. Not too late."

"No, sir. I won't let you down. And I'll carry a whip."

"People talk. Apprentice riding in the Middleton? Not

even carrying a whip? Trainer must be crazy. Makes the owner look bad. Understand?"

"Yes, sir."

"See you at the weighing room."

The crowd gathers. I watch the first race from the jockeys' stand. I tell myself that I want to get a sense of how the horses are traveling on the ground today, but I know I am just killing time — my mind is on the race ahead.

Two races before mine, I change into the prince's colors.

When I weigh out, Mr. Wilkinson is there to take the saddle. Standing outside the weighing room, he tells me to let the mare settle and not to make my move too soon. "We don't know whether she stays this distance. Her speed is what matters. Horse to beat. Touch of Class. Good handicapper. Stays on."

There is a phrase racing commentators on TV like to use: "caught the eye in the paddock."

Manhattan certainly catches the eye. She looks bigger, paler, prouder than the other runners, almost as if she belongs to a different species.

I am in the center of the paddock, tapping my whip nervously against my leg as Mr. Wilkinson and Mr. Webber discuss Ishtagah, one of the prince's other three-year-olds, who is not even racing today. Looking up at them, wearing the prince's colors, I feel like a small, exotic bird. I long to be out on the racetrack, on Manhattan's back.

When the announcement "Jockeys, get mounted" is made, Deej leads Manhattan to us.

Hey, girl.

She looks around and then snorts, her nostrils dilated.

"You're in the mood to race, aren't you?"

She seems to arch her back slightly as I am legged up. Deej leads us around the paddock, and I am distantly aware of the spectators looking at us.

I hear a child's voice in the crowd. "Look at that one, Mummy."

I look down and smile at a boy, about eight years old. Yes, look at this one.

We are last of the six runners on the racetrack. I notice Manhattan's right ear is twitching, as if she can hear a distant sound.

All right, Hat. Relax, girl.

"She's not right," I say to Deej. "Something is bothering her. I can tell by her ears."

Deej reaches to unhook the lead rein and glances back at her as he holds her by the rein.

"She's fine." He looks up at me and smiles. "Relax. Just treat it as if you're on the gallops at home." He lets us go. As I turn Manhattan to canter down to the start, he calls out, "Look after yourself, Bug."

I turn and click my teeth, expecting Manhattan to launch herself as she usually does. Instead she trots slowly, then canters, stiff-legged and reluctant. A man in the crowd laughs. "Glad I didn't put any money on that one," he says loudly.

Come on, Hat!

Not thinking, I slap her gently on the shoulder with the whip. Her reaction is immediate. She goes even more slowly. Both ears are half-back now. She has become the Manhattan of old. The mare who hates racing.

I have such difficulty getting her down to the start that the rest of the field is already circling behind the stalls when I arrive.

A couple of the jockeys glance at me coldly. What, they are wondering, is a girl apprentice doing in a race like this?

I check my girth. Manhattan's attention is on me, not the other horses or the race. Her ears are trembling as if there is some kind of electric current going through them.

I think of Deej's words. Treat it as if you're on the gallops at home.

Suddenly, I understand.

I call to one of the starter's assistants. As he approaches, I hold out my whip.

"Could you hold this for me, please?"

The man takes it.

Is that better, Hat?

I sit forward in the saddle, laying both hands on her shoulders so she can feel that they are empty. Then, slowly, firmly, I trace a heart on her right shoulder.

We stand motionless for several moments. One of the jockeys nods in my direction and says something as he lowers his goggles. Somebody laughs.

Manhattan's ears stay back, trembling slightly.

It's gone, Hat. No whip. Just me.

I'm not getting through. I can feel it, the tension in her.

You're a princess. Remember that.

One of the other starter's assistants takes Manhattan's head to lead us toward the stalls.

"Hey, jockey." I hear a voice behind me. "What about your stick?"

"I'll get it later."

Beside me, one of the other jockeys looks at me in surprise.

"We won't need it, will we, Hat?"

We are first into the stalls, and while the other five runners are loaded, I drop the reins, hold each side of her neck, palms flat against her coat.

It's gone, Hat. No whip. Understand?

There are two more horses to go into the stalls. I gather up the reins and feel Manhattan tremble beneath me.

A click, then a crash of metal as the gates are opened and the racecourse stretches before us.

The horses on each side of me are quickly out of the stalls and into their stride.

Manhattan is flat-footed. For a crucial couple of seconds, she seems frozen to the spot.

"Come on, Hat!" I shout.

Then she is out of the stalls, a good five lengths behind the last runner.

The five is soon ten. Manhattan is sticking her toes in. With every stride, the rest of the field is moving farther away from us.

There is an almost irresistible temptation to scream and

ride her out. Instead, I crouch lower in the saddle, placing a hand on each side of her withers.

It must look ridiculous, a jockey sitting low in the saddle, still and motionless as, with every stride, her horse loses ground.

OK, Hat, game over. It's your time now.

I feel the slightest easing of movement below me as her muscles are slowly relaxing. The field is now fifteen lengths ahead of me, approaching the bend.

"It's all right, Hat. We're going to win."

A group of onlookers is standing on the inside rails. Strangely, the face of one of them — a man in his forties — comes into focus as I pass him. He is laughing at us.

We're going to win. We're going to show them, Hat.

We must have run three furlongs before Manhattan begins to remember where she is. She takes a light hold of her bit, stretches her legs. Her ears relax, going forward and back with every stride.

Time, Hat. Time.

I'm tempted to let Manhattan make up the fifteen lengths down the back stretch, but I know that the effort of doing too much too early will make her tire at the end of the race.

She is beginning to enjoy herself now. Her ears are pricked, as if she has heard a distant sound that is calling her. She feels as full of her own strength as she did when we were out together, alone on the heath on those cold February afternoons.

Her giant, effortless strides are eating up the ground.

Wait. Wait. Wait.

By the end of the back stretch, the two stragglers of the field, both under pressure from their jockeys, are five lengths in front of me.

Not so fast.

As the bend approaches, I am aware that we are making up ground. Manhattan has started to race.

We pass them as if they are standing still, then take the bend well. The four other horses are a good eight lengths ahead of us. Their jockeys are beginning to ride them out.

Beyond them, the grandstand looms into view. I hear the sound of the crowd, still as low as a murmur.

Two furlongs. I switch Manhattan to the outside. She sees the lush green of the finishing stretch ahead of her and begins to lengthen her stride.

One furlong. Now it is as if there are two races taking place. In one, four horses with barely a length to separate them are involved in a driving finish. Four lengths behind them, on the wide outside, a great gray ghost, her ears pricked, is coasting forward, showing the world, for the first time in her life, what she can do.

Go, Hat.

I crouch lower in the saddle, like a cat about to pounce.

Three lengths adrift, two. We pass one horse, another. The two leaders are battling it out ahead of us. Manhattan is still accelerating but the winning post is approaching fast.

The crowd's roar is a cauldron of sound all around us, and Manhattan responds to it.

Half a length. A neck. We are stride for stride with the

two horses for what seems like no more than a second, then the winning post flashes past.

"Photograph." I hear the racecourse announcement as I begin to pull up, but I know in my heart what the result is.

To my left, one of the jockeys is punching the air.

I pull up, gasping with exhaustion, my muscles screaming with relief.

So near, girl. So near.

A jockey canters past me.

"That one was finishing like a train," he calls out, looking at Manhattan.

"She was."

He laughs, and I know that, like everyone who was watching the race, he will have one thought in his mind.

The girl left it too late.

Deej is ahead of us. He grabs Manhattan's reins and slaps her on the neck.

"That was more like it." He laughs. "If only you'd started racing earlier."

"The whip," I manage to say. "I shouldn't have carried a whip down to the start."

As we make our way through the crowds toward the winners' enclosure, I sense a curiosity among racegoers. I hear someone saying, "She should have won."

When we enter the winners' enclosure, Deej leads Manhattan to the position for the second-place horse. With one last pat for Manhattan, I slip my feet out of the stirrups and dismount.

Mr. Wilkinson approaches, looking displeased.

"Try to do it hard way. Too bloody cocky."

"She wasn't racing, sir. She only started taking an interest about four furlongs out. It was the whip. I should never have carried it in the paddock."

Behind him, Mrs. Wilkinson raises her eyebrows.

Mr. Webber pats me on the back. "The prince will be relieved," he says. "That's the first time she's even been involved in a finish. At least we know she isn't completely useless."

I take off the saddle and glance at Manhattan. She looks pleased with herself, but not exactly tired. I give her a pat on the neck, tip my cap to the Wilkinsons and Mr. Webber, and run up the steps to weigh in.

As I sit on the scales, I hear the racecourse announcer giving the result of the photograph.

"First, number two, Touch of Class. Second, number nine, Manhattan. Distance: short head." There is a moment's pause. "Stewards' inquiry."

Trouble.

On.

The.

Way.

BEGINNER'S LUCK

It is like a trial. On our way upstairs to the stewards' room, Mr. Wilkinson tells me that the racecourse officials—the stewards—will be asking us why I allowed Manhattan to lose the race by allowing her to be tailed off early in the race.

"Leave it to me," he tells me. "Been here before. I do the talking."

In a small room, three middle-aged men in suits sit behind a desk. Standing nearby is another younger man who tells us he is the stewards' secretary. Behind them are four television screens, which show the race from different angles.

The chief steward, Mr. Thompson-Smythe, is a tall, military-looking man in his fifties. "Not a very satisfactory race, jockey." He speaks in a slightly bored voice. "This inquiry is to establish whether your horse, Manhattan, ran a true race. Should she have won? Let's have a look at it."

The starting stalls appear on the screens. We watch as Manhattan starts slowly, then loses ground early in the race.

It looks bad, because I am sitting still, allowing the rest of the field to get away from us. Then, at about the halfway point, it is as if Manhattan has decided to take an interest. Her ears go forward. She starts to gallop. We make our run. Too late.

The screens freeze as we pull up.

The four men are looking at me.

"What on earth were you playing at, Barton?" asks Mr. Thompson-Smythe.

"She doesn't like the whip, sir. I left it at the start, but it took a while for her to realize that I wasn't carrying it. That was when she began to race."

There is a disbelieving harrumph from one of the stewards.

A cold smile appears on the chief steward's face as he turns his attention to Mr. Wilkinson. "Clive? Any comment?"

The trainer looks irritated. "Tricky mare. Not genuine. Barton knows her well. Ridden her all winter. First time we've seen what she can do."

"Well, she didn't do enough to win," the third steward says. The men make notes.

"Girl's inexperienced." Mr. Wilkinson nods in my direction. "Promising. But a long way to go."

Mr. Thompson-Smythe looks up. "Any particular reason why you put an inexperienced girl up on such a difficult ride, Clive?" he asks.

"Horse goes for her," says Mr. Wilkinson. "Bit of a gamble."

"I imagine the stable jockey will be getting the nod from now on," he says with a knowing smile.

There is a low rumble of anger from Mr. Wilkinson. "Why would you imagine that? Girl got the horse running. Can't ask for more."

There's another thoughtful silence. The second steward murmurs, "Beginner's luck."

"Well, young lady," Mr. Thompson-Smythe says in a patronizing, adults-know-best tone, "you're lucky to have such a supportive boss."

"And such a very good horse," says the second steward. "Got you out of trouble there."

Mr. Thompson-Smythe reaches for a printed manual in front of him. I see on the front of it the words *Procedures and Penalties*. He waves it at me. "Book of rules," he says. Opening it, he reads. "Here's rule 45.1.2: 'A rider must take and be seen to take all other reasonable and permissible measures throughout the race, however it develops, to ensure the horse is given a full opportunity to achieve the best possible placing.' You didn't do that, did you?"

"I—"

Beside me, Mr. Wilkinson clears his throat loudly.

I take the hint. "No, sir," I say.

"Well." Mr. Thompson-Smythe glances at his fellow stewards, then delivers his verdict. "If you were more experienced, you would be facing a fine and ban under rule 45.1." He pauses. "As it is, we'd like you to take this as a friendly but serious warning. Do not fall asleep at the start of a race. And"—a cold smile appears on his face—"most jockeys find it's quite a good idea to carry a whip."

"But—"

"But what?" snaps the chief steward.

"Nothing, sir. Yes, sir. I will."

As we leave the office and head downstairs, Mr. Wilkinson glances down at me.

"Journalists. Will want a word. Say nothing."

He turns out to be right. Four men, notepads and tape recorders in their hands, stand before us as we return to the weighing room.

Ignoring Mr. Wilkinson, they start talking at me. What were my tactics? Why was I not carrying a whip? Would I ride the race differently if I had another chance?

Mr. Wilkinson holds up a hand. "Talk about the horse. With me. Jockey has to go to the stables."

He pushes me forward, and I make my way into the weighing room, ignoring the shouted questions.

By the time I have changed, the journalists have gone. I walk toward the stable, just another jockey, and once I put my saddle in the horsebox, just another lad.

Deej is on the course, watching Mr. Wilkinson's other runner. I walk into Manhattan's stall, where she is munching hay as if she has been there all the time.

There's my girl.

I run a hand down her neck, then under her stomach. She is only slightly warmer than usual.

You're all right, aren't you? You've hardly broken a sweat.

She turns her head toward me, as if expecting a carrot.

Just beaten in a Group Two race. You're safe now. You showed them that you could race.

It might be my imagination, but I sense an air of

disappointment to her. She is a princess. Princesses don't come in second.

They said I was lucky to be riding a good horse. And I suppose I was.

She nudges me with her nose, impatient with this chat. I give her a carrot, which she munches with her eyes half-closed.

I lean toward her, my forehead resting against her neck. She ignores me, returning to her hay.

Just.

Another.

Day.

UNREASONABLE

The next morning there is a picture of me on the racing page of one of the national papers. It shows me at the finish line, my hands on Manhattan's neck, my mouth open as if trying to scream my horse across the line.

It is a strange photo. I look tiny on top of Manhattan. She has her ears pricked, like a horse who is ignoring the speck of humanity that happens to be riding her. There is desperation on my face.

The report of the race adds to the big joke:

> Apprentice Jay "Bug" Barton had a race to remember when her second professional ride, on the "Magic" Wilkinson–trained 33–1 shot Manhattan, narrowly failed to edge out hot favorite Touch of Class in the Middleton Stakes.

First the 16-year-old seemed to have forgotten to carry a whip. Then she allowed the mare to dwell at the start and inexplicably made no attempt to make up ground, appearing to go to sleep completely when her horse tailed off down the back straight.

Only when the field turned for home did Manhattan begin to race. Remarkably, she almost won, in spite of her jockey's unusual tactics.

After the stewards let off Barton with an official warning, veteran trainer "Magic" Wilkinson loyally defended his young employee's tactics, but declined to say whether Jay would be riding for him in the near future.

As for Manhattan, the trainer said he would be discussing future plans with her owner, Prince Muqrin. She will be worth following, with a more experienced jockey in the saddle.

It gets worse. A journalist has the bright idea of looking at the TV footage of the race. Under the headline WHAT WERE YOU THINKING, BUG? a series of photographs are published. Down at the start, eyes closed, both hands on Manhattan's neck, like a person praying. Halfway through the race, at the back of the field and looking as if we were out for a morning canter. The crazy finish. Trotting back with a look of desperate disappointment on my face.

It is a great story. Big horse. Little girl. Hope. Fear. Inexperience. Disappointment.

What fun people must be having as they read it and laugh at the pictures.

Surprisingly, the lads don't tease me. Angus is almost friendly toward me. Laura tells me I did all right, which as near to a compliment as I'm ever going to get from her. The others in the yard know the truth about Manhattan. They don't like one of their own being laughed at. They feel sorry for me. "I told you, she's got a jinx on her, that mare," Liam says one morning. "Even when she runs well, something goes wrong."

As for Manhattan, the race has changed her. She has shown the world that she can race, and now that is all she wants to do. Her eyes are brighter. She eats her food up as if needing all the energy she can get.

A couple of days after the race, I am crossing the main yard after third lot when I notice that Mrs. Wilkinson is standing on the path leading from the house to the stables.

"Jay." The voice is low, drawled.

I walk over to her. "Mrs. Wilkinson."

She holds up a freshly lit cigarette in her hand. "I'm having a quick ciggie break. Do you indulge?"

I shake my head.

"Very sensible." She takes a puff. "Hope you're not taking what you read in the press seriously."

"Not really."

The trainer's wife looks at me more closely. "Tougher for girls," she says. "If you'd been a boy apprentice, no one would have thought twice. They'll get used to it in the end, but for the moment we just have to live with it."

"I know I rode as good a race as I could," I say quietly.

"And so do we." She speaks the words almost jokingly. "Mr. Bucknall thinks we should run her again soon. At the moment, she is low in the handicap and won't have to carry too much weight."

"She could run again anytime. It's as if she didn't have a race."

"The prince isn't keen on running her too soon. And I—we—think he's right."

I'm curious. "What does he want to do?"

She smiles, takes a last drag of her cigarette, then throws the butt into a flower bed nearby. She covers it, pushing the earth with the toe of her elegant boot.

"He has a plan," she says. "I'll let you know. Just keep your nose clean and you can make those journalists eat their words."

But I don't.

Late that night, just as I am drifting off to sleep, the cell phone Uncle Bill gave me purrs gently on the bedside table. It is the call I am dreading.

"Hi, Uncle Bill."

"Not bad, girl, not bad at all. Would have been better if you'd won, but I put a bet on you each way, so your coming second on the gray was just fine. Good odds too. You did all right."

"She ran well. She's a good mare."

"And?"

"And what, Uncle Bill? I'm sorry, I'm really tired. I need to get some sleep."

"That's not how this works, doll. I need another tip. Pronto."

I groan. "I can't do this. The Wilkinsons have been really good to me. I think we should stop this right now."

"And what about me? Haven't I been good to you?"

"Of course. But . . . I think I've done enough."

"No." He snaps the word angrily. "You haven't. Not nearly enough. In fact, we've only just started, girl."

"I feel like a traitor."

There is a long silence during which the only sound is Uncle Bill breathing heavily.

"I was looking at Dusty today," he says eventually.

"Dusty? What's he got do with this?"

"Expensive business, keeping ponies. Bit of a luxury, really. If you don't help me, I'll be forced to make some savings. The other horses have gone, but Dusty's too old to sell. At least for riding."

"How do you mean?"

"Yeah." Uncle Bill sounds almost sorrowful as he ignores my question. "Still, I can still get a few pennies for him. There are cattle trucks that go to southern Europe. Horses and ponies being exported for meat."

"No."

"To be honest, it's not a great end for a sixteen-year-old pony—crammed into a truck with no water or food for a few days, then killed for meat."

"You couldn't do that. Not to Dusty."

"I'm not doing it, love. You are."

I stay silent, trying not to believe what I'm hearing.

"And the way they kill them out there. Oh dear, oh dear. Barbaric isn't the word."

I lie in my bed, eyes closed. I remember something my uncle once said to me as he drove me back from pony racing one day. He said that the reason he got his way was that everyone knew that, if he had to, he would go further than most other people would dare. He said he didn't do reasonable. In fact, he did *un*reasonable. And he liked it.

"Well?" There's a growl in his voice now.

So I say it, just to get him off the phone.

"All right. I'll call you tomorrow."

Something about the way Manhattan ran at York seems to lift the stable. She and I are at the front of first lot every morning. Normally, the Wilkinson horses can seem a bit sad compared to the glossy two-year-olds and three-year-olds of the bigger, smarter Newmarket yards. Now their lads look at us and take notice.

Mr. Wilkinson begins to have winners. The prince's horse Ishtagah finishes third in the first Classic of the season, the 2000 Guineas. Drive On now wins a valuable race at Kempton Park. Horses that last season seemed useless are now picking up races across the country. There is talk in the racing papers about the "in-form Wilkinson stable."

All this is excellent news for Uncle Bill.

Most evenings, I tell Auntie and Laura that I need a

walk to clear my head. I make my way to the park nearby, sit on a bench on my own. Then I call Uncle Bill.

Every time I sit there, my eyes darting around to check that I am alone, I feel a twinge of guilt. Then I remind myself of the race I was supposed to lose on Poptastic. If big trainers are breaking the rules, why shouldn't a lad?

I dial. Uncle Bill picks up on the first ring. "OK, doll," he says. "What you got?"

I tell him in a quiet robot voice which horses are going well at home, if they like the ground soft or hard, who we expect to win.

"Good girl." I hear the scratch of his pencil as he makes notes. "Keep 'em coming. Dusty's well, by the way."

It is easier to be a spy than you might think. The trick is to divide your life. I become two people. There is Jay, riding out in the mornings, chatting with the lads, wondering if the guv'nor is going to give her a ride in a race soon.

Then, for a few moments every day, there is Barton, sitting in a park alone, spilling secrets into her cell phone.

Barton looks at Jay as if she were another person.

Jay tries not to think about Barton.

The.

Stranger.

The.

Spy.

A Bit of a Plan

A h. The gray mare. How is she?"

It is evening stables, two weeks after the Middleton. Mr. Wilkinson, with Bucknall and Angus, lingers in Manhattan's stall. Suddenly she matters to the stable.

Manhattan is looking impatient. I have stripped off her blanket, and the cool late-spring air is making her restless.

Mr. Wilkinson runs a hand down her back, over her rib cage and then, carefully, down one front leg, then the other. She flattens her ears and swishes her tail, but the trainer holds his ground.

"Stop it. Silly mare." His voice sounds almost affectionate.

"She's just showing off," I say.

"And how's Bug?" he asks.

"Fine, sir."

"Forgotten what the press wrote?"

"Yes, sir."

"Just words," he says. "Never trust words. Down with words."

"Yes, sir."

"Free tonight? After dinner? About nine?" The trainer doesn't bother to wait for a reply. "Mr. Webber coming to dinner. Prince taking an interest. Plans for the mare. May involve you."

"Me, sir?"

He gazes at me for a moment. "Scrub up a bit. Try to look your best."

A long time ago Uncle Bill once told me that I looked like a junkyard dog.

"Lean and mean, like a junkyard dog" were his exact words. Tonight after dinner with Auntie and Laura, I prepare to go and see Mr. and Mrs. Wilkinson, and I hear his voice, the way he laughed.

I catch a glimpse of myself in a full-length mirror on the back of the closet door. Even now, out of my work clothes and in my best (all right, only) jeans, I look like a skinny teen nobody.

My skin is hard and dry from riding out in the wind and rain. Between my eyebrows is the shadow of the scar caused by my fall from Norewest. I am thin and fit and strong, like someone you might see carrying something heavy out of a van.

I have the look of a delivery boy.

In the closet, there is a pink round-necked blouse I

bought in town before going out with Deej and Laura but in the end didn't have the nerve to wear.

Too soft, too girlie, I thought at the time. They would laugh at me.

Now I put it on. No more games. No more trying to fit in. I am beyond caring. In the top drawer, there is some makeup I brought with me from home but have never worn. Eyeliner. Mascara. Some lip gloss. Even a pair of small earrings in the shape of butterflies.

For this meeting, I am not going to be a lean, mean junkyard dog. I am not going to be Bug. I am me.

I am sneaking out of the hall when Auntie sees me.

"Oh, my," she says. "The girl's looking smart for a change." She stands between me and the front door. "Let me see you."

She puts her big hands on my shoulders. Her eyes take in my makeup, my earrings.

"Very nice." She smiles. "Quite the young lady."

"I'm going to see Mr. and Mrs. Wilkinson. Prince Muqrin's racing manager is there tonight."

Auntie is staring at my feet. I'm wearing a pair of old sneakers—the only shoes I've got apart from my riding boots. "Oh, no," she says. "You can't go out in those."

I laugh. "I don't have a choice."

"Wait." Auntie trots heavily up the stairs. When she returns, she is carrying a pair of small, black leather shoes with laces and raised heels. "Jas gave them to me." She wipes off the dust with a handkerchief, then shines them. "I used to wear them on special occasions."

"No, Auntie."

"Go on, girl. My feet are too fat for them these days."
She kneels down and unlaces my sneakers.

Her smart, heavy black shoes make me look as if I'm
going to church, and the hard leather rubs against my ankles
but, as Auntie ties up the laces and gives them one last wipe, I
have to admit they look better than my sneakers.

"Perfect." Auntie stands back and smiles. "They could
have been made for you. Off you go."

I lean forward, give my landlady a kiss on the cheek,
and I'm gone.

It is almost dark by the time I reach Edgecote House, and I'm
beginning to regret borrowing the shoes. Every step is agony.
I hobble my way up the path.

When she opens the front door, Mrs. Wilkinson is looking different too. She is wearing a black evening skirt, and has
even more makeup on her face than usual. A glass of wine is
in her hand.

"Jay, how nice." The voice is less fierce than usual.

I follow her across the hall, Auntie's shoes clacking
loudly on the stone.

Mrs. Wilkinson looks back. "Are you injured?" she asks.
"You seem to be going a bit lame."

"New shoes," I say. "They're not exactly comfortable."

Mrs. Wilkinson laughs. "We have to suffer for our
beauty, don't we?"

She leads me into the sitting room, where Mr. Wilkinson
and Mr. Webber are seated on each side of the fireplace. To

my surprise, they stand up as I enter, almost as if I'm a proper guest.

"Jay." Mr. Wilkinson waves in the direction of an armchair. I sit, nervously. "Or Bug? Not sure."

"I don't mind, sir."

"You remember Mr. Webber."

"Yes, sir."

The prince's racing manager gives me a cool, professional smile. I get the sense that he is weighing me up, assessing me as if I were at some kind of interview.

Mrs. Wilkinson pours herself another drink at a table in the corner. "Wine, Jay?"

"Just something soft, please."

She pours me a fizzy water, gives me the glass, then ambles over to the desk in the corner, where she takes up her usual place. She watches us, as if from a distance, now and then sipping at her wine.

"The prince wanted me to thank you for the way you rode Manhattan the other day," says Mr. Webber. "She can be a tricky ride."

"She's really cool once you get to know her." I blurt the words out, then realize that I am sounding a bit girlish and overenthusiastic.

"Cool?" mutters Mr. Wilkinson. *"Cool?"*

Mr. Webber sits forward in his chair. "D'you think we saw the best of Manhattan at York, Jay?"

"No!" I almost shout the word, then bite my lip. "Sorry, but no. She hardly had a race. She is so much better than that."

"The prince thinks so too. He wants to give her one more run—a real test, then retire her. If she doesn't disgrace herself, he'll keep her as a mare and breed from her. Otherwise, she'll be sold."

I nod, now nervous as to what I am about to be told.

"Plan." Mr. Wilkinson takes a long sip of his whiskey. "King George. Run her. Prince wants you on board."

"He was most impressed by the way you rode," says Mr. Webber. "And also the way you haven't been upset by what has been written in the papers. We thought that was very professional of you. Quite grown-up." He frowns. "Are you feeling all right?"

For the first time, I realize that I am sitting, mouth open, with a stunned smile on my face. I actually feel slightly sick with excitement.

"No. Yes. Thank you. I'm . . . fine, sir."

"The press thing is important." Mr. Webber glances at his watch. "Prince Muqrin has been having one or two problems at home. There are people in Saudi Arabia and other parts of the Middle East who don't exactly approve of girl jockeys."

"Saudi women aren't allowed to drive cars," says Mrs. Wilkinson from the shadows behind me. "So you can imagine what people think about a prince allowing a girl jockey to ride his horse. It has been a bit of a scandal."

"Keep your ride quiet," says Mr. Wilkinson. "Secret. Good at keeping secrets, Bug?"

For a brief moment, an image of me sitting in a park

talking into a telephone flashes through my mind, and then is gone.

"Yes, sir."

"We'll announce it. Last minute. Keep 'em guessing. No fuss about female jockey."

Mr. Webber stands. "I'd better be on my way back to London," he says.

Something about what I am being told confuses me. "Who's King George?" I ask. "You mentioned something about Prince Muqrin and King George."

The three of them laugh. I sit there, feeling foolish.

"It's the race," says Mr. Webber. "The King George VI and Queen Elizabeth Stakes at Ascot. In July. Up for that, Jay?" He shakes my hand. I nod dumbly. "I'll see you again soon."

As Mr. and Mrs. Wilkinson see Mr. Webber to the front door, I sit, taking in what I have just been told so casually.

"King George." I say the words out loud. "*That* King George."

In the racing calendar, the King George VI and Queen Elizabeth Stakes is one of the biggest races of the season. It is where the best of the year's three-year-olds race for the first time against the cream of the older horses.

I am thinking of the great champions who have won the race in the past. Ribot, Dancing Brave, The Minstrel, Shergar, Lammtarra, Nijinsky. It was the race where Petite Etoile was the hot favorite and got beaten.

"Not bad news, eh?" Mrs. Wilkinson appears at the

door. "We thought you'd be pleased. Now, you won't be riding in races until then. We want you to concentrate on the mare. The prince is very important to this stable, and he still seems to believe that Manhattan can win a decent race."

"So do I, Mrs. Wilkinson."

"We're quite aware of that." She smiles at me.

Back in his armchair, Mr. Wilkinson mutters something to himself, then reaches for his whiskey. I'm about to stand to leave when Mrs. Wilkinson holds up a hand. "There was just one other little matter we wanted to ask you about since you're here. Absolutely in confidence."

I sit back in my chair, suddenly on my guard.

"Are you sure you don't want a glass of wine?" she asks.

"No, thanks, Mrs. Wilkinson."

She laughs. "Don't look so worried, Jay. We just thought you might be able to help us with a little problem we've got."

"Something happening. In the yard." Mr. Wilkinson gazes at the fire, the glass of whiskey held between his hands. "Tips. Getting out. Bookmakers. Money. Not helping."

"Tips?" My mouth is suddenly dry, my voice strangled. "What kind of tips?"

"Over the past few weeks, money has been going on our horses," says Mrs. Wilkinson. "We're pretty sure that someone working for us is leaking information."

"Bad for the yard," mutters Mr. Wilkinson. "Owners asking questions. Suspicions. Bad smell around the place. Whenever one of the horses runs. Stewards ask questions. Think we're in the pocket of the bookies."

Mrs. Wilkinson's eyes are fixed on me. "Jay, I'm afraid we have a spy in our midst," she says.

I breathe evenly, my eyes not flickering in the slightest as I stare at her. When I speak, my words are as calm and cold as any spy could make them. "What makes you think that?"

"Never mind that. You haven't heard or seen anything suspicious? None of the lads have said anything?"

"No. Not at all."

Mrs. Wilkinson smiles, drains her glass, and stands up. "Just a thought since you were here. If you hear anything, let us know, will you? These things need stamping out. A yard depends on trust."

I stand. I say good night to Mr. Wilkinson. He looks up, grunts, and a look crosses his crumpled features that might almost be a smile.

I follow Mrs. Wilkinson to the front door. We say good night. The door closes behind me. I stand for a moment, gazing across the stable yard lit up by moonlight.

I think of a conversation I had with Mr. Wilkinson when I arrived here. He said he expected two things above all from his lads — that they were punctual and they always told him the truth. "Don't have to be the best," he said. "On time. Straight with me. That's what matters."

I trudge slowly down the steps, Auntie's shoes knocking on the stone like the crack of doom.

Liar.

Liar.

Liar.

Liar.

Family Heritage

The world closes in. It should be the best moment in my life, and yet it is the worst.

Every day I ride a great gray miracle of a horse. Together we feel as if we can conquer the world.

Every week I take her out on Wednesday afternoons to work away from the prying eyes of the journalists and tipsters who watch the morning gallops through binoculars from the road. Manhattan covers five or six furlongs with the best sprinters in the yard and makes them look slow. When she gallops over longer distances with the milers and Classic hopefuls, Ishtagah and Drive On, she is pulling my arms out at the finish.

Every morning I awake long before the alarm goes off and lie there, taking time to believe the impossible. I, Jay Barton, am going to ride a brilliant horse in one of the biggest races in the British racing season.

And yet, always within me, there is the knowledge that it could all disappear if it is discovered that I am a traitor.

Uncle Bill talks to me now in the way that I heard him doing to his business partners and enemies back in the old days. He's in a dangerous thank-you-and-good-night mood.

I beg him to leave me alone. Surely, I say, I have done enough to save Dusty.

"Never mind Dusty," he says. "You stop helping me, and I'll tell my pal Clive Wilkinson about what you've been doing."

"But that will incriminate you too."

"Got nothing to lose, girl."

"What proof have you got?"

He laughs as if I have said something genuinely funny, then drops his voice. "You must think I just got off the bus, love. I've been recording these calls. I've got evidence here, on my phone." He pauses. "So, no more funny business, eh? What can you tell me this week?"

I'm trapped, Hat.

I can't talk to Laura or Deej or Auntie. They are all good friends now, but none of them can help me.

I talk to a horse instead.

"We'll win. That will be my escape. Once we've shown the world what we can do, I'll be strong. I'll tell Mr. Wilkinson. I'll come clean. Whatever he does then, he won't be able to take away what we do at Ascot."

Manhattan looks at me, ears pricked, as if to tell me I've got nothing to worry about.

"Oh, Hat. I wish you could understand."

She makes me feel ashamed. She has come through by being strong, being herself. I have betrayed everyone, including myself.

Michaela calls more often, and that's not the only surprise. She talks less about herself than in the old days, asking questions about my life.

We have been through some tough times. We've both been selfish in our own way. But a friend is a friend, and Michaela, for better or for worse, is the best I've got.

Sometimes I have a niggling sense that she is trying to find out something about me. Could she be acting for her dad? Nothing would surprise me with him, but surely Michaela wouldn't play Uncle Bill's game. Perhaps that's what happens with spying. We catch it from each other without noticing.

One night I'm talking to her just before I go to sleep when she mentions something in a suspiciously fake-casual tone of voice, that she has a project at school about family history.

"Project?"

"Yes, why not?" Michaela is on the defensive. "After exams, we had to choose some project to keep us busy until the end of term. I chose family heritage."

What? I can imagine Michaela choosing many projects (boys, parties, dancing), but family heritage would be pretty near the bottom of the list.

"I've been researching my dad and your mum," says Michaela. "It's kind of interesting, actually."

She is right about that. Bill and his younger sister, Debs,

were left alone in the world when he was twenty-two and she was nineteen. Their parents, taking their first vacation alone in years, were killed in a crash with a truck in northern Spain. Their house was sold, and the money made from it was divided between Bill and Debs.

"What really surprised me," Michaela is saying, "is that they were really close as children."

"But he's always so mean about my mother. And so is Elaine."

"He's been talking about that recently. This whole situation he's in has made him a bit more open about the past somehow. He says that he and your mum were both really hit hard. He says they each reacted differently. He invested the money in houses and stuff and became a full-time businessman."

He turned into Uncle Bill.

"And she, your mum, went a bit crazy. It was as if nothing mattered to her. She spent the money on having a good time. That was when she and my dad drifted apart."

I remember Debs's parties, how I learned to be invisible, like a cat. There were mornings when she was ill from drinking too much the night before. Now and then, I found myself having breakfast with a man I had never met before. It's a part of my mother that I have tried to forget.

"I'm glad she had fun," I say quietly. "While she could."

"It was your dad I was wondering about."

"My dad?" I tense up. Mention of my father makes me feel vulnerable in a way I really don't want to be right now. "What about him?"

"What did your mum say about him?"

"Just that he was foreign—Polish. He was a musician of some kind. She said that they loved each other very much, but when she found she was going to have a baby, he suddenly disappeared from her life. He was gone before I was born."

"Maybe he's in Poland now and we could find him. You might have half brothers and sisters. How cool would that be?'

I have heard enough. "Michaela, what is this? What's going on here?"

"It's just interesting. How we become what we are."

"Yeah, well I'm concentrating on the present. I've got a race to think about."

There is silence on the other end of the phone.

"I'd better turn in, M."

"Just stay strong, Jay." She speaks quietly, and just for a moment I wonder if she has a suspicion about the calls that her father makes to me. "That's what I keep thinking when I'm working on this family heritage thing. We have to be ourselves—whatever the pressure."

We say good night. I switch off the light, and in the darkness, thoughts of my mother crowd in. I could do without Michaela investigating our family past right now, but I begin to wonder about my father—where he is, what he is like, whether he ever thinks of me, if he even knows I exist.

Locked.

Door.

Opened.

GOOD GIRL

In June, something unexpected happens.

Prince Muqrin's three-year-old Ishtagah runs a brilliant race in the Derby at Epsom.

In the Wilkinson yard, we thought the colt had a chance. He had improved since he ran well in the 2000 Guineas, and the longer distance—the Derby is half a mile farther—would suit him.

The experts, on TV and in the press, disagreed. A brilliant Irish horse, Mountain High, unbeaten both as a two-year-old and this year, started as the hot favorite, while a French-trained runner, Positano, was also tipped to win.

Ishtagah, they said, had "something about him" and was "as game as the day is long," but lacked the class. One journalist mentioned that the Wilkinson yard had not had a Group One winner since the last century.

I watch the race in the packed bar at the Racing Center with a few of the other lads from the yard—Amit, Laura, Tommy, and Liam.

There is a strong pace, which suits Ishtagah, and as the field sweeps around Tattenham Corner, he is about eighth or ninth but hopelessly placed on the inside rail.

O'Brian is waiting for the gaps to open up as they enter the stretch and horses begin to tire.

They do, but too late for Ishtagah. Three furlongs from home, the Derby has become a two-horse race, with Mountain High and Positano going six, seven, eight lengths clear from the rest of the field.

Watching as O'Brian tries to find a way through the pack, we curse the bad draw our horse has been given.

Then, a furlong and a half from home, he sees daylight and bursts his way to freedom.

Now the bar is roaring him on, the horse from Newmarket challenging the best from Ireland and from France. With Mountain High and Positano locked together on the rails, the Wilkinson horse is storming up the center of the track, with O'Brian riding a wild, showy finish.

As the three horses flash past the winning post, it is impossible to separate them, but the TV replay calls it before the official result of the photo finish has been announced.

Positano has won by a short head from Mountain High. Ishtagah is a neck away in third place.

After the race, Prince Muqrin is asked by a TV interviewer if this is the best horse he has ever owned.

He thinks for a moment. "Certainly one of the best." There is laughter in the winners' enclosure.

I glance at Laura, and we both smile. We know the prince was not joking.

The next morning after second lot, I am in Manhattan's stall when Mr. Wilkinson pays an unscheduled visit.

"The mare. How is she?" he says, looking over the stall door.

"She's full of it, sir. Can't wait to get back on the racecourse."

The trainer opens the door, glancing behind him as he does so. I know Mr. Wilkinson well enough by now. He has something to tell me. He sniffs. "Other horse going to run in the King George," he says. "Ishtagah. Time to take on the older horses."

I must have gone pale because the trainer watches me for a moment through his hooded eyes.

"Sporting owner. The prince." He speaks even more softly than usual. "Wants to run both horses. Pat's made his choice." He actually smiles, a rare and slightly worrying event. "You still up to ride the mare?" he asks.

"Yes, sir."

"I'll announce it tomorrow."

He walks to the stall door and lets himself out.

"We've been thinking about her shoes," he says. "Can't run in a big race without plates."

"She'll sulk if Ivor does them."

Mr. Wilkinson shakes his head. "Mare doesn't like men. Mrs. Wilkinson had an idea. Woman farrier. She found one. Jean. Coming tomorrow. By the time of the race, they'll know each other."

He is about to go when he remembers something else.

"Journalists. Don't talk to them. Understood? Think they know best. They'll look at the field. See Ishtagah's in with a chance. Manhattan? Never won a race. She must be running as Ishtagah's pacemaker."

"Pacemaker? You mean she would just be there to make sure the race is run fast enough to suit Ishtagah?"

He silences me with an odd twitch of his facial muscles. "Might tell Angus same thing. Mare's in the race to help Ishtagah, I'll say. Word spreads in the yard. Gray mare's a pacemaker for the colt. Confuse our spy. He'll leak the wrong information."

"So she's not just a pacemaker? We're in the race to win it."

"Too right we are. Secret between us. Not even Mr. Bucknall will know. So keep your bloomin' mouth shut. Understood?"

The next day, when the newspapers report that Prince Muqrin will have two horses in the big Ascot race, every single one of them assumes that Manhattan is only there to make the pace for her brilliant stablemate Ishtagah.

The lads are excited too. There is a plan. Manhattan will take the King George field at a brisk pace. Ishtagah will stay on as she fades. In the string, there's talk of teamwork, tactics.

They watch Manhattan with more interest now—her springy step, her gray coat that in high summer seems to glow like hot metal, the way she looks around. As if she can sense that a great test is ahead of her, she is more of a handful when we work, and now and then I have difficulty pulling her up.

"There's a skill to making the running," Angus tells me as we take the horses home one morning after second lot. "Too fast, and they'll all ignore you, let you run your own race. Too slow, and you're not doing your job." He manages a craggy smile. "But she'll be a great pacemaker, the mare."

I say nothing, hating the secret I have to keep. It feels as if I'm betraying the brilliant, bright horse beneath me. Even at a walk, she is telling the world that she is not the type to fade at the end of a race in order to help another horse to victory.

She is a winner and always will be, whatever games the humans may be playing.

I concentrate on the big race. I ride out three lots. Manhattan does her work once a week in the afternoon. Most evenings I am in the gym, working on my strength and fitness.

Then I stop taking Uncle Bill's calls. I stay strong, as Michaela has told me. This turns out to be a mistake.

Outside the racing museum. 2:50 pm tomorrow. Be there or you'll regret it.

This text from my uncle arrives late one night, and I know that a no-show tomorrow is not an option. Uncle Bill is not someone you can ignore and hope will go away.

When he arrives, I notice that his small car has a few

more dents than it had the last time I saw it. When I get into the passenger seat, I almost gag at the sour smell of stale tobacco and human sweat.

"Hello, Uncle Bill."

Without looking at me, he accelerates away from the curb.

"I have to be back by four," I say. "Evening stables."

He reaches into the top pocket of his shirt and takes out a cigar, smaller and thinner than the ones he used to smoke. He lights up. As the inside of the car fills with smoke, I open the tinted window.

"Keep it shut." The voice is low, threatening. "Security." He inhales deeply from his cigar, then breathes out.

I cough; my eyes water.

As we leave town, he looks at me for the first time. His eyes are red. There is a cut on his cheekbone. A bit of tobacco sticks to his lower lip. "Michaela thinks you're going bonkers," he says. "All you can talk about is that Manhattan thing."

"That's not true. I also talk to her about her family heritage project."

Driving fast, he turns onto a smaller road. "Yeah, don't know what that's all about."

"She's interested in finding out more about my father."

He looks across at me, frowning. "The less you know about him, the better."

"Where are we going?"

He takes the corner of the small country lane too fast

and swears quietly to himself. "Are you?" he asks. "Going bonkers?"

"No." I look at the countryside through the darkened window. "No more than usual anyway."

"Not taking my calls. People don't do that to me. You'd have to be bonkers to even think of it."

"I've got a race coming up quite soon. I'm concentrating on that."

"Yeah?" He looks across, and I see rage in his eyes. "Well, you're going to have to do a bit of multitasking, then." He glances in his mirror, then swerves into a gateway leading to a field. There is not a house in sight. He switches off the engine and turns toward me. "Remember what I said about being a good girl? Doing what you're told? Do you recall what I said would happen if you didn't?"

"Dusty?"

"Nah. I gave that nag to a local farmer to run with his sheep. Michaela got all emotional about him being sold for dog meat. I worry about that girl sometimes."

"You said you'd tell Mr. Wilkinson."

"That's right. And now you're not doing what you're told."

I turn toward him. "Please, Uncle Bill."

"I need money. And for money, I need tips. If you don't give some information now, I'll send the recordings of you talking to me by e-mail in the morning. You'll be out so fast, your little feet won't touch the ground." He puffs on his cigar and blows smoke in my face.

Blinking, I hold his stare.

"Believe me," he says quietly. "I'm a man of my word."

And I do believe him. Sooner or later, my uncle will send the tapes to the Wilkinsons. They'll know me for the traitor I am.

"Manhattan's running in the King George at Ascot."

"Yeah, yeah." Uncle Bill is unimpressed by this information.

"She's not the pacemaker."

He looks away. "That's not what the press is saying."

"She's there to win."

Uncle Bill turns toward me. A spark of curiosity is in his bloodshot eyes. "But she's the outsider of the field. Something like eighteen to one. Are you telling me she's got a chance of winning?"

I hesitate. Then say the words.

Very.

Good.

Chance.

LIFE'S NOT RACING

There is a whole chapter in *Great Ladies* about how Petite Etoile got beaten in the King George VI and Queen Elizabeth Stakes of 1960.

She was a hot five-to-two favorite but failed to beat the 2000 Guineas winner, Aggressor. At the time, some experts said that she lacked the stamina. Others thought that Lester Piggott had ridden an overconfident race on her and had left her with too much ground to make up. There was a rumor that one of Lester's great rivals, Scobie Breasley, who was riding one of the less-liked horses in the race, had boxed him in as an act of revenge.

One thing was sure. After being beaten in the King George, Petite Etoile was never quite the same.

Now, as this race approaches, I notice that Manhattan has become calmer, as if she can sense that the days and weeks of waiting will soon be over. She has even relaxed about her feet being touched since Jean, the farrier, visits her once a week.

The racing press says that this will be one of the greatest King Georges of modern times. The first three horses involved in an epic finish for the Derby — Positano, Mountain High, and Ishtagah — are to meet again. Against them will be the winner of last year's Arc de Triomphe, a brilliant French-trained four-year-old called Sweet Dreamer; two other winners of French classics, Mon Desir and Tartuffe; and an unbeaten colt from Japan called Rock Island. Then there is that rank outsider in the race, Ishtagah's stablemate Manhattan.

We are the curiosity of the race. Journalists write about Manhattan's "sporting owner Prince Muqrin" — it's their way of saying he doesn't know what he is doing. Then there's "Magic" Wilkinson, "the wily old-timer" — which means he's over the hill. As for Manhattan, the words they use are always the same. She's "moody Manhattan," "mercurial Manhattan," "the mare with a suspect temperament."

Of course, there is a bit of curiosity about the "pint-size girl jockey" who will be riding the "giant mare." One newspaper — strangely, it seems to me at the time — writes about "the growing controversy in the Arab world of a Saudi prince using a girl jockey."

Noise. Rumor. Gossip.

The best advice Mr. Wilkinson has given me is to avoid talking to anyone from the press. In the days before the race, I get used to strangers calling out my name as I ride past with the string, or even on the street.

Two days before the race, I am collecting my tack for second lot when I find a copy of a trashy tabloid in the tack room. It has been left open on the show-business page.

There is a photograph of me, riding Manhattan on the way to the heath. I must have been surprised by the camera, and I'm looking at the photographer with a scowl on my face. The caption beneath the picture reads:

TENSION GETTING TO YOU, BUG?

Riding the mercurial mare Manhattan in Saturday's clash of champions at Ascot, girl apprentice Jay "Bug" Barton, 16, seems to have been taking lessons from her horse. Sources at racing HQ say that the teenager refuses to talk about the race and has taken to snubbing the ordinary folk of Newmarket.

"She acts like she's a celebrity these days," a former friend has revealed. "Just because her name is in the papers now and then, she seems to think she's too good for the rest of us."

And what exactly are the chances of the touchy teen winning tomorrow? Bookmakers are quoting 18–1!

I shake my head, reading this nonsense. There is a world out there, looking for exciting, entertaining stories about fame and happiness and heartbreak. Almost always, the stories are lies.

* * *

It is evening stables the day before the big race. When Mr. Wilkinson visits Manhattan's stall, he is grumpier than usual. I have stripped the mare down, and she seems bigger than ever, glowing with strength and arrogance. The trainer gives her no more than a glance, then nods. "Put her blanket on and let her down. Need to talk, Jay. Now."

He walks out of the stall without another word.

He knows. That is my first thought. He has discovered that I am the stable spy. It is the end.

With a sick feeling in my stomach, I throw a blanket over Manhattan's back and fasten the straps. I give her a pat and leave the stable to face my fate.

Mr. Wilkinson is standing on the green in the middle of the yard. He is gazing downward at the grass, deep in thought, his hands in his pockets. As I approach, he looks up at me. To my surprise, it is not anger I see in his eyes, but sadness, maybe even embarrassment.

"Jay. Wanted to talk to you," he says. "Disappointing news."

"News, sir?"

He clears his throat and sniffs. "Change of plan tomorrow. Putting Dermot Brogan on Manhattan."

The words are muttered hurriedly in a matter-of-fact voice, and at first I think I must have misheard.

"Not my decision," he says. "Owner's."

"Are you saying I'm being jocked off? The day before the race?"

"Prince Muqrin. Problems back home." Mr. Wilkinson seems to be talking to himself. "Crisis. Got enemies. Religious stuff. Demonstrations. Death threats. Big fuss. They're saying member of royal family? Putting up a girl jockey? Not right? Bloomin' sinful."

"I don't understand."

"Read the papers, girl! Get off the blinkin' racing page now and then. Saudi Arabia. Funny sort of place. Women should stay at home. Marry. Bring up children. Know their place."

"Ah."

"Life's not racing, Bug." He sighs. "More's the pity. My view." He tries for a smile but manages no more than a wince. "Your time will come. Mr. Webber called this afternoon. Lucky for us, Brogan's available. Former champion jockey. Couldn't ask for better."

"But—" I'm feeling so sick to my stomach that for a moment I'm afraid that I might throw up right there, in the middle of the yard. I try to think of something to say, but the only words I can think of—"It's not fair," "You promised," "Please, please, please"—seem pathetic and childish.

"Nothing more to say. Announcement's been made. Don't talk to the press." He looks at me, and I can see the sorrow in his face. "You be all right to lead her up at Ascot?"

I nod.

"Good girl." He walks away, across the yard, leaving me standing there.

Never.

More.

Alone.

King George

I feel the eyes of the crowd on me as I lead Manhattan around the paddock at Ascot, before one of the biggest races of the season. Now and then I hear what is being said.

That's her. That's the girl in the papers. Poor kid. She must be so disappointed. Looks like she should be at school.

I stare ahead. The world has gone slightly crazy since the announcement was made yesterday that Dermot Brogan was going to replace an unknown girl apprentice on Manhattan.

Last night, as I walked through the door at my digs, the phone was ringing. It continued until Auntie took it off the hook. Anyone could guess that I was upset, but the papers seemed to want know exactly *how* upset. They needed a taste of my misery to share with their readers.

Looking through the racing pages as we traveled to the races in the horsebox this morning, Deej told me a few of the experts had decided that if the great Dermot Brogan was riding Manhattan, she may be a bit more than a pacemaker. One or two of them suspect a clever tactical plan by the cunning old fox Magic Wilkinson.

In the paddock, Manhattan is striding out so fast that sometimes I have to stop her to avoid walking into Positano in front of us. She loves a crowd and is picking up on the excitement of the moment.

The seven other horses in the paddock are some of the best Thoroughbreds in the world. Standing nearby, the royalty of racing has gathered—successful trainers from England, Ireland, France, and Japan, the sheikhs, princes, and millionaires who own them. Above us, the stands are packed. The queen is here.

This is as good as it gets. The King George VI and Queen Elizabeth Stakes. All eyes are on us. And I am utterly numb.

We stop the horses as the eight jockeys enter the paddock. I see Marcel Dessaux, the French champion jockey who is riding the favorite, Sweet Dreamer, and Johnny Finnegan, a veteran who has ridden more Classics winners than anyone riding today. Pat O'Brian and Dermot Brogan walk in together, both wearing Prince Muqrin's purple-and-white silks but with Pat in a white hat and Dermot in a black one. They laugh and chat as easily as if they are taking a stroll down to the pub for Sunday lunch.

The bell rings. I lead Manhattan to where Mr. and Mrs. Wilkinson stand with Prince Muqrin and Mr. Webber. They gather around Ishtagah, who is being led up by Deej.

When Dermot Brogan walks toward Manhattan, he nods in my direction with the smallest of smiles. He is a man in his forties who has won big races in the past and has a good reputation in the racing world.

As I stand in front of her, a hand on each rein, I hear a familiar voice behind me. "And how is Jaaaay today?"

Prince Muqrin.

I half turn, giving a polite little nod. "I'm all right, Your Highness. Thank you very much."

"I'm so glad." He sounds almost concerned.

Brogan is given the leg up by Mr. Wilkinson. I lead Manhattan away, watching her face, her ears. She is caught up in the excitement of Ascot on big race day. She looks around, ears pricked, ready to show the world what she can do. Brogan pats her.

As we make our way out toward the racecourse, he looks down at me. "Sorry about the ride and all that."

I shake my head. "Not to worry."

"Is she any good, this one?" he asks. "They say she can be tricky."

"She's got a lot of speed but doesn't like to be bumped around in a race. You want to give her a clear run. And you mustn't carry a whip."

"Not carry a whip?" He laughs as if I have made a joke, and I feel smaller than usual.

"If you do," I say, "don't let her see it."

Brogan is staring at the racecourse ahead. I no longer exist for him.

"That," he says, as if talking to himself, "is going to be up to her."

I let slip the lead rein.

Go, Hat. Do your best. Today's your day. Do it for me.

I am standing on the course, watching her walk away from me as the runners parade in front of the grandstand, when someone takes my arm.

Deej.

"Let's get a place in the stand," he says.

We climb the steps to the part of the grandstand reserved for stable staff and watch in silence as the runners turn and canter to the start. Manhattan's ears are still pricked, and she seems to move across the turf like a ballet dancer in a way that reminds me of a famous photograph of Petite Etoile and Lester Piggott. I notice that Brogan has his whip tucked under his arm.

Deej nods in the direction of the betting ring. "The public seems to like Dermot. I've heard that a lot of money's going on Manhattan."

"Yeah?" At the back of my mind, I register that Uncle Bill must be at work, getting his money on Manhattan at the last moment. Right now I'm past caring. "I told Dermot about the whip. He thought I was being a silly little girl, worrying about her horse."

"No, he didn't." Deej nods in the direction of the runners. "Did you see the way he was carrying the whip on the way to the start? Keeping it out of her line of vision. He's not stupid."

She is one of the first to be loaded into the stalls and for the briefest moment, I am there in my mind: Manhattan trembling with anticipation beneath me, I am gathering up the reins.

"They're off!" The announcer's voice breaks in. I look down the track and see that she is one of the first to break. "It's Positano and Manhattan making the early running."

"Not too soon," I murmur.

Brogan settles her, allowing the other runners to overtake him one by one. After three furlongs, she is going easily, near the back of the field.

Beside me, Deej is watching Ishtagah, who is in third place, tight on the rails. "What's Brogan doing?" he mutters. "I thought he was supposed to be making the pace."

The eight runners turn away from the stand, taking the long right-hand bend into the back stretch. Positano is sharing the lead with the Japanese colt, Rock Island, and, behind them are Mountain High and Ishtagah. Going easily on the rails is Marcel Dessaux on Sweet Dreamer.

As they approach the final bend, Dessaux begins to make his move, switching his horse to the outside.

A couple of lengths behind him, Brogan is tracking him on Manhattan.

The crowd roars as the field enters the home stretch. Rock Island is falling back, and for a moment, Deej grips my arm as Ishtagah improves his position. But it is Sweet Dreamer who attracts the eye as he glides up to Positano and hits the front two furlongs from home. Dessaux is looking around, like a jockey who is surprised by how easy the race has been.

Suddenly Manhattan is there, passing Mountain High,

Rock Island, Ishtagah, Positano, no more than two lengths behind Sweet Dreamer. Her ears are forward, and she is gaining with every stride. She is loving it, enjoying her moment. The roar of the crowd is deafening. This is what they have to come to see, a battle to the finish by the best of England and Ireland against the best of France.

It is then that Brogan, following a jockey's instinct, makes his big mistake. He pulls through his whip to his left hand and begins to ride a finish.

"No!" I say the word so loudly that Deej looks at me for a moment.

Within a couple of strides, Manhattan is a beaten horse. Her ears go back. Her easy action is gone.

Suddenly aware that he is losing ground, Brogan makes things worse. He brings his whip down hard on Manhattan's hindquarters.

The tail starts turning. Ahead, Dessaux is riding out Sweet Dreamer. It is Ishtagah who, with every stride, seems to be pulling him back. The noise of the crowd is deafening. At the post, I'm aware that the French four-year-old has won, just ahead of Ishtagah, but my eyes are on Manhattan. She finishes fifth, some six lengths behind the winner.

Moments later, I am on the course, the lead rein in my hand. The runners canter back down the course toward us. As Sweet Dreamer, Ishtagah, and the third horse, Positano, are led through the excited crowd toward the winners' enclosure, Dermot Brogan dismounts and takes off his saddle.

Before he heads back to the weighing room, he glances in my direction. "Race was too far for her. Didn't stay the distance," he says, then walks off, casually twirling his whip in his hand. For him, it is just another spare ride that didn't work out.

I lead Manhattan back to the stables. There is a look on her face that I know well. The human world has let her down again, and she has turned in on herself. If winning races means having a small man on top of your back waving a stick and then hitting you with it, she is not interested.

I don't know, Hat. What can we do with you? You're the world's most impossible animal.

"Mare all right, Bug?" It is Bucknall, who has come to see how she is.

I tell him that she seems fine.

"Brogan said she didn't stay."

I keep quiet.

"A mile and a half was too far for her."

"He shouldn't have used his whip. He would have won if he had ridden her out with his hands and heels."

"Hah!" Uninterested, Bucknall sinks his hands in his pockets and wanders off.

What.

Might.

Have.

Been.

GOOD HORSES DON'T HAVE EXCUSES

The sun is shining on the yard of Magic Wilkinson. The trainer's grumpy face appears in the papers. According to one big article about him, he is "the old-style master craftsman of Newmarket." In an age when racing has become a business, he is a real character. He understands horses and what makes them tick. He kept the faith through hard times, and now he and his main owner, Prince Muqrin, have a brilliant horse in the yard.

Its name is Ishtagah.

As for the mare Manhattan, the newspaper says that she is an example of Magic's patience. Any other trainer would have given up on her. Instead, he kept the faith and it very nearly paid off.

The business of my losing the ride at the last minute was another example of the trainer's cunning, apparently.

The master of Edgecote House allowed the world to think that Manhattan was in the big race as a pacemaker for Ishtagah. To make sure no one thought the mare was a serious contender, Magic let it be known that an unknown girl apprentice would be on board. Then, using "political pressure" on the horse's owner, Prince Muqrin, as an excuse, the clever old tactician put top jockey Dermot Brogan on board 48 hours before the race. It was a masterstroke only he would have dared, and it very nearly paid off.

Good old Magic.

The lads are cheerful. We have already had more winners during the season than the three previous years put together. Sometimes the muscles on Mr. Wilkinson's face move into a position that almost looks like a smile.

But Manhattan and I have lost our place in the sun. When we train, she still looks and feels like a world beater, but now there is something a bit pointless about her brilliance.

She is all show, people say. Her best performances only happen at home, out of sight, when nothing is at stake. And what good is that?

The first time I am able to speak to Mr. Wilkinson after the King George is on the Monday evening two days after the race, when he does evening stables. He looks at Manhattan and then asks, in a slightly bored way, how she is.

I tell him she is fine, eating well. As he is about to leave, I say in a quiet voice, "I think she could have won if he hadn't used his whip."

He looks at me steadily. "Lost the race," he says quietly. "All that matters. Good horses don't have excuses."

"What will happen to her?"

"Autumn sales. Sell her as a brood mare. Proved she's good enough to breed from. But not for the prince. Had enough." He glances at me, almost sympathetically. "Get you a ride sometime. Another lads' race. Missus is looking for a suitable race for you. Eh?"

"Yes, sir." After he has gone, I realize that it is the sort of thing a trainer says to a stable lad with crazy dreams of making it as a jockey.

I am now just waiting for the dream to end. My life as a lad. My ambition of riding as a jockey. Racing Manhattan.

Uncle Bill has left several messages on my phone asking me to call him, but even if he wanted me to continue after giving him such a bad tip, my days as a spy are over. I think of him, his hard blue eyes staring over the fields at Coddington. Anytime now, he will dial Mr. Wilkinson's number.

The following afternoon, I am in my room at Auntie's, getting some rest before evening stables, when there is a light knock on the door.

"Jay, love," Auntie calls out. "Sorry to disturb you, but you have a visitor. At the front door."

I groan wearily. At this point in my life, a visitor can only be bad news.

"It's Mrs. Wilkinson," Auntie whispers through the door.

I get up, slip on some shoes, brush my hair. When I get to the front door, Mrs. Wilkinson and Auntie are chatting like old friends.

"Jay." The smile leaves Mrs. Wilkinson's face as I approach. "We need to talk."

Auntie steps back into the house. "Make yourself at home, Mrs. Wilkinson. You have a good old chat in the sitting room."

"Sweet of you, Auntie. Thank you so much, but"—she looks to the blue sky above us—"it's such a glorious day, I thought Jay and I could go for a little walk. All right, Jay?"

It's not a question. I nod. "Yes, Mrs. Wilkinson."

We walk down the street. To break the silence, I mutter something about Auntie being quite a character.

"Yes," says Mrs. Wilkinson. "Isn't she?"

When we reach the end of the road, she looks around. "Is there somewhere we can sit down for a chat?" I lead her to the park. We sit at the very place where I used to phone Uncle Bill. My spy bench.

"This is nice." Mrs. Wilkinson looks around her, then fixes her cold smile on me. "I wanted to talk about where we go from here."

And suddenly I know it is all over. Uncle Bill has made the call he threatened to make if I let him down. *I'm a man of my word,* he said, and he is. I glance at Mrs. Wilkinson now. Her face seems sad somehow—disappointed I have let her down, and Mr. Wilkinson and the yard. I have betrayed everyone. Sitting here in the park, watched by the cold eyes of the woman who once believed in me, I feel the guilt washing over me.

"I'm sorry!" The words come out in a shout. "I didn't have a choice."

Mrs. Wilkinson frowns. "Sorry?"

"I hated doing it, but my uncle was in trouble. He told me I had to give him information from the yard. First he said he was going to sell the pony I ride for horse meat in Spain. Then he threatened to tell Mr. Wilkinson that I had been snitching secrets. I was trapped."

"Ah."

"It was me who was the spy, Mrs. Wilkinson. I know I've let you down and I've lied and everything. I just didn't know what to do."

"Really," she says quietly.

"That was what you wanted to talk about, wasn't it?"

She shakes her head. "I actually wanted to talk to you about your future. I wasn't expecting a confession."

"What?" I shake my head. "I assumed Uncle Bill called you."

"No. We haven't heard from your uncle for a while now." She smiles coolly. "What was all that stuff about a pony and horse meat?"

"Dusty. He's the best pony in the world. I won my first race on him."

To my surprise, Mrs. Wilkinson laughs. I've heard her

angry laugh and her I'm-just-being-polite laugh, but this one sounds genuine. She looks at me, shaking her head. "A pony?"

I nod.

"Sometimes I forget how young you are." The smile leaves her face. "You have many talents, Jay, but lying is not one of them. We suspected the spy must be you when a lot of money went on Manhattan at Ascot. Only one person could have leaked the information that she wasn't a pacemaker."

"Was that why I was taken off Manhattan?"

"No. It was as we said—the prince had problems at home. It was political."

A woman with a terrier is walking down the path behind us. She looks at me disapprovingly, as if she knows my secret.

"So. I'm finished." I close my eyes. Right now, I feel as if I want to sleep for a million years.

"My husband certainly wanted you to go. As you know, he has an old-fashioned belief that people should tell the truth. He trusted you. All the suspicion was bad for our reputation. He was all for kicking you out."

I shrug miserably.

"I disagreed with him."

"You did?"

"And that means you're staying. I don't want to lose you. You can work out this season as a lad. Maybe we could get you a few rides over the winter. Then go for the apprentice races next season."

I must be looking uncertain, because Mrs. Wilkinson

adds in a quiet, girls-together voice, "Don't worry. Clive agrees with me. He always does."

"I'm not sure. After all that's happened."

Mrs. Wilkinson brings her hands down onto her knees in a brisk, impatient movement. "This is what I wanted to talk to you about, Jay. You've done pretty well since you've been at the yard. Everything has been against you, but you've kept going." She looks me in the eye. "You've got drive," she says. "Lots of people can ride nicely, get horses going well on the gallops, but the best jockeys are not always great horsemen. They've got drive. If you've got both horsemanship and that will to win, then just possibly you might make it as a jockey. I think you can."

"Thank you, Mrs. Wilkinson."

She looks away, like someone embarrassed by what she is saying. "You've been a tonic. For Edgecote. The way you've ridden, how you've stayed loyal to that impossible mare. I don't know quite how you've done it, but you've shaken us all up. Just being you." She looks at me and smiles. "You're too important to the yard for us to let you go. And if you tell anyone I said that, you really will be fired."

We sit in silence for a few moments.

"I know it's been tough, Jay. Tougher than if you were a boy."

I nod, relieved that she understands. "It's as if I have to be twice as good as the others. And the way I look is such a big deal. No one worries what boys look like. If I complain, they say I can't take it—I'm being girlie."

Mrs. Wilkinson sighs. "That," she says quietly, "is the game we have to play."

"Some game," I mutter.

She turns to me. "Who d'you think decides which horse is running where for the Wilkinson yard?" she asks. "Who does the horses' work schedule? Who buys the yearlings on behalf of owners? Who is actually running things behind the scenes?"

I'm surprised by the sudden emotion in her voice. There is an angry blush on her cheeks.

"You?"

"That's what we do. The game. And I play it pretty well. I don't mind being the little wife of Magic Wilkinson. Not a bit. It works. We're a team. He talks to the press, calls the owners, appears at evening stables. I do the rest. I'm the trainer at Edgecote. You have to build your power slowly, out of sight, when no one is watching."

"Seems a bit unfair."

"It's the way the world works, Jay." She pats me on the arm and stands up. "Think about it. Maybe between us we can put this behind us."

"I will."

"Can I give you a lift to the yard?"

"No, thanks, Mrs. Wilkinson. I'll walk."

Without another word, she strides toward the park gate.

"And thank you," I call out.

Without turning around, she gives a small wave over her shoulder.

* * *

I sit there on the bench after she has gone.

The game we have to play. The way the world works. Those words echo in my mind.

I think of the men who have played a part in my life. Uncle Bill. Mr. Wilkinson. Prince Muqrin. Angus. Bucknall. Dermot Brogan. Pete. Even Deej. Then I think of those of us on the other side of life's great dividing wall. My mother. Mrs. Wilkinson. Laura. Michaela. Auntie. Manhattan. Me. It is as if we are all part of some great male plan, and the best we can hope to do is to fit in with what they want.

And in that moment, I know what I have to do. I have never played the game according to other people's rules before, and I am not going to start now. An idea has been lurking at the back of my mind for days, but I have been trying to ignore it.

Until now.

No.
More.
Games.

SQUARE PEG

She can tell. When I ride her out the next day, Manhattan is quieter than usual, as if she knows what I have decided. Although we are at the head of the string as usual, her ears are half-back. There is no spring in her step.

You'll be all right, Hat. You have a future now. You'll be a great mother. Whoever owns you will look after you.

Back in the stable, I rub her down for the last time. Even when I wash under her stomach, she hardly reacts. She accepts a carrot from me, but moodily.

After I have put her blanket on, I pat her, tug one of her ears.

I'll be back this afternoon, girl.

Late that morning, I catch Laura as she's on her way to lunch. I walk with her for a while. I must be a bit quiet because she asks if everything is all right.

"It's fine," I say. "But I need to ask you a big favor."

She looks at me, raising her eyebrows. "Now what?"

"We're friends, right?"

She laughs. "Just get on with it."

"It's about Manhattan."

During the early afternoon, I write some notes and put them in envelopes. Mr. and Mrs. Wilkinson. Prince Muqrin. Deej. Even Angus.

Downstairs, Auntie is catching up on some daytime TV in the kitchen. When I appear at the door, she glances up, sees the backpack over my shoulder and the look on my face, and says, "No, Jay."

I nod. "I need to go home."

She switches off the TV. "What happened? Are you in trouble?"

"Not really. I think I've discovered that racing isn't for me. Too rough."

"But you're good with horses."

"It's not the horses. It's the humans."

Auntie shrugs. "Humans are human, what can I say? They can be a tricky business."

In my mind, I see Pete, a pitchfork in his hand. I see Bucknall, leaning back in his chair. *Jyaaasmine.* Angus watching me, eyes narrowed. Mr. Lukic, hands in pockets and shoulders hunched angrily, as I ride into the winners' enclosure on Poptastic. Dermot Brogan looking down at me as I lead Manhattan up at Ascot. Uncle Bill, his face close to mine, in his tiny car. Mrs. Wilkinson smiling sadly on the park bench.

Hatred, amusement, suspicion, rage, pity, contempt,

disappointment—I have seen too much of them all. When I was supposed to lose, I won. When I should have won, I lost. I've lied and spied and let people down.

"To tell the truth, Auntie, I feel a bit broken right now." I sniff, wipe my nose with the back of my hand.

"You're not broken, Jay." Auntie smiles. "You're just a bit cracked." She puts her hand on mine, holding tight as I try to pull away. "You know what they used to say about my Jas?" She looks into my eyes. "They said he's a square peg. I didn't understand then, but now that I'm older, I think I do. The world is full of round pegs with their sharp edges smoothed off, but we need a few square pegs too. Where will you go?"

"Back to my uncle's place. I need to talk to him and sort things out, then move on. New chapter."

Auntie stands up and does what I feared she was going to do. She puts her arm around me. I lean away but she holds me closer, and after a few seconds, I give up resisting and relax.

"You're such a good girl." The words are in my ear. I try to tell her that I'm not, I really am not, but the words won't come. "You've done so well. Are you saying there will be no more horses for you?"

"Probably not. For the moment anyway."

"Will you come back and see us?"

"Of course."

She stands back and looks me in the eyes. I manage a smile.

"Bye, Auntie," I say.

*   *   *

The yard is quiet when I arrive. I go to the tack room and leave the envelopes on the central table. I take one last look at the List:

1st Lot

MANHATTAN Bug

Manhattan is having her afternoon nap as I enter the stall. I put down my backpack, walk up to her, drape an arm over her neck, then push my face against her, feeling her warmth, breathing in the smell I have come to love.

This is it, Hat. From now on, you'll have a new lad. Laura. You like her, don't you?

She stirs slightly, and for a few moments I think of the journey we've been on together — the dramas, the gallops, the ups and downs. I see us together, alone on the heath, a skylark singing high above us, when we were happy.

Manhattan turns to look at me, surprised by all this emotion in the middle of the afternoon.

You're right. It's your sleeping time. I should go.

My eyes are wet. I wipe my face on her neck, then stand back. Slowly, I trace a heart on her shoulder. I look at the mark my finger has left on the beautiful dappled coat.

Remember this. Remember this forever.

Then I smooth it over. Life moves on. I have a train to catch. Manhattan nudges me. I give her the last carrot in my pocket, pat her neck, and leave the stable, glancing back at her as I go.

Just.

A.

Horse.

HEARTBROKEN TEEN

Coddington Hall has changed since I was last here. The stables are empty and quiet. The only sign that there have been horses there is the manure heap. Grass is growing on it already. The fields need cutting, the hedges are whiskery. Harry, the farmer next door, used to look after them, but now that there is no money to pay him, they are neglected.

The house is silent too, with odd gaps where the best bits of furniture used to be. Michaela is away, staying with a friend from her old school whose parents have a house in France. Uncle Bill wanders the place, holding onto a cell phone that these days never rings. He is away from the house a lot more often than he used to be, and there is a bad atmosphere between him and Aunt Elaine.

She is now the resident victim at Coddington, moping around the place, occasionally putting things in boxes. She no longer bothers with makeup and has decided to let her dark hair, which used to be dyed crow black, grow gray.

She was not exactly thrilled by my return. "Oh, great, that's all we need," she said when I appeared on the doorstep late one evening.

I gave her the 130 pounds I saved while I was in Newmarket. "Household expenses," I say. She nods and, without a word of thanks, walks off to put the money away somewhere.

Why are you back? I see that question in her eyes, and it is one I ask myself. To her, I'm an unwelcome outsider. Uncle Bill thinks I have let him down. And I remember too well what Michaela once thought of me.

The fact is, I have little choice. The cash I have just given to Aunt Elaine would hardly have kept me in food and rent for a week. There is nowhere else for me to go.

Rest. Think. Plan. Then move on as soon as possible. That is what I shall do.

"You'll need to find some paid work," Aunt Elaine says soon after I return. "You can't sit around here all day."

She is right about that. I think about it every day in that first week as I go for my early-morning run. Somehow my body can't get used to my own life. I wake up at six and I know I have to tire myself out, just to keep sane.

What job? My racehorse management apprenticeship must have come to an end when I left the Wilkinson yard. I wonder if I could become a vet and work with animals. No. I'd need to go to college for that.

I try not to think of Manhattan or what is happening in the yard where I worked. It is the past. That door is closed.

* * *

One evening about two weeks after my return, Uncle Bill knocks on the door of my room.

He has been in London and throws an evening paper on the bedside table. I look up from *Great Ladies,* which I happen to be reading.

"You're in the news, doll," he says.

I look down. There is a photograph of me riding Manhattan, and a headline: HEARTBROKEN TEEN QUITS RACING.

I pick it up and read the article:

> The last-minute decision of Newmarket trainer Clive "Magic" Wilkinson to replace the young apprentice Jay "Bug" Barton with the more experienced Dermot Brogan on Prince Muqrin's Manhattan for last month's prestigious King George VI and Queen Elizabeth Stakes has ended the teenager's career. The 16-year-old has left her job at the Wilkinson stable, vowing never to work in racing again.
>
> Tipped as a future professional jockey by racing insiders, Barton was "devastated" by her boss's change of heart, according to a close friend. "Bug's a proud person, and she was particularly humiliated by having to lead Manhattan up at Ascot as a lad. That was the final straw as far as she was concerned."
>
> A spokesman for the Wilkinson yard

confirmed that Barton no longer works there, but claimed that she was taking a temporary break from racing.

I throw the newspaper back on the table.

"Keep it as a souvenir, babe." My uncle wanders toward the door.

"Why are you avoiding me, Uncle Bill?" My question sounds more aggressive than I intended. I really am just curious.

He stops at the door. "What you talking about, girl?"

"I've been wanting to say I'm sorry about your losing all that money on Manhattan. I think she would have won if I had been riding her."

He gives a little laugh, which is not entirely friendly. "I got to give it to you, doll. You don't doubt your own abilities."

I look down at my book. "I just wanted to say that, so you know. You were right. I do owe you a lot for what you've done since Mum died. I'll leave here as soon as I've found a job, and we can all get on with our lives." I frown, pretending to read, and turn a page.

To my surprise, Uncle Bill walks back and sits on the side of the bed. "We'd have made a good team." He says the words in a quiet, gruff voice, staring ahead of him.

"I couldn't do it anymore." I stare at the book. "The tips. The secret calls. The spying. It made me hate myself."

"The thing is, doll, we're not that different, you and me. The rage thing? I get that. Winning? That's me too."

"Was that why you didn't phone the Wilkinsons like you threatened to do? Because you thought we could carry on, like a good family team?"

My uncle is staring at me. There is an expression on his face that I have never seen before. "You don't get it, do you?"

"Get what, Uncle Bill?"

"You won. You took me on, and you beat me. It may feel as if you've lost, but you've won."

"I haven't won anything."

"I really thought I could get you to do what I wanted, just like I can do with everybody else. But I couldn't." He laughs, shaking his head. "It's true, I was going to put the call through to old man Wilkinson. I thought I could—I'm Bill Barton—but it turned out I was wrong."

"Why?"

"I remembered my sister, Debs. I thought about you. How you've kept going. I suddenly knew I couldn't take you down with me. I told myself that it was because you're a kid, but the truth is simpler. You're tougher than I am."

I shrug, feeling weirdly embarrassed by what my uncle is saying. "I don't feel tough."

Uncle Bill looks at me. I can tell that he has already said more than he wanted to say. "You're going to be all right. Proud of you, doll."

Without another word, he gets up and walks to the door.

"Uncle Bill," I call after him. "There was just one other thing."

"Yeah?"

"I'm not a doll."

He gives a bark of laughter and is gone.

I have thrown the newspaper away. Am I a heartbroken teen? Not really, but I am numb. I am tired. For these past few days, I have been telling myself it is time to grow up, to forget my mum's crazy dreams for me. They have brought nothing but trouble. Earn a living. Get by. Move on. Don't look back.

It is beginning to work. I am becoming a new, more realistic Jay Barton. No longer riding high in the saddle. Grounded.

Then something happens that changes my life forever.

When Michaela returns from her vacation, she is tanned yet weirdly distracted. France was great, she says, but she's glad to be home — particularly now that I'm here. Our first evening together, she tells me that she needs to show me something.

After supper, we go to her room. She sits at a little table and switches on her laptop.

"Prepare yourself for a bit of a shock," she says as the computer comes to life.

"Is this your family heritage project again?"

"Hm, sort of." Michaela is never more annoying than when she's got a secret. She taps at the keyboard. A file marked *JDad* appears on the screen.

"JDad?"

She opens the file. A list of documents scrolls down the page. I see the words *Genealogy, Letters, Helldawgs, Crazy Jerzy, Fan sites, Jim, Polish builders.*

"What is this, M?"

"Right." Michaela turns toward me. "Confession time. I wasn't really doing a family heritage project for school."

"*No*. You mean you *lied* to me?" My best I'm-being-totally-sarcastic voice goes right over her head.

"I just thought, after the whole Jean-Paul thing, I owed you one. We all owed you one, really."

I'm still suspicious about where this conversation is going. "Are you telling me you found out something?"

"I asked my father about our grandparents. And about their childhood. And your mum. I said it was for my project. He gave me a big folder from his filing cabinet, marked FAMILY. It was full of photographs and letters and quite a bit of legal stuff about their will after their parents died. Then there were some letters from your mum to my dad."

"I never knew."

"The letters are quite short, and not exactly friendly. When I started asking questions, Dad suddenly realized what he had given me. He took back the folder and locked it up." Michaela's eyes are sparking with excitement. "But not before I made a discovery. Seventeen years ago, she mentioned Jerzy—that's your dad, right?"

I nod.

"He was a musician in a metal band. She writes about

the 'Jerzy problem,' how they had been a bit careless. There's something about 'my little accident.'"

I begin to see where this is going. "Seventeen years ago. The accident is me."

"There's nothing more from your mum for a while, but there is a copy of a letter from my dad to a Mr. J. Turkowski."

"My father."

Michaela nods. "It says that if Mr. Turkowski agrees to leave the country immediately, he will not be reported to the police."

"Reported? For what?"

"My dad discovered that he was in this country without the right papers. He was an illegal alien—he could have been in big trouble."

I'm confused now. "So why didn't my mother tell me any of this?"

"Because she didn't know." Michaela gives a little embarrassed wince. "In the letter, it says that if Jerzy agreed to leave the country immediately, my dad would support you and your mum. All Jerzy had to do to give you security in the future was to go home—disappear. He couldn't tell your mum because she would want to go with him."

"You mean he did it for us?"

"Looks like it."

"So all that stuff about him being a coward and running away was a great big lie?"

"Maybe his life back in Poland wouldn't have been such a great life for a young English mum and her baby?"

Suddenly I feel overcome with sadness—for my mum, for me, for my Polish dad who just wanted the best for his family. Even Uncle Bill probably thought he was doing the right thing. "It gets better," says Michaela, as cheerful as ever. "I became a detective and started searching online for Jerzy Turkowski. It turns out he was in a Polish heavy metal group called the Helldawgs that was quite successful at the time. Your mum and Jerzy must have met when the band was touring in England. I got onto one of those chat forums. Someone had asked whatever happened to 'Crazy Jerzy Turkowski of the Helldawgs?' I scrolled down and found this." Michaela taps a link to a website called Metalchat.com. "Jerzy is now an American citizen and works as a builder in Oregon under the name of Jim Thurston. No longer on the music scene."

I sit in silence. I'm really not sure I like the direction that Michaela's Sherlock Holmes act is taking us.

She clicks on the keyboard. Two photographs appear on the screen. One is of a rock band posing moodily for a publicity shot, all long hair and makeup. The lead singer, a little dark-haired guy trying to look tough, is at the front, sneering at the camera. The second photograph is of a thin, balding man in his forties. He has a neat mustache, and his arm is around his wife. In front of them stand two boys, age about ten and eight.

It is the eyes that tell the story. Everything else is different—clothes, hair, attitude—but they have remained unchanged. Crazy Jerzy of the Helldawgs and Jim Thurston, the family guy in America, are the same man.

I am looking at my father.

Over the next few days, we find out more about Jim Thurston. There is a website for his building business with other photographs of him—standing in front of a newly built house, or looking at some plans, or up a ladder in a hard hat.

How do I feel? Not much. After the shock of hearing the news, I start to look at Daddy/Jim more coolly. The truth is I feel no connection to this serious little Polish guy in America. He is a stranger. In my room at night, I think of my mother and the past she never really discussed with me. What were they like together, Jerzy and Debs? In my imagination, I see them as only a bit older than I am now.

They were young, happy, in love. And then I came along.

I look at the photographs of my father at work and with his family. He once dreamed of being a rock star. Now he is a builder.

And perhaps, it suddenly occurs to me, there is a lesson there. I must try to stop thinking of the past—about Manhattan and what might have been. I'll look forward, not back. Perhaps I should be a vet's assistant. I could work my way through college until I get the right qualifications.

Working with animals. A serious, secure job. I imagine myself, one day, posing like Jim with my little family around me. It will be good. It is all going to be fine.

There is a contact e-mail address on the Jim Thurston website.

I'm nervous, but Michaela insists that we have to contact him. It's better to know who my father is—even if he doesn't want to meet me—than to live all my life not being sure.

"We've got to be cunning," she says. "We can't just come out with it. Men are scared of stuff like that."

She is good at this, Michaela. She pretends to be someone called Carrie, a great Helldawgs fan. Carrie sends an e-mail asking Jim Thurston if he is Crazy Jerzy, the lead singer of "the Dawgs." Is he in touch with the other Dawgs? Are they planning a reunion?

It is impressive. Reading it, I'm completely convinced.

Within a couple of days, Jim Thurston is in touch.

Hey, Carrie,
Yup, I'm Helldawgs Jerzy, but I'm not crazy anymore! There's a fan website you can find online for all Helldawgs-related stuff. You'll find it at www.real-helldawgs.com.
Thank you for your interest.
Jim Thurston

There is nothing left to do now but tell the truth. Jim Thurston is Jerzy Turkowski, and Jerzy Turkowski is my father.

I talk it through with Michaela. Then she writes the e-mail. She isn't really Carrie, she says. She is Michaela. Her best friend is Jay, who was born Jasmine Barton sixteen and a half years ago. Her mother, Deborah Barton, tragically died when Jay was nine, and Jay really wants to be in touch with her father. She has reason to believe that you are that father. She doesn't want anything from you, just contact. She needs to know for certain.

We send the e-mail late at night. An answer is waiting for us when we switch on the computer in the morning.

> Oh, my God. There's hardly a day when I don't
> wonder what happened to Jasmine. Thank you
> from the bottom of my heart, Michaela. Please ask
> my daughter to write to me as soon as possible!
> Yours very happily, Jim

Just like that.

I'd been expecting silence, maybe lies, but it turns out that there has been a gap in my dad's life too. He starts sending me e-mails. He says he has talked about me in the past to his wife, Linda. He has missed me for the past sixteen years, even though we have never met. He asks me to send him photographs, tell him everything about me.

Whoa, there. Easy does it. One step at a time, right?

I tell him about my mum, about school. I give him a tidied-up version of my life as a stable lad. He decides to look for me online and finds stories and pictures of me on Poptastic and Manhattan. At this stage, he becomes a bit overenthusiastic. He is proud of me, he says. So young, and already I have achieved so much.

He writes about his life in America. His wife, Linda, is "the apple of his eye." He adores his "two little handfuls,"

Barney and Jared. His business is "pretty darn hunky-dory" thanks to improvements in the economy. And so on.

At the end of every e-mail, he says how pleased he is that we're in touch.

Your loving father, Jim. That's how he signs off. Personally, I don't see how you can love someone if you've never met them, but then maybe my dad is a bit free and easy when it comes to love.

He certainly was seventeen years ago.

Now and then, the four of us — Uncle Bill, Aunt Elaine, Michaela, and me — are all at Coddington and manage to have dinner together, just like in the old days. It is on one of those rare occasions that we break it to Uncle Bill and Aunt Elaine that Michaela has found my father and that I am getting e-mails from him. They surprise me by being quite relaxed about the whole thing.

"Never liked the guy," says Uncle Bill. "Jumping around onstage. Didn't do the right thing by my sister. She was a fool to fall for him."

"Is it true you made him leave the country?" Michaela asks.

Uncle Bill shrugs. "I was helping my sister. What kind of future would she and her baby have had with a long-haired illegal immigrant?"

"He seems nice now," says Michaela.

"It broke my mum's heart." I say the words softly.

A look of annoyance crosses Uncle Bill's face. "Family comes first. I was trying to help."

"But why was everyone so rude about my dad? He thought he was doing the right thing. I grew up thinking he didn't care about me."

There is a heavy, guilty silence around the table.

"Hey." Aunt Elaine smiles, as if a thought has suddenly occurred to her. "D'you think he might want you to move over there, Jay?"

"I'm not sure that—"

"Nice place, Oregon. Lots of horses there. You'd love it."

The telephone rings in the hall and Michaela goes to answer it. She returns after a brief conversation, looking puzzled.

"It was someone asking for Jay," she says.

"Speak of the devil, it's your daddy!" Aunt Elaine laughs cheerfully.

"No, he had a funny accent—sort of weird and posh. He said he was going to drop by here tomorrow afternoon."

Uncle Bill looks worried. "Here? I don't want strangers turning up uninvited, thank you very much."

"I couldn't quite get his name. Mackerel? Mucking? He had a funny nickname too. Prince."

I'm aware of a thumping in my chest. It has to be Prince Muqrin.

"He definitely thought Jay would know who he was," says Michaela. "He said, 'Just tell Jasmine that the prince called.'"

"I really don't like the sound of this guy." Uncle Bill is staring hard at me. "When I was a kid, one of the local tough guys called himself 'the Duke.' Ended up in prison. Is this boy in some kind of gang?"

"Prince? What kind of name is that?" Aunt Elaine shakes her head. "He sounds very unsuitable."

"Who is he, Jay?" asks Michaela.

All.

Eyes.

On.

Me.

A Line in the Sand

By the time a big black car about the size of a small tank is kicking up dirt on the driveway the next day, Coddington Hall has changed.

As soon as Aunt Elaine discovered that our visitor was a real member of the Saudi royal family, she went into action. Books that had been packed up have been returned to the shelves. The best china is making a rare appearance. She has borrowed a few magazines from a neighbor—*Vogue, Country Life, Horse and Hound*—and they have been left, ever so casually, on the table in the sitting room.

Uncle Bill and Aunt Elaine have spent a lot of time talking about what they should wear. Now, as we wait for the royal arrival, my uncle is in his green country-gentleman suit, and around his neck is a red spotted scarf-thing of a type that I have only seen in pictures of Prince Charles when he is out shooting.

Aunt Elaine is in a tweed coat and skirt and pearls. Rather oddly, she has a scarf on her head, which she told Michaela is because the prince is a Muslim and women need to have their heads covered. The fact that she hasn't had time to go to a hairdresser is probably just a coincidence.

Only Michaela and I look even halfway normal.

Through the window, we see the prince's car as it sweeps up to the front door. Two men, each the size of a wardrobe, jump out. One looks around as if a sniper could be hiding in the stable, while the other opens the back door. Prince Muqrin, wearing a dark suit, steps out. He says something to his security guards. They remain standing watchfully by the car as he walks toward the front door.

Aunt Elaine opens it as he approaches.

"Prince Muqrin," she says, a big cheesy smile fixed on her face. "What a pleasure this is."

The prince extends his hand and glances toward me.

"This is my aunt Elaine," I say. "This is Prince Muqrin."

My aunt actually does a little bob as she shakes his hand. "Your Highness," she says humbly.

"And this is Uncle Bill."

"Welcome, Prince," he says. My uncle winks as he shakes the prince's hand.

"And here's my best friend, Michaela."

"Michaela, charming name." The prince smiles as he shakes her hand, then turns to me. "And how's my friend Jay?"

"I'm fine, thanks, Your Highness."

Prince Muqrin addresses us all. "I apologize for having

to bring my colleagues." He nods in the direction of the two giants standing by the car. "There have been one or two security issues recently."

"Shall we have some tea, Your Highness?" asks Aunt Elaine.

"Please," says Prince Muqrin. "Call me Tariq."

We take tea in the sitting room. It is the most awkward ten minutes I have ever had to sit through. Aunt Elaine, perched on the edge of her seat, makes panicky small talk. When Prince Muqrin asks Uncle Bill about his business, there is a brief, awkward silence.

"Import and export—tough old business, Tariq," he says.

"I'm sure."

The prince, I notice, drinks his tea rather quickly. He nibbles politely at a cucumber sandwich.

"What fun this all is," he says when there is a pause in the conversation. "Now I know where Jay gets her perfect manners."

I can't help glancing at Aunt Elaine. Her smile wavers just for a second. "We do our best, Tariq," she says. "She's a good girl. In her own way."

"Now, Elaine and Bill, Michaela." The prince's general smile is like a full stop on the conversation. "I have one small request. I mustn't take up too much of your busy time. Could I possibly have a moment with my friend Jay? I need to discuss something rather private with her."

"Of course, Tariq. Feel free." Aunt Elaine sits back in her chair.

"Private," Michaela murmurs. "That means without us."

"Sorry, Your Highness." Aunt Elaine stands up suddenly. "We'll leave you two to chat."

The prince stands. "How kind you are." When we are alone, he sits down again. "What a nice family." He smiles at me and seems to relax.

"Yes. They are. In their own way."

He laughs, then considers me for a moment while sitting very still. It is as if he has been told that if you are a prince, you should never make any sudden movements. "I hope you don't mind my descending on you unannounced," he says softly. "I needed to talk to you about something rather important, and I didn't want other people involved. This is just between you and me."

"Right."

"I think you are aware that I have been having a few problems back home."

"Yes. I heard."

"I belong to an absolutely maaarvelous family. Al Saud, the House of Saud. Very important in Saudi Arabia. Quite powerful, I suppose. A bit like your royal family, the prime minister, and Parliament all rolled into one."

"Great." It's not quite the right word, but it is the only one that comes into my head at this point.

"Great, indeed." He gives a sad little smile. "Tradition is very important in my country. Certain things are expected of one."

"Yes."

"No need to go into details. I have been very lucky. For

my twelfth birthday, the king gave me a ring containing one of the biggest diamonds in the world."

"Nice."

He laughs. "Not really—I wanted a PlayStation. So now I've grown up and I have a choice. To be me, living the life I want to live, or to be Prince Tariq Muqrin bin Rashid al Saud, the keeper of tradition like my father and grandfather and his grandfather before him."

"I see."

"When I saw you on the gallops and watched on TV how you did with Manhattan at York, it was a moment of revelation for me."

"It was?" Something in my voice tells him that I am wondering what all this family history has to do with his visit today.

The prince sweeps a crumb from the table. "It wasn't the horse I admired, although I love the rascal dearly. It was you."

I sit back in my chair, slightly worried now.

"You've broken out. I've heard all about your dad disappearing, how your mother passed away when you were young. You haven't been terrifically successful at school, I gather."

"Well—" I'm about to start making excuses when he holds up a neatly manicured hand.

"You've escaped from your past." He pauses for a moment, then leans forward slightly, fixing me with his dark eyes. "No one has been on your side. The world has been against you. You've just kept going." He looks around and suddenly seems a bit small in his perfect suit and cuff links and sober tie. It is as if they have been there all the time, waiting for him to fill them. His cage.

"I didn't have much choice," I say. "I just like riding horses. It wasn't complicated."

"Not complicated maybe, but difficult—challenging." The prince frowns, silently discouraging any discussion of the matter. "And now," he says, "you've given it all up."

"I've done enough. It's time to move on now that Manhattan is safe." A thought occurs to me. "She is safe, isn't she?"

"Of course. The mare will be fine, whatever happens. You saved her from a nasty end." He looks out of the window. "My family wants me to give up too. They think I'm not serious. The press seems to agree."

"'The playboy prince.'"

"Exactly." He smiles sadly. "Some people in my country are very worried about me. They think I have been corrupted by my life away from Saudi Arabia. I actually want a woman jockey to ride one of my horses. A female! Back home, women are supposed to be at home, being good wives, raising a family."

"Bit sexist," I say.

He shrugs. "We have different values. Unfortunately, my family saw the idea of you riding a horse owned by me as a slap in the face to our great traditions, our culture. They said I would be giving ammunition to the enemies of my family. Look at al Saud, these people would say. They are as immoral as Europeans, even Americans." He gives an angry laugh and sits staring at his fingernails for a moment. "It is why I made the decision I did over the King George."

"Manhattan went well for Dermot Brogan. If he hadn't shown her the whip, she might have won."

The prince gives a small, dignified shake of the head. "I've seen how she goes for you. Something magical happens when you ride her. You bring out the best in each other."

"But maybe—"

He gives me a look that freezes the words in my throat. "Here's the position," he says, suddenly business-like. "Ishtagah has been invited to run in the Breeders' Cup Classic in America. The best horses in America, three-year-olds and up, will compete. Two European horses have been invited. Sweet Dreamer—the French colt who beat us in the King George—and my horse. Ishtagah's not going that well at home now though and has never liked traveling. I asked the Americans if I can run the mare instead. They have agreed."

"That's great."

"I've been thinking a lot recently, Jay. I have to be true to myself, like you—escape from the past. If I compromise now, more compromises will follow. Tradition isn't everything. I want to show the world that there is a new generation in the House of Saud. I am prepared to run Manhattan in the Breeders' Cup Classic . . . but only if you ride her."

I must be looking scared by this speech because the prince smiles.

"It isn't just politics. I also want to win one of the biggest races in the world," he says. "But I shall absolutely understand if you refuse. If that is the case, I shall probably sell all my horses." I must be looking shocked, because he adds, "There's more to life than horses and racing, isn't there?"

I can't think of anything, but I nod politely.

"What happens on a racecourse in America—a woman jockey riding for a Saudi prince—could bring change," says the prince. "I will have shown that the House of Saud is not the slave of the past, that it can make history as well as follow it. We could make history—you, Manhattan, and me. We could draw a line in the sand—the desert sand."

"No pressure, then."

He laughs. "You can handle pressure, Jay. I've seen that. However the horse runs, everything will have changed by the simple fact that you rode it."

"What about all those protests?"

"Saudis love racing. It will be the perfect way to change attitudes. Sport can go where politics can't." He looks at a large gold watch on his wrist. "That's it, really. I just wanted to tell you personally that, between us, we can do something extraordinary."

"I don't do extraordinary things. I just ride. If I do come back, it won't be for some great cause in the world. It will be for me."

"And for Hat."

I laugh. "Yes. And for Hat."

He stands up, reaches into his top pocket, and takes out a heavy, embossed business card and lays it on the table. "Call me if you want to discuss this."

He walks to the door and opens it. Aunt Elaine is in the hall, fiddling with some flowers in a vase. I'm pretty sure she has been listening at the door.

"Elaine," says the prince. "This has been such fun, but I must bid you farewell."

Uncle Bill and Michaela appear as if by magic from the kitchen.

"Just one question," says the prince. "How would the three of you like to go to America?"

Clever.

Clever.

Man.

AMERICAN DIRT

I am on Manhattan with her easy, graceful gait as she trots past the grandstand at Santa Anita Park racecourse, near Los Angeles. There are people bringing in gigantic flower displays. Already the warm air is full of the sweet smells wafting from the concession stands under the grandstand—hot dogs, popcorn, chocolate sauce, and caramel. There are people everywhere, going about their business: groomers, exercise riders, hot walkers, clockers, jockeys' agents—the world of American racing.

Manhattan shakes her head and gives a low dragon-snort. There has been no change quite as exciting as this. At first, she is on her guard, remembering bad experiences in her life, but then, as she sees how different it all is, every day becomes an adventure.

She loves it here in America. We have been in the stables—"the shed row," it is called—for three weeks now, and I have never known her to eat so well. The color of her coat has grown lighter in the West Coast sun, and her mane and tail almost seem to glow when we are on the track. She senses that the people milling around the racecourse have noticed her and has a new haughty look in her eye.

The dirt beneath Manhattan's hooves is different from anything she has worked or raced on before. To my eye, it seems more suitable for motorcycles or stock-car racing than horses, but this is the American way. An artificial track is preferred to turf.

I have read that one of the reasons why so few European horses have won the Breeders' Cup Classic is that they are not used to this surface. It is tougher, faster, and kicks up in their faces.

Behind two other English horses, which are running in other races at the meeting, I canter down the back stretch. Since she has been here, Manhattan has been getting a feel for the surface. Today, I've been told to let her stride out with the other two horses down the home stretch. The American exercise riders call it "breezing," and I like that word. On Manhattan, I feel like I am riding the breeze.

Ahead of me, one of the jockeys looks around. "Here we go!" he shouts. They turn. I follow five or six lengths behind them. And we're off.

"Time to show them your paces, girl."

Manhattan's ears go forward as she breaks into a canter and then, head down and pulling hard, goes through the gears until we are moving at a good half-speed gallop.

The sound of her hooves on this surface is louder, yet more muffled, than on grass. Manhattan likes it. It is as if she can sense that a track like Santa Anita favors a strong gallop, and speed at the finish.

She knows today is little more than a warm-up and is happy to pull up behind the other two horses.

We turn back to Clockers' Corner, where the trainers are waiting. I give Manhattan a pat on the neck.

"You like it in America, don't you, girl?"

Deej and Laura are looking after Manhattan in America, and it is Laura who leads her back to the barn. I walk beside them both, past the walking ring, the saddling paddock, the receiving barn. As we go, photographs are being taken, and there is a buzz of interest among the people who seem to hang out on American racetracks throughout the day.

According to Laura, the story of Manhattan and her young girl jockey has attracted the attention of the American press.

There are horses in the Breeders' Cup Classic who have won the greatest races in the world — the Dubai World Cup, the Kentucky Derby, the Arc de Triomphe — but none has a story like Manhattan's.

A public fairy tale has grown up around her. She was once a wild and flighty filly who, in the hands of the legendary Magic Wilkinson, has been tamed. Over three years, he has persisted with her, believed in her. It was his clever idea, the story now goes, to put an inexperienced stable girl on the mare, so that she felt she was in charge. It was a masterpiece of patient old-fashioned training — or so the papers say.

Then, as in all good fairy stories, the trouble began. Some say Magic lost his nerve before the King George and played it safe by putting up an older, male jockey. Others say Prince Muqrin made the decision.

I, the little stable girl who dreamed of being a jockey, was heartbroken and left racing, they say, until Magic gave me the call.

Deej tells me that the American press have latched on to my story—the mystery kid, the rookie teen girl taking on the best jockeys in the world. Over here, apprentices are sometimes called "bug boys," and so there are headlines about "the bug girl called Bug."

From the moment we arrived in Los Angeles, there have been photographers at every turn. At the airport, I was wearing my hoodie as I walked beside Mrs. Wilkinson, but one photographer caught my face as the cameras flashed like a fireworks display. I look wide-eyed, scared and excited, more like a kid at Disneyland than a jockey arriving to ride in a great race.

I get used to cameras clicking as I pass, to strangers holding tape recorders and shouting questions at me.

They are there now when I meet up with Mrs. Wilkinson an hour after Manhattan has worked, to be taken back to the hotel. As we make our way to the car, I walk quickly, head down.

"They won't follow us far," Mrs. Wilkinson murmurs. She is right, but when we arrive at the hotel, a couple of photographers are by the front door.

In the lobby, Mrs. Wilkinson buys a racing paper at the newsstand. Standing behind her, I glance down at the magazine rack and find myself staring into my own eyes.

On the front cover of a magazine called *Celebrity Confidential* is the photograph of me taken at the airport. The headline reads: JOCKEY TEEN BABE FLIES IN.

Teen babe? I pick up the magazine. The background to the picture has been faded and makeup has been put on my face. I have been made to look as if I'm posing, like some celebrity on a red carpet.

When I open the magazine, there is an old picture of me at a pony race, standing beside Uncle Bill.

"Don't bother with any of that." With a brisk movement, Mrs. Wilkinson takes the magazine from me and, with an arm around my shoulder, escorts me toward the elevator. "The world outside doesn't exist until after the race."

"Why do they do that?" I'm muttering. "Why do they make me look different? They've Photoshopped the photograph."

"You're successful, young, and"—she gives one of her reluctant smiles as we wait for the elevator—"passably good-looking. They'll make you look like a celebrity, even if you don't want to be one."

"They wouldn't call me a teen babe if I were a boy."

"No." The elevator arrives, the doors open, and we step inside. "They probably wouldn't."

My hotel room is enormous. Everything is crisp and white. The bed could fit a couple of families in it, and someone has left a towel on the pillow, cleverly folded in the shape of a swan.

One entire wall of the room is a window facing toward Los Angeles. I stand, looking down at the world below. The cars move silently along the freeway in the brightness, like a slow-moving silver river. The sun reflects off the windows of high-rise buildings. In the distance, a plane is coming in to land.

Tomorrow Michaela will be flying in with Uncle Bill and Aunt Elaine. Just for a second now, I remember the look on their faces when, standing in the hall, Prince Muqrin told them that if I agreed to ride in America, they would be his guests. The three of them looked at me almost as if a stranger had taken my place.

Funny little thing. Stable girl. Family charity case. Not anymore.

There have been times over the past two months since I told Prince Muqrin I would return to the yard to prepare for America when I have wondered whether I was doing the right thing.

The news that Manhattan, ridden by a girl apprentice, was to take on the best horses in the world was suddenly all over the racing press. The bigger story, that a young member of the Saudi royal family is to stand up against the protest and threats and demonstrations, was on the news pages.

Journalists who had nothing to do with racing asked for interviews. Photographs of me appeared in news stories about the Middle East, about the rights of women, about political things I don't understand.

I longed to be invisible once more. Every time that I was recognized by a stranger, I felt less like myself, as if something was being taken from me.

It was racing that kept me sane. Mrs. Wilkinson issued a

statement saying that Jay "Bug" Barton would give no interviews until after the Breeders' Cup Classic. When photographers appeared on the gallops, the lads made sure they didn't get close to me. Even Angus was on my side.

"The racing world protects its own," Deej said to me one day as we rode out, and it was true. For all the fights and problems of the past, I was one of them. Together we were strong.

To my surprise, there has been one person in the outside world who has understood all this almost instinctively. When the story first broke, I began to get excited e-mails from Jim Thurston. We could meet up in America, he said. He would fly to Los Angeles. He was so proud of his daughter. He was in touch with Michaela and was making plans to see her and Bill and Elaine.

I wrote one e-mail:

Let's get the race done first. Afterward we can meet.
I need to concentrate on this. I hope you understand.
Jay XX

And he did. He left me alone. He wrote me a short e-mail. He said he was the same as me when he was building a house. It's the people who focus in this world who get things done. We had the rest of our lives to get to know each other.

For the first time, I feel close to my father. He understands.

In my hotel room, I turn away from the window and close my eyes.

Only.

One.

Thing.

Matters.

A Piece of Work

My head is resting against hers, forehead to forehead, our little daily ritual. Today is the day.

We have been out on the course in the early morning. Laura and I have groomed Manhattan together. Standing on the straw in the barns, the mare seems to have grown over the past few days. The color of her coat is lighter than it used to be. She glows with health.

I have asked Laura to give us a few moments together. Laughing ("Blimey, you two"), she has gone for breakfast.

Manhattan has lowered her head to take a carrot from me. I lean toward her, and now, for a few seconds, we are head to head. The next time I see her will be in the paddock before the Breeders' Cup Classic.

"Oh, Hat. You rest well today. Ours is the last race. They're noisy, the barns, but you can sleep through it. You can sleep through anything. We've come this far, you and I. Let's show them. Nothing else matters. Not the past. Not the future. Not the world outside. Not what people say. It's just the two of us, doing the best we can."

It's quite a good speech, I think, but she seems unimpressed. She nudges me with her nose.

I give her another carrot, a quick pat on the neck, and leave her to it.

See you later, girl.

As I emerge, one of the older American groomers sees me. "You show 'em today, Bug," he calls out. One or two of the others in the barn wish me luck.

I'm waiting at the door of the barn where I have agreed to meet Mrs. Wilkinson when one of the exercise riders, Amy, wanders up to me.

A wiry, olive-skinned woman who must be in her forties, she has the look of a woman who has given her life to getting up early to ride horses and doesn't regret it one bit.

"Hey, Bug." She stands beside me as we both look toward the racecourse. "Ready for your big day?"

I nod. "Yup."

Amy has been friendly to me since I have been here. She says she has been an exercise rider at Santa Anita since she was my age, which was almost twenty-one years ago. She has talked about how the track's surface has changed over the past ten years. How it favors some horses and not others. "You can only tell when they race," she has told me.

She asks me if I have been studying the other runners.

I shake my head. I just know that my post position is

12. I should be able to keep out of trouble. "Manhattan runs her own race. You can't be tactical with her."

Amy turns to me and moves a little closer, glancing back into the barn. "Word to the wise, kid," she says quickly. "Watch out for Pablo Dominguez. One of the older jockeys."

"Is he on one of the favorites?"

"No way. That's the problem. He's on La Punto, a good four-year-old who qualified at Churchill Downs early in the season, but he's not in this class, and Pablo knows it."

"I don't understand, then."

"He's a piece of work, Pablo. Bitter, right? Once they thought he would be a Hall of Fame jock. Didn't work out— falls, broken bones, booze. He doesn't like young jockeys. He doesn't like foreigners. And he's got a thing about women riding in races."

"Ah."

"He's been talking about you to the other jocks— saying stuff about your not having the experience to ride in a race like this."

"He may be right."

"My guess is that if he manages to make you look bad today—stops you from having any chance in the race—that will be as sweet as any winner for old Pablo."

I look at her and see she's not joking. "Thanks for the tip," I say.

"Just watch out for him." She winks, then ambles away, hands in pockets, muttering almost as if she is talking to herself. "He's in the purple colors."

* * *

The heat has gone out of the California sun by the time we are all in the paddock before the last and biggest race of the day, the Breeders' Cup Classic.

They stand in a semicircle in front of me, the people who make up Team Manhattan: the trainer, the trainer's wife, the racing manager, and, dazzling in the white robes he wears for public appearances, the owner.

They are making small talk about the race that has just been run. Apparently there was a rough finish, an inquiry, a change in the result. Mr. Wilkinson tells me not to jump out of the stalls too quickly.

"Keep out of trouble in the early stages," says Mrs. Wilkinson. "But stay in touch with the field. Don't give the mare too much to do in the homestretch."

I listen, my eyes following Manhattan as she is led — with Deej on one side of her head, Laura on the other — around the walking ring. She is how I like to see her — curious, looking around, relaxed, saving herself for what lies ahead. I look across the paddock to where a small hunched figure in purple silks with white stripes is listening to his trainer. Pablo Dominguez.

The bell rings. Manhattan stands before us. Mr. Wilkinson is speaking, but by now I have zoned out. Everything has already been said.

In the saddle. Ride around the paddock. The outrider leads us toward the track. Close, yet only a distant voice in my mind, I hear Michaela's voice calling out, "Good luck, Jay!" Glance down, smile. Four people looking up at me.

Four?

Uncle Bill, then Aunt Elaine, then Michaela, then a small, tanned man with a mustache.

Who? Could it be? As we pass, I look back. The man smiles, and I know in that moment who it is.

The race. Concentrate. My hand on Manhattan's neck. The noise around us is deafening. A band is playing somewhere. It is like a party, a festival. Manhattan senses the excitement of humans.

To the start. She is pulling hard. As we approach the stalls, a horse passes me, too fast and too close. Its jockey, hunched in his purple colors, makes a weird, animal-like hissing noise but keeps his eyes straight ahead.

Circle behind the stalls. None of the jockeys is talking now. Stand for a moment. I see Ted's face when he taught me the heart trick. *Takes their mind off the job.* Slowly, calmly, I make a heart on Manhattan's shoulder. Then again, for luck. I pull down my goggles. We are led into the stalls. Wait. Manhattan is trembling with excitement. I gaze down the dirt racetrack. From a distance, I hear the commentator.

"The horses are loaded for the Breeders' Cup Classic."

There is a click, then the gates clang open. A bell rings.

The crowd gives a mighty roar of excitement. A surge of horsepower beneath me.

Off.

And.

Running.

THE BIG QUESTION

It is a faster pace down the stretch in front of the stands than I was expecting. Dirt is kicking in our faces. The noise—thundering of hooves, jockeys screaming and cursing as they jostle for position—is deafening. For a few seconds it feels more like going into battle than riding in a race. Manhattan's ears are flat against her head.

Easy, girl. It's just another race.

Neither of us has experienced anything like this before. From a distance, I hear the racecourse commentator's voice.

"And Manhattan is dead last. She . . . is . . . dead . . . last."

Keep calm. It's just you and me and a race to win. We're doing fine. Settle, girl. Wait.

She begins to relax into her stride. As we approach the long leftward turn away from the stands after the first quarter pole, we are trailing by some fifteen lengths behind the leaders.

She takes the bend well, tight against the rail. I'm expecting the pace to slow a bit as the race reaches the halfway pole down the back stretch, but there is no letup. The two leading horses, several lengths ahead of the rest of the field, seem to be having a private battle.

But Manhattan feels good beneath me. She likes the feel of dirt beneath her hooves. She is relaxed, almost sleepy, poised, ready for the moment when she has to answer the big question.

The runners have spread across the track down the back stretch.

Not what we wanted, Hat. I was going to take you on the outside.

I see the purple colors in front of me. If I go outside him, Dominguez can easily carry me wide around the last bend so that I will have lost too much ground to recover in the stretch. I take the inside.

Let's keep this simple, Hat.

I let her quicken so that now we are on the inside rail at the back of the field, which has bunched up as we approach the turn.

Ahead of me is a horse whose jockey is beginning to get to work on him.

I am about to pull out and ease my way past him when, to our right, someone yells and swears. Like an out-of-control bumper car, his horse swerves inward, moving in a matter of strides from the outside of the field to beside me, holding me against the rails. It is like a door being slammed shut.

Out of the corner of my eye, I see purple.

"Cozy here, eh, *chiquita*?"

The voice is a low growl. Around the turn as we head for home, the jockeys ahead of us are coming alive, pulling their whips through, shouting, "Hah! Hah!" at their horses. I am completely boxed in. The jockey on the horse in front of me glances over his shoulder, then suddenly begins to lose ground. Dominguez, on my outside, could overtake him, but instead moves back with him, taking me farther and farther away from the field. It is like a cork being slowly pulled from a bottle. In a shock of realization, I see that the two jockeys—one in front of me, another beside me—are working together to take me out of the race.

"You ain't going nowhere, honey," says Pablo, eyes straight ahead.

He has his horse leaning toward me, pinching me against the rails. We are so close now that his boot is rubbing against mine. Ahead, the field is moving away from us.

We're trapped. If I pull back sharply to get around Dominguez, I will be so far behind that my race will be over, yet we're losing ground with every stride.

"Do something, Hat!" I scream the words into the wind.

Manhattan's ears go back. No other horse has dared to rub up against her like this on a racetrack. She likes it even less than I do.

Suddenly, without breaking her stride, she lunges, teeth first, to her right.

Dominguez's horse is so startled, it throws its head up in alarm. For a second, there is a gap to our right.

It is all we need.

Head down, Manhattan barges her way like a battering ram between the horse in front of her and Dominguez.

I hear a curse, and at the moment we see daylight, there's a crack and, just for a few strides, Manhattan loses her action.

As we enter the home stretch, she hits her rhythm once more.

Yes, Hat. We can do this.

But can we? As we pass the last quarter pole, the runners are like a wall ahead of us. We must be almost twenty lengths behind the leading horse.

I had wanted to save Manhattan until the last furlong, but now I have no choice. We are beyond tactics now.

OK, Hat, let's go.

A gap between the two horses ahead of us widens as they tire. We go for it, parting them like an ax splitting wood.

There are still eight or nine horses in front of us. Low in the saddle, I push Manhattan through the field, worming our way past the tiring horses. Ahead of us, three horses are locked in battle.

No choice, girl. Got to go on the outside.

I check Manhattan for a stride, then switch her to the right. Now we have a clear run to the finish line. There is an explosion of sound from the crowd as they suddenly see us, poised to make our challenge. It is like hitting a wall of noise, but Manhattan, her ears pointing for home, dives into it.

We are in the final furlong. The two leaders, locked

together, are still four lengths ahead of us, but we are pulling them back to us with every stride.

"Now, Hat, now!"

From somewhere distant, the hysterical voice of the racecourse commentator is screaming: "And now Manhattan's on the charge!"

"Go, Hat!"

I hear my own roar as, from somewhere, Manhattan finds more strength, more speed. We reach the two other horses fifty yards from the post. She seems to lower herself to the ground and stretch for the line.

And suddenly I know. The winning post flashes past me. The sound all around changes from screams and yells to cheers and celebration. The commentator is saying, "Unbelieeeevable, we've never seen a race like that. Manhattan takes the Breeders' Cup Classic!"

We pull up around the bend after the winning post. Manhattan slows to a canter, then a trot. She is spent. Some of the other jockeys are shouting across to me, but I can't hear what they're saying in the frenzy of noise. I smile and nod. We turn to head back to the grandstand.

We trot for a few meters but then, without warning, Manhattan slows to a walk. I pat her. She is drenched with sweat. Looking behind the saddle, I see that her flanks are heaving with exhaustion. She can hardly put one foot in front of the other.

Easy, Hat. You've run your race now. They can wait for us.

The outrider who will lead us back is cantering toward

us. We stop, standing at the end of the track, taking in the crazy scenes in front of us. Down the track, lead rein swinging, Deej is running toward us, the biggest smile I have ever seen on his face. Beyond him, the Wilkinsons and Prince Muqrin are surrounded by people congratulating them. In the grandstand, thousands and thousands of faces are looking at us, cheering, laughing, waving banners that read GO, GIRLS!, MANHATTAN FOR ME! and WE LOVE BUG! Somewhere in there, my best friend, Uncle Bill, and Aunt Elaine will be laughing with joy. With them will be my father. A band has started playing. The racecourse commentator is gabbling with excitement. A woman with a microphone, followed by a cameraman, is walking toward us.

Manhattan snorts, amazed by what she is seeing. She lifts her head high, her ears pricked. Her body is shaking and she is blowing so hard that I feel her moving beneath me with every breath, but she stands tall, her feet planted in the dirt, the queen of Santa Anita Park.

These few seconds are our moment, and somehow I know it. Frozen in time. Never to be forgotten. I trace a heart on her sweat-drenched shoulder.

We did it, girl. You and me.

Then we walk on, toward the noise and the waving and the people.

Let.
The.
Madness.
Begin.

CHANGES

It is not much to show for a life. On a small slab of con-crete, part of a long wall in a cemetery garden, the words are written:

Deborah Ann Barton
1982–2008

I look along the length of the wall. So many names with their dates, each with their own memories of happy days, sad days.

It has been six crazy months since my life changed on the Santa Anita racetrack. Every day I have thought about Debs and wondered what she would say about her daughter's fame. What would she make of the decisions I took? How would she react to the reappearance in my life of the old Helldawg, Jim Thurston?

Jim. I smile at Mum's stone. The next time I'll be here, he will probably be with me. He is bringing his family to England later this summer for their vacation. He said he wants to pay his respects to my mother.

There will be a few days spent at Coddington. "Completing the circle" is what Jim calls it, although, to tell the truth, the family circle has a few dents in it these days. After he returned from America, Uncle Bill was arrested for not paying his taxes. He was found guilty, and a judge told him he had to repay his debt to society by doing two hundred hours of community service.

It's quite possible that the first sight Jim Thurston will have of Uncle Bill in his homeland will be through the window of a car as it passes a gang of yellow-jacketed litter pickers as they repay their debt to society.

I thought about what Uncle Bill has done in my life, the good as well as the bad, and how Michaela found my father, and I reached a big decision. I would use some of my winnings in America, plus the money I have earned for interviews and personal appearances since then, to help the family keep Coddington. I made one condition — that they brought back Dusty to live out his days in the field next to the house.

Uncle Bill is going to pay me back, he says. The litter-picking thing has given him time to think up a few new plans. Three words to my uncle: include me out.

The big family reunion is not exactly a red-letter day in my diary, but my father has told me I needn't worry about what happened in the past. Nobody's perfect, he says, and I guess he should know.

When I visited him after Santa Anita, he told me several times that "families are what it's all about." My face must have given away more than I thought because he quickly started talking about how great his kids, Barney and Jared, were, how lucky he had been to find Linda.

"I thought I had a perfect life," my father said. "But it just got even better."

There are voices behind me in the crematorium garden. A family—mother, father, and bored-looking daughter of about twelve—are searching along the wall for the name of their dead loved one.

As I pass them, the mother does that little double take that I have come to know. She recognizes me from the papers.

A taxi is waiting. I drive in silence to the station. When it arrives, the train is fuller than I expected. It is the start of summer vacation, and families are returning from the seaside.

Now and then, one of the adults, knowing who I am, catches my eye. I give them my public this-far-and-no-further smile.

I gaze out of the window, watching the fields of barley and corn as they glide by.

The madness started that day in California last October. Maybe you read or heard about me somewhere. How someone thought they saw me in a swanky new London club. How a Hollywood star was rumored to be going out with me. How a friend of mine, who preferred to remain nameless, revealed that I wanted to be an actress. How surprisingly shy I was, or how nice, or how I was the most impossible person in the world.

The newspaper stories, the weird and crazy fantasies, rolled out whatever I did or said. They were about a stranger I didn't even know. For a few weeks after my return from America, I played the fame game, appearing on TV, doing interviews, listening to men in suits as they explained how much money could be made if I agreed to exploit something they called my "brand."

But as winter turned to spring, I knew in my heart that, with every new celebrity item about me, I was leaving behind what I really loved. The more I became a brand, the less there was of me.

I learned to say no. I stayed in Newmarket, out of sight, riding out at the Wilkinson yard. With the new season, Mr. Wilkinson began to give me rides. I had some winners, and for other trainers too. I'm doing well.

Now and then, I stay a weekend at Coddington. Michaela has fallen in love with a boy from her college, and so a lot of listening and sympathetic nodding has to go on. Uncle Bill talks racing to me. Aunt Elaine asks how Tariq is. We might almost be a family.

They say that when you ride a race, you should never look back, and that is true for life too. But now and then I think of what was said about Manhattan after she won in America.

She was hailed as one of racing's all-time greats. She had it all, they said—speed, strength, and courage. With that one great performance, she proved herself to be a true champion for our time.

There is no Manhattan in the string this year, but, riding

out, I am reminded of her every day. A two-year-old might stand stock-still, as she used to. Another might prefer to be at the front of the string. There could be something about the way a colt carries his head while working, or a filly might pretend to be fierce in the stable.

The train slows as we approach Newmarket, and soon I am stepping onto the platform where it all began.

I catch glances from strangers as I make my way through the station, but no one tries to talk to me. I like this town, where jockeys and lads, the famous and the unknown, are together, united by the strange business of working with horses.

It feels like home.

Up the main street. Turn right toward Edgecote House. The drive and the house are more spruced up, less tired, than they once were.

There have been changes this season. The Wilkinson yard has become almost fashionable. Prince Muqrin is still an owner, although he spends more time these days in Saudi Arabia. He is a minister in the government now. In the newspapers, he is no longer the "playboy prince" but the "new face of the House of Saud."

In the end, what happened at Santa Anita might have only made a small difference. A woman rode one of the prince's horses, and the whole of civilization did not come tumbling down. It's not everything, but it's something.

I stand at the entrance to the yard for a moment. It is midafternoon, and there is an air of sleepiness to the place. Officially I am still a lad, but these days I spend so many days racing that I don't have my own horses to "do" but help out Laura and Chloe — one of the new girls — with their horses.

I walk across the yard, into the tack room. Deej is at a table, working out the List for the following day. As I enter, he looks up and gives me a big smile.

"Hey," I say. "It's the head lad at work."

He laughs. "It never stops," he says, but there is no complaint in his voice.

Soon after the Breeders' Cup Classic, Angus took early retirement. His old riding injury was acting up, he said. There is a rumor that Mrs. Wilkinson encouraged him to make the move. Now and then he visits the yard, looking older but happier.

Deej became head lad. A few weeks later, Harry Bucknall announced that he was to run a small yard of steeplechasers down in the West Country. Another rumor has it that Mrs. Wilkinson told him that his services were no longer required.

I like these rumors. I believe them.

She is there every day, first and second lot, still the trainer's wife but no longer in the background. Sometimes Mr. Wilkinson remains at home. More rumors. Change is in the air.

Deej and I chat easily about the yard, its latest winners, how there are more girls working there than there used to be, how Laura is getting along since she was promoted to traveling head lad. The way he talks these days is more confident. He is stronger now, waiting for his moment. One day, I just know, he will be a trainer.

"I'd better get this stuff done," he says, nodding at the chart in front of him. "D'you fancy going out later?"

"Sounds good."

I walk through the back yard, down a lane leading to the paddocks at the back.

There are three brood mares grazing in the afternoon sun. Leaning on the gate, I give a low whistle.

One of them, a big gray, looks up. She is broader than she used to be, and her stomach shows the first signs of the foal growing within her. She holds her head high, ears pricked, and stands motionless for a moment, looking toward me.

Then she gives a low neigh of welcome.

Hey, Hat.

She.

Trots.

Toward.

Me.

ACKNOWLEDGMENTS

I have been exceptionally lucky in the writing of this book.

The great trainer Sir Mark Prescott was generous with his time and patience, allowing me to visit, nose around, and ask impertinent questions at his yard in Newmarket. I am deeply grateful to Mark; to his assistant trainer, William Butler; head lad, Colin Nutter; and to all the lads and staff at Heath House.

I would also like to thank Duncan Gregory at the British Racing School in Newmarket and Matt Mancini at the Racing Centre for their helpful advice and information.

Thanks are also due to my nephew Dan Blacker, a trainer in California, who provided expert assistance and advice on American racing and slang.

Three books were particularly useful to me: Susan Gallier's *One of the Lads* (London: Stanley Paul, 1988), Rebecca Cassidy's *The Sport of Kings* (Cambridge: Cambridge University Press, 2002), and Elizabeth Mitchell's *Three Strides Before the Wire* (New York: Hyperion, 2002). I am indebted to the TV production company Matchlight for their documentary *Jockey School*, which was first shown on BBC's Channel Four in 2014. Terry McNamee's informative 2013 blog post, "The Tetrarch: England's Spotted Wonder," was of great help when I was researching Manhattan's bloodline.

My agent, Caroline Sheldon, has, as ever, been a source of tough good sense and encouragement; I'm truly a fortunate author to have had the benefit of her wisdom and drive throughout my career.

I am grateful to Charlie Sheppard of my British publisher, Andersen Press, for the insight, understanding, and commitment with which she edited the original version of this book.

It has been a great pleasure to work once again with the team at Candlewick Press. I would particularly like to thank my editor, Carter Hasegawa, for his enthusiasm, wisdom, and efficiency.

I was hugely helped by three good friends—two professional writers and my former editor—who read earlier drafts of this book and provided constructive criticism and encouragement. Warm thanks go to Tania Kindersley and Will Buckley, and also to Marion Lloyd, who has been telling me I should write this book for many years. I hope she feels it was worth the wait.

Thanks are also due to Lydia Alexander, who typed every draft and was with me for every step of Jay and Manhattan's journey, often helping with a cheering comment when I was flagging.

The dedicatee of this book, Paul Sidey, was enthusiastic about the story from the moment I told him about it and, despite being very ill, was characteristically generous and supportive while I was writing it. I wish he were here to see it in print.

Angela Sykes was a perceptive, kind, creative presence from the first spark of the idea that became *Racing Manhattan* to its final full stop. I thank her with all my heart.